In Plain Sight

a novel

Edmund Okocha

Book design by Jaelyn Jackson

Book edited by Charlene Taylor

To my family, I refuse to imagine life without them

chapter1

I t sounded like something from a dream. The thumping was rhythmic, but after many seconds of no response, it became erratic, close to the point of madness. Rapid successions of exasperating knocks ensued. The noise yanked me cruelly from a slumber, which had only begun two hours ago. Perturbed, I glanced at the clock on the iHome speaker resting on a brown Oakwood stand.

Brazenly, it read, 4:32 a.m.

"What the fuck?" I muttered in a near whisper, as I annoyingly shoved the thick blanket off my body. It made a rustling sound as if it too was displeased with the nuisance.

I slid into the blue slippers that were by the side of my California king-size bed. My night robe that was tossed mindlessly on the floor a few hours earlier was now recovered with care as my arms glided tenderly through its sleeves.

"Hold on! I'm coming!" I yelled towards the door in response to the unrelenting knocking.

I maneuvered my way expertly through the shadowy space of my four-bedroom beach house. The last door before the front entrance squealed flippantly as I

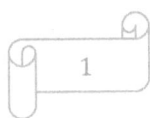

nudged it forward. It was as if the door was letting out frustration for not being repaired as I had planned over four months ago. In about a week I would rejoice for procrastinating on this repair because it would save my life.

When I got within an earshot range, I almost yelled, "Who is it?"

"Open up it's the FBI!"

"FBI?" I whispered.

My mind raced through the events of the past twenty-four hours, desperately combing through any activity that might have piqued the interest of the Federal Bureau of Investigation. My friend Tim and his girlfriend, Jasmine, had reached out for a spontaneous night on the town. Outside of editing a few manuscripts and preparing for my show on Wednesday—which was in three days—there was nothing pressing on my schedule, so I yielded to their request and joined them. Unbeknownst to me, they showed up with Cassandra—Jasmine's best friend and former college roommate. I should have known this would happen because their past acts of spontaneity had followed a similar sequence. Their hope of a romantic match however, due to no fault of Cassandra's, was to no avail. She was a striking beauty: attractive face, long legs, shapely butt, big boobs, everything... and from what I gathered over dinner, she was an ambitious woman. If not for her close relationship with Jasmine, I might have attempted to invite her to my place for sessions of intimate exercise. We parted ways around 1:15 a.m. with all parties, at least from my deduction, having enjoyed the evening. I exchanged numbers with Cassandra, but doubted I would call and I doubted if she would either.

None of the mentioned activities warranted an FBI investigation.

"Who are you looking for?" I asked, now fully awake.

"We're here for Ebenezer Cosmen," a deep baritone sounded at the other side of the door. "Don't be alarmed, you are not under arrest. We're just here for some questioning."

"Can this wait till the morning?" I pleaded, even though I already knew the answer, "I'm operating on two hours of sleep here. I will be more useful later."

"I'm sorry it can't sir." This time I heard a wimpish voice through the door. Like that of an unsure teenager.

Before opening the door, I looked through the peephole and saw the oddest-looking pair I've ever seen in my life. Everything about them was the complete opposite. The smaller of the two was white, short, and fat with sandy-colored hair. He looked like a wigged basketball with protruding arms and legs as an afterthought. His physique looked entirely fictitious. The other agent was black and ball-headed like Michael Jordan. He stood about 6'4" with a muscular build. I found it odd that they were both dressed in blue stylish suits at four-thirty in the morning, but only the black man looked flattering in it.

At least one of them is a brotha, I thought, as I unlocked the door.

"Ebenezer Cosmen," the muscled man said in his deep baritone, "I'm Special Agent Tristan Taylor, and this is my partner Special Agent Earl Tomkievich. We are following up on an investigation and we would like to ask you some questions. May we come in please?"

I eyed both men for a second, and then took a little longer scrutinizing the badge handed to me before stepping aside. I felt the cold breeze pierce through my body as I stood by the door. The temperature had dropped significantly since the time I was out with my friends, and this development made me even more upset.

"Have a seat," I said a bit rudely.

Earl sat on one end of the three-seater couch and Tristan sat at the other end. Earl reached in his coat pocket and fetched a pen and notebook. I flipped the switch next to the door to provide a little lighting. The

room was dimly lit, but enough to make out relevant facial expressions.

"So, what is this about?" I asked, impatiently.

Tristan heaved a heavy sigh before he began.

"First of all, we would like to apologize for being here so early," Agent Tristan said. "We would not have done this if we did not think it was important."

He paused for a response, but there was none forthcoming. Remnants of my anger still lingered and I was unwilling to absolve them of anything as of yet. Although, I was suddenly interested in what they had to say. It had to be serious for them to interfere with my schedule this early in the morning.

I nodded my head and waited for him to continue.

He didn't.

He allowed the silence to linger instead. It felt odd and discomforting like moments following a mistimed joke. He stared intently at the floor-to-ceiling white linen curtains before him, and then slowly, his gaze moved across the room. The curtain was the kind of white touched by hands devoid of dust. A cursory look to the right revealed the hidden cords that were used to open and close them. There was a television, two bookshelves, a few Basquiat paintings, a dining table and four chairs arranged around the bespoke fireplace which leapt with a gas flame. The floor was a high-polished wood, dark and free of either dirt or clutter. He concentrated his stare on one of the paintings perched high above the bookshelf to his left. It was as if he was seeking approval from the artwork before continuing. These delays added to the intensity of the moment and I began formulating different tales in my head on what this visit was about.

"Your book a decade ago," Tristan began slowly, "was any of that a true story? I mean did you draw inspiration from real life events to write that book?"

I stared at him quizzically. I was certain this early morning imposition was not for a fireside chat about a book I wrote ten years ago. I truly believed this peculiar line of questioning would lead somewhere worthwhile or else, I would consider some legal schemes as compensation for my troubles.

"It was all fiction," I managed to say. "I don't know anyone like that in real life. Why do you ask?"

Tristan paused again.

I hated these pauses. I wondered if it was an FBI approach to summon a certain level of emotion out of me. As a booklover, I have read my fair share of police procedurals to know that detectives at times summoned these tactics to lure out feelings and sentiments.

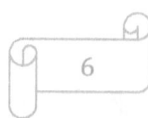

"Okay," he said. "So all the details in the book were ideas you came up with on your own? Are you certain that there—"

"What's this about?" I interrupted impolitely, no longer able to contain my irritation. "Why don't you guys just come out and say it?!"

The fury in my voice did very little to influence their calm demeanor. It felt like talking to a deaf person. The basketball shaped agent had been quiet the entire time. He maintained an expressionless look on his face and this added to my rage.

"There is no easy way to say this," Tristan said.

"Say what?"

He sighed heavily.

"We believe you might be in a unique position to assist us on a case."

"What case?" I asked, in a tone consistent with my anger, "And why do you believe that? I have no experience in law enforcement or anything remotely close to it. Everything I write about is purely fiction and I doubt—"

"Sir!" said Tristan, in an authoritative tone, "we know all that and we are still interested in bringing you on."

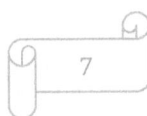

"Why?"

"This is concerning the stabbing deaths that have been occurring lately around town," Tristan said. "During our investigation, we've gathered that we might have a copycat in our midst. We've uncovered clues that strongly suggest the killer was inspired by similar events ten years ago. The details are eerily similar. Therefore, we would like to pick your brain to see if you can guide us towards the right path. It seems like the killer is ahead of us at every turn."

"I'm confused," I said, "am I a suspe—"

"No, no, no," Earl, with his wimpish voice, blurted out before I could even finish my sentence, "You're not too hard to find, so we've been able to rule you out as a suspect. The different places and times of death did not match your movements. This visit is just a reach out for assistance because we seem to be lost, and like Agent Tristan said, this killer is using the same methods from ten years ago."

"Okay," I said, a little relieved that I was not a suspect, but a question still nagged at me, "Why couldn't this wait till much later in the day? It's not even five o'clock yet!"

Both men traded stares, and I saw Earl yield to Tristan by nodding his head.

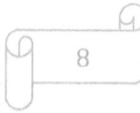

"The killer's latest victim is Jennifer Gibson," Tristan paused again. This time, it was to allow the severity of the name to weigh on me a little before continuing.

I noticed the stress lines on his forehead. His eyebrows converged and his nose flared as he breathed weightily. I wanted to chuckle at his antics, but that would be highly insensitive following what I was just told. Jennifer Gibson was the daughter of the Senator from Delaware, Terry Gibson, a crafty charismatic politician with lofty goals of running for the highest office in the land. Although I was still a bit confused as to how I could be of any use to the investigation, I didn't share my concern. I figured I would get more information as the days went by.

"Can I sleep on it?" I asked, "I really meant it when I said I was only operating on two hours of sleep. I need to make some phone calls and check my schedule."

Both men appeared to be in deep thought.

"Okay," Tristan finally said, "We will contact you later today. Here's my card just in case you need to reach us."

"Thank you for your time," Earl added.

I let the men out and more cool breeze in. The idea of going to sleep was no longer feasible. I walked to the kitchen and made coffee with my French press. I sat in the same spot Earl occupied moments earlier, and turned on the television. While I waited for the TV to come on, I placed a call to the only person that might bring a little understanding to this tale. As the 65-inch screen winked to life, I navigated to the local stations for news about Jennifer Gibson. Now, I too was curious with how this ordeal mimicked ten years ago.

The phone kept ringing.

chapter2

I like to think I'm a man of workable intellect. Rarely am I the smartest in the room, but certainly never the dumbest. Regardless of the subject matter, if it's rooted in logic, I can either converse fluently from a rational stance, or ask relevant questions to gain lucidity on the topic. Either way, I'm never lost in a room.

This belief had been my guiding light to most things I had embarked upon. I graduated with a Bachelor of Science in Computer Technology in 2004 from the University of Delaware, the largest public university in the second smallest state, and I quickly gained employment with an instrumentation company in Northeast Philadelphia.

The job was sufficient. It provided enough challenge to deter monotony.

My bills were paid.

Immediate needs, met.

My savings account accrued at a bearable pace, and sometimes I had enough to interact with the characters of the night. I maintained an above average credit score and a slightly lopsided work-life balance with the tilt towards work. I lived in the Spring Garden area of

Philadelphia, walking distance from the revered rocky statue and the art museum steps. In the winter, when the tourists had dwindled to a few hundreds, I partook in a yoga class held at the top of the art museum steps.

It was fun.

Forty dollars per session well spent.

Also, in the winter, I dabbled in a little bit of writing. The discipline and rigor of computer programming made me invest more of my free time in writing. The freedom and the open path to stretch as far as my imagination could take me was something I enjoyed to no end. I loved the flexibility of it. The idea that I could make up things... I could create a rodent with three legs and the ability to lift a car and then conveniently compartmentalize it as science fiction. To know that such autonomies were permissible if I was able to concatenate words and phrases to convince readers of its veracity thrilled me. I began writing short stories and sharing some with my friends. Their reaction was that of surprise and disbelief, but I was unsure of its authenticity.

"Oh my God!" they would exclaim, "You code and you write! Both sides of your brain really work!"

Their open-mouthed awe was often met with a dismissive wave. But as time aged, I too began to observe the growth in my writing. This was always my gift—and a curse— depending on the vantage point. Being the last to realize my capability, I believed, preserved my humility. It invited a much deeper appreciation for my talent. But I still maintain this later realization robbed me of key early opportunities.

I began spending all my free time on this new shiny art form.

Still, I enjoyed coding and its indemnity, the belief in logical reasoning, and the assurance in knowing that mathematical truths would surely lead me to my desired result as long as its guidelines were obeyed. This was a certainty about coding I would never give up in my life, but there was something new and exciting, and perhaps dangerous about writing. Writing was like the bad gangs my parents warned me about.

Lawless.

Unruly.

Its anarchistic ways made it appealing. I wanted to be part of the movement. To tell fantastic stories to people living in despair of a brighter day when they could lace up their clique with diamond roles like Nas said in "*If I Ruled the world.*" In a little over a year, I completed seventeen short stories. Each of about eighty-pages with slightly over twenty-thousand words.

I allowed my imagination to roam freely like an uncaged lion—free to scour the depths of my thoughts and regurgitate its contents via words. But even with this progress I was incredibly reluctant to publish them. My friends would scream and holler at my unwillingness to circulate my work, but their concerns were steadily met with, "Once I feel it, I'll publish it."

I finally felt it in the summer of 2006. I decided to use a self-publishing company I researched online. They were responsible for the book's binding and cover artwork. They kept twenty-five percent of all sales. I was still a full-time software developer because the book sales were never a financial plan of mine. It just felt fulfilling to say I was a published author. The fame and fortune were not things I cared for. At least not for that project. The reviews were mild from paltry news publications. I did receive an inspiring analysis from the Delaware News Journal. The author of the article, who later became my friend, professed that my writing style was unique, and with a little more time honing my craft, I might have what it takes to be mentioned in the same sentence as Walter Mosely.

I saved the article.

I used it as an inspiration when I began my next project. This time I was no longer interested in short stories. My sight was set on a full-fledged novel with all the nuances and details needed for the reader to feel completely present in the story. Every weekend in the summer of 2007, I rented a cabin in Seaford, Delaware from an elderly black couple I met at a bookstore. The cabin was just off of DuPont Highway. The cottage backed onto a picturesque lake, and at low tide, the stairs could take you to the shoreline for a breathtaking view of the tall trees that stood at a distance. It was a spacious one-bedroom post and beam where you could smell cedar as soon as you stepped on the porch. The scenery and deafening stillness were what I envisioned in my mind when I began this project.

It was called *Tilted Grin*...

...a story about a makeup artist for a local play in Elkhart, Indiana. By day he produced wonderful mimics of animals and clowns, but during the small hours of the night, he went around killing women and children. And with the unique skillset he earned from his cosmetology degree to disguise himself, he was able to elude the authorities for decades. The killer's trademark was a slanted smiley face, which later on, following his arrest, authorities observed that the slanting faces he sketched at his murder scenes bore a distinct resemblance to his pictures as a child. To properly describe the perpetrator's mind, I embarked on some very dark study about psychopaths. When the book was done, I hired an editor and an artist for the book cover. In the wake of some modest publicity from my first book, I was able to secure a small advance from a publishing company to help with its distribution. An equal measure of optimism and trepidation consumed me upon the book's publication, but the truth landed somewhere in the center. The reviews were somewhat promising. I attracted about one hundred and fifty people for the book reading in Barnes and Noble in the biggest mall in the largest county in Delaware. The sales were underwhelming, and after a few months, I returned to the rigid demands of my job as a computer programmer. I was certain that my career as an author would not chart the same course as some of my idols like Mosely, Morrison, Follet, or Connelly, but I found solace in knowing that I survived the process with my dignity, more or less, still intact. I wrote when I found the time, but I spent most of my days enhancing my skills as a computer programmer. Occasionally, I would get an alert of a book sale. It made me smile, albeit, short-lived. In all, I sold a total of 351 books—half of which, I'm convinced, were to my friends and family members. Of course they never admitted to it.

My life changed forever the day I was visited by two officers from the Philadelphia Police Department. It was a meek Saturday morning. A cacophony of blaring car horns, barking dogs, and screaming children, filled the air outside. I had spent a chunk of the past two months working on a localization software to translate our main interface into seventeen languages, so I was exhausted and desperately needed that day to be stress free. My friend Tim promised he would visit later in the day with his dog, so that was all I had planned for the day.

"Who is it?" I said grudgingly.

"Is this Ebenezer Cosmen?" A brash voice sounded at the door.

"Yes," I responded feeling irritated.

"This is Captain Disher," the voice said, "and I'm with my partner, Lieutenant Stottlemeyer, we are with the Philadelphia Police Department, and we would like to ask you some questions."

"About what?" I retorted, on the brink of being incensed.

"Sir," the captain continued calmly, "I'd rather not talk about this in the hallway. Can we please come in? It shouldn't take long."

There was a pregnant pause, then I blurted out, "Do you have a warrant?" Recalling something I might have heard in an episode of Law and Order.

"Sir, we didn't think we needed one," the captain said, maintaining his cool, "You're not under arrest. This is just a visit to obtain information for an ongoing case."

Another pause.

My hesitation stemmed from the myriad of news reports, literatures, movies, all highlighting the troubling relationship between the police and the black community. Although, my experiences in life were yet to witness this turmoil, I was cognizant of it, and I knew it would be a soaring display of stupidity if I didn't at least consider it.

"I'm opening the door now," I said slowly.

Standing before me were two middle-aged white guys. One of them had a mustache that almost covered his upper lip and the other was clean-shaven with a round bulging belly. I immediately noticed their holstered guns and prayed it remained that way throughout their stay.

"Ebenezer?" The mustached man confirmed.

I nodded and stepped to the side for them to come in.

"So, what is this about?" I asked.

"First of all," the captain said, "can you confirm that you're the author of this book?"

He held up a copy of *Tilted Grin*.

"Yes," I said, my frustration now turned into confusion.

"Okay," the captain heaved a heavy sigh. "I think we have a killer out there that's using the methods you laid out in this book to carry out his killings. He is using specific details—"

"It's not me," I interrupted, hoping to secure my innocence early in the conversation. "This is all fiction. There's nothing about—"

"Sir, sir, sir," the captain tried to calm me down, "we know that. No one is saying you did this. We know it's a fictional novel, but there's someone out there using it for real life killings. The makeup, the smiley faces, some of the clues left behind. This is not the first time we've seen copycats like this, but we're just trying to cover everything. You know, leaving no stone unturned. You know what I'm saying?"

I did not react to the stupid smirk he had on his face.

"During the course of our investigation," Lieutenant Stottlemeyer spoke for the first time, "we realized the book sales were low. So we think you might know who bought the books. We would just need their names so we can rule them out as suspects, too."

Reminding me of my measly book sales, I felt was a bit of a low blow, but I didn't show it. My facial expression remained indifferent throughout his speech.

"No," I said plainly.

"Wha—what, I'm sorry?" he stammered.

"I don't know who bought my books," I clarified.

"Sir," the captain took back the reigns of the conversation, "I'm sure you have friends and family that bought your book. We would at least like their names just to rule them out. That's all."

I liked the captain. For one, he was kind and mindful with his word choices. And he wasn't an asshole about my miserable book numbers.

"Okay," I said hesitantly. I had no reason to believe that any of my friends and family were roaming the night killing women and children. I wrote down the names of five friends and eleven family members I knew for sure bought my book. I had a few more names in mind, but I couldn't say with any level of specificity that they bought it. I wanted to exist in the bliss of not knowing.

When the cops left, I immediately placed a call to my literary agent and childhood friend, Reynald Muhammad, in Baltimore. I called him Ray for short. We had not seen each other since the day of my book reading over five months ago.

"E CEEEEEEE!" he said in a rehearsed show of enthusiasm. "I was thinking about calling you later today. How've you been man?"

I knew he was lying, but I didn't care. The visit from the cops was the only thing on my mind. I told him everything they told me and sought advice on how to proceed. I've known Ray since the third-grade. We were eight years old and the only black kids in our classroom. Our friendship formed effortlessly and it had been one of my best life decisions. With the exception of my father and my baby sister, Caroline, Ray was the only other person on earth I trusted with my life. We've been in countless fights both as allies and as adversaries, but our friendship had endured through it all. Ray learned at an early age of his gift of the gab and he used it to manipulate any situation he found himself in. He once talked his way out of getting a ticket for speeding in a school zone.

"Are you serious?" Ray was ecstatic.

I couldn't tell if he was back to his normal self or still playing the rehearsed role of an enthused agent.

"Yes," I said, "but why do you sound like you're happy. Someone is out there killing people using my book as a guide!"

"Yea, yea, yea, I get that," he said glibly," but can't you see what's happening here?!"

"No!"

"Come on E," he said, excitedly, "I swear I wonder what you'll do without me. You said the cops just left right?"

"Yes."

"Ok, I don't trust those mo'fuckas so I aint talking on this line. I'm coming up there right now. I'll see you in a few hours."

And without warning, the line went dead.

I stared at my phone for a few seconds, *what the fuck just happened!?*

For over five months, since the disappointing turnout at the book reading, I've been trying to get Ray to accompany me to some local bookstores in Philly or Baltimore for another stab at it, and his response was always that of an extremely busy man, so his reaction to this news was completely foreign to me. While I waited, I called my friends and families, whose names I gave to the cops earlier, and informed them of the visit. In what felt like an era, I finally heard the tap on my door.

"Yo! Wuddup bro!!" Ray exclaimed as he reached out for a hug.

Ray stood only at about 5'7", but his personality gave him the presence of a giant. His body was well sculpted, and his skin was the color of dark roast coffee. He kept his hair closely cropped and his hairline perpetually sharp.

"So, what's this idea that you can't talk over the phone?" I asked, edgily.

"Damn, chill, E," he said as he walked past me towards the kitchen.

He fixed himself a tall glass of water. He downed the first two, before walking out with a half-empty glass from the third pouring.

"Damn!" I said, "Y'all don't have water in Baltimore?"

"Whatever man," he said, "It's hot as balls out there. I gotta stay hydrated."

"So, what's up?" I asked.

He knew how badly I yearned for what he had to say, and he did everything he could to torture me.

"You think the Sixers gon' make some noise this year in the—"

"Yo, fuck the Sixers," I interrupted, with my facial expression stuck somewhere between a sneer and a smile, "let's talk man!"

He exploded in an uncontrollable laughter.

With nothing else left for me to do, I joined in.

When he realized his act could no longer continue without really upsetting me, he decided to share his plan.

"We gon' put this out there." His voice dropped rapidly to almost a whisper, "We'll let the media know that there's a killer using the details in your book to kill people. This will drive up sales because people are fucked up like that. They have a morbid fascination for this type of thing. They love that murder and serial-killer shit. They'll buy your book even if it's just out of curiosity. This is the exposure we really needed. See, it's not that your book sucked, we just didn't have the funds to properly market it. The advance we got was only enough for a few tours and to pay the editor and artist. This time however, we have free exposure. And it's happening in real time!"

There was nothing sophisticated about Ray's line of thought, and yet I was mad as to why I did not think of it first. Perhaps I was concerned with the moral aspect of it all: The uneasy idea of profiting from actual deaths.

"What about the families that are actually affected by this?" I asked. "They are suffering while I'm out here trying to benefit from their misery."

"No, no, no, ma brotha!" Ray said, wagging his index finger like a mother admonishing a child. "Whether you leak it or not, the dead *is* dead. You can't bring them back. One might argue, that if you bring more publicity to this, you can help catch this asshole quicker."

I felt like he had a point, or maybe it was just remnants of the grudge I held for not selling as many books as I secretly thought I would. I really believed *Tilted Grin* was a product of my best effort, so to witness the sluggish sales was disheartening. I told myself, and everyone else willing to listen, that I was okay with the sales numbers. I repeated this mantra until it became the dominating voice against all forms of doubts swirling in my head. And soon it was baked into my brain as the truth. Now, with this rare opportunity before me, I believed the true worth of my work would come to light, and I could enjoy the glory I truly deserved.

"Who you gon' call?" I asked.

"Ghostbusters!" Ray sprang up and pantomimed a dance move.

"Seriously man," I cracked a smile.

"All of 'em man!" he almost yelled. "CNN, FOX, MSNBC, ABC, CBS, NPR, NBC, New York Times...all the alphabets! Shit even Oprah! Yo, if you make it to Oprah's Book Club, you know that's like printing money. You'll be certified!"

✱✱✱

I never did make it to Oprah's Book Club, but the story found its way to the lips of newscasters and radio personalities, and the pages of newspaper articles all over the country. My friend at the Delaware News Journal helped immensely with the circulation of this story, and his efforts made him a finalist for the Pulitzer that year. In two weeks, my book sales leapt from 351 to over 173,000 copies. And by the fourth week, I was number six on the New York Times bestsellers list. The small publishing company I was using was unable to keep up with the demands, so I switched to a bigger company that was used to that level of attention. Ray remained my agent, but I switched my editor.

I tried valiantly to hold on to my computer programming position, but the demands from my overnight success were too much to handle. I was on

Larry King, Leno, Letterman, and even had a two-episode role on Law and Order SVU. I was offered a reoccurring role on a True Crime show on the ID Network. I was first used to provide expert commentary on a six-part docuseries about psychopaths and murder. The ratings exceeded their expectations, so they hired me as a fixture on their Wednesday primetime lineup. Ray negotiated a pay of $412,000 per year. I was twenty-six years old and was enjoying a level of success I never envisioned for myself. In the summer of 2008, at the height of my celebrity, the serial killer faltered and was caught in Tyler Texas. For selfish reasons, I felt bad for his capture. I hated that I felt that way, but I guess I wasn't above the allure of greed.

chapter3

"**Y**ou messing with me right?" Ray said, in response to what I just told him about the FBI visit.

"No, I'm serious," I said. "This feels like Déjà vu!"

"But, what else did they say? Ray asked.

"Nothing really," I said, "Like I told you, the main differences this time are these guys are FBI, not Philly PD. And they want to hire me as a consultant, so I'll be close to the case. Oh, and the Senator's daughter is the victim this time, so it's major."

"Yo! You have to be the luckiest writer ever!" Ray said, "How fucked up are you that all these mo'fuckas wanna copy your work. You said you haven't given them a response, right?"

"Yes."

"Good," Ray said, "keep it that way for now. I'll make a few calls and I'll call you back later. In the meantime, get some sleep bro. The next few years might be another whirlwind of cash flow and exposure."

"What are you thinking?" I asked, unwilling to end the call.

"I'm not sure yet," Ray sounded sincere, "I'm thinking we play it a little differently this time. Instead of doing all the media blitz like the last time, I think we can get another book from this. It's time for *Tilted Grin* to rest. I don't know if you've been reading the literary blogs, but they're beginning to call you a one-hit-wonder because your last two short stories have been extensions of Tilted Grin. They're saying you got lucky with it because of the serial killer. Working closely with the FBI will surely give you some inside information and unique knowledge for a new book. We can leverage this with the publishing company when it comes time to negotiate your advance."

"That sounds fucking awesome," I said with a huge grin on my face, "I think that might work. And as for the critics, yea I've been reading what they're saying, and to some extent, I agree with them. I think it's time for something new. I like your plan. Let's go with it."

"Cool," Ray said, "but get some sleep please. I will call you later. Let me make a few calls and confirm some things."

Despite Ray's repeated warnings I only managed two hours of sleep before the eagerness to know what laid ahead crept all over my thoughts. I laid still in bed for about half an hour then the sound of my phone belligerently demanded my attention.

"Hello," I said, without screening the caller.

"Mr. Cosmen," the baritone voice was remarkably formal, "this is Agent Tristan Taylor and I was just following up on our discussion from this morning."

I cursed at myself for not screening the call before answering. I had nothing.

"Umm," I said, trying to organize my thoughts. "Can...can you please.... Umm, call back in... about two hours?"

"Sir," Tristan remained formal but persistent, "we will need to know something by today. I don't want it to—"

"Call me in an hour," I said forcefully, derailing his thoughts.

That seemed to do the trick. He agreed, and the line went dead. Now fully awake, I walked out to the living room and tried to distract myself with belated tasks until I heard from Ray. I glanced at a manuscript I was working on, but it didn't appeal to me, so I tossed it aside. I checked the notes emailed to me from the producers of the show on the ID Network, but that too was dull. I needed to hear from Ray. The idea of writing a new book, this time with full access from the FBI's point of view, was exhilarating. So far, the reports on this new killer detailed the sloping smiley faces at each scene, and his victims have been women and children. But that was it as far as the similarities go. I was sure the FBI had more information, but that was all that was released to the media. I longed to be with the FBI behavioral specialists to glean some of the methods used in building a feasible profile. In Tilted Grin, I glossed over this part of the story with mountains of colorful words and clichés obtained from innumerable television shows and rudimentary google searches. To listen to the lingo directly from the source, I believed, would lend a level of credibility I desperately needed to be taken seriously in this genre.

I waited for almost an hour before my phone finally buzzed to life. It was Ray.

"Hey," I said eagerly, "so what's the plan?"

Ray noticed the seriousness in my voice, and he too went straight to business, "Let's do it! We'll get a new book out of this. I floated the idea with some of my contacts at the publishing company, and they said if you can gain that level of access with the FBI and you are able to intertwine that in a well-written novel, the advance will be huge, and so will the sales. They said you might even make it to Oprah's Book Club with that one. No pressure."

That's exactly what I wanted to hear. Not Oprah's Book Club, though that would be great too, but I wanted his plan to mean a new book. I was itching to get started.

I believed I was ready to prove to the world that *Tilted Grin's* success was not a fluke.

"I'm ready," I said calmly, hoping to suppress my excitement. "I'll call the FBI and let them know I'm in."

"Before you do," Ray lowered his voice, "just remember it is important you get a lot out of this. So, it'll help if you can befriend one of the agents. You know, like a buddy or something. Someone to talk to informally, and hopefully get some really juicy details, because you know they will not grant you access to everything they do. They will make sure—"

"I know, I know," I said, not in the mood to be lectured. "I'll get what I need for the book, trust me."

"Okay," he said. Then he added, "By the way, you know the 10th anniversary of the original killer's death is in five weeks. Do you think this is related somehow?"

Ray's words caught me off guard. The killer from ten years ago committed suicide while in custody in Texas. It bothered me why I had not remembered this fact, and it created a new question in my head as to why the FBI agents didn't mention it during their visit.

"Yea, I knew that," I lied, "but I'm not sure how this is related, but when I see what they have, I can make a better connection."

"Well," Ray continued, "I was thinking about a few media runs to mark this anniversary. I can get you a spot on Fallon, Noah, or Colbert, and maybe talk to the publishing company for a 10th anniversary release of *Tilted Grin*. Maybe change the book cover?"

"Ok," I said half-heartedly, "but I don't know what my role as a consultant fully entails, and I'm not sure how they'll feel about it. I know I won't be talking about the new case, but the similarities between both cases will definitely draw attention to it. What do you think?"

Ray thought for a minute, then said, "You're right. I can scratch the television angle, but still do the 10th anniversary release. We have to profit somehow from this anniversary."

"But it's not even the 10th anniversary of the book's release," I said, "It's for the killer's death."

"Yea, I understand that," he said dismissing my concern, "but we can still spin it somehow. We won't specifically call it the 10th anniversary of the book release, but we also won't call it 10th anniversary of his death either. That would sound like we're celebrating his life. Don't worry. We'll find a way to market it."

The morality issue I felt ten years ago had since disintegrated. Ray's relentless pursuit of ways to profit from this ordeal had blinded me from all the principled stances I once took. My life had completely changed from what it once was. I now own three homes: a condo in Brooklyn and Los Angeles, and a four-bedroom beach house in Rehoboth Beach, Delaware. The beach house was a suggestion by the mature black couple that rented out their cabin during the creation of *Tilted Grin*. The property was not as secluded as the cabin, but during the off-season, it provided a serene and charming backdrop I deemed apropos for writing.

"Okay," I said reluctantly, "but besides a new cover, what would make people buy the same book?"

"It won't be exactly the same," the haste of his response implied that he anticipated my question. "We'll add information about the real-life killer from ten years ago. We can gather news reports and include that in the new print to give it a little more edge. People will gobble that shit. That will hold them till the new book comes out."

I sat in awe and marveled at the ease at which the ideas came to him. I knew what I was getting with Ray, but I found myself continually amazed seeing him in action.

"I can't even argue that," I said, surrendering, "that makes perfect sense. I'll just—"

I heard a beeping sound on my phone. It was the same number I had failed to screen earlier.

"Hey, Ray, this is the FBI agent calling. I'm gonna switch over. I'll talk to you later okay."

"Cool," Ray said, "remember to call Palmer, and don't promise them anything. Just keep your—"

"Ray, I gotta go," I said, and switched over before he had time to further protest.

"This is Ebenezer," I said, in a tone lower than I intended.

"Hi, this is Agent Taylor," the familiar baritone sounded. "You said you would call in an hour. I waited and sir—"

"I'm sorry about that," I merged in smoothly, showing remorse. "I had a few projects that made me lose track of time. Anyway, I will be willing to come on as a consultant. How does this work? Will you be here with the papers or do you have an address where I can meet you guys?"

"Papers?" Agent Taylor sounded confused. "What papers?"

"I'm sure you know I'll need to sign a contract before any of this can happen. And I'll need my lawyer to look over this contract."

It was clear they were not ready for this development. An uneasy minute was wasted before the baritone materialized on the line. This time, his words fled his lips with a reluctance that seemed new to him.

"Umm ok. I...I guess we can do that. Can you stop by with your lawyer around 3 p.m. tomorrow?"

"Well," I began, "I'm in Rehoboth and my lawyer is in Queens, New York. I can let him know about it as soon as we end this call, but I can't guarantee how fast it'll take. It's about a four-hour drive."

"Well," the confidence in the baritone voice reemerged, "can you let us know? Tuesday at 9 a.m. would be the latest we can do."

"Good," I said, "I'll be heading back to New York by Tuesday evening for my show on Wednesday anyway."

He gave me the address and added, "Okay, talk to you soon."

As promised, I placed the call to my lawyer, Matthew Palmer, and I gave him a quick rundown of what was happening. To my surprise, he happily accepted the offer and promised to be at my place in five hours.

I called the FBI agent, and then my agent, and brought them up to speed with the information I deemed useful for their roles in the development before finally trudging up the steps for a well-deserved rest.

chapter4

BLAINE GRUBBER stepped out of the sunlight and into Sláinte Pub and Grill, a dimly-lit bar and restaurant near the 30th Street train station in Philadelphia. The space was filled with patrons dressed in all shades of green, partly due to the Irish beginnings of the establishment, but mostly due to an unfailing loyalty to their beloved Eagles. On multiple TV screens across the busy expanse was the game between the Philadelphia Eagles and the Seattle Seahawks. It was the fourth quarter with less than two minutes left on the game clock. Blaine was well versed with the inconsistent relationship between game clocks and actual clocks. He knew, depending on how close the contest was and how many timeouts each team had, two minutes could stretch as long as fifteen minutes in real time.

He was unbothered. Patience was one of his greatest strengths.

He walked up to the bar and managed to get the bartender's attention. He too was fully engrossed in the head bashing on the screen.

"Let me get a Guinness stout," Blaine's voice was low, close to a whisper, but he knew the bartender read lips well. He had been here many times, but as a different person.

"You got it," he said, then quickly added, "need a glass?"

Blaine shook his head no.

As soon as the bartender walked off to tend to his order, the room erupted in a thunderous roar. The Eagles had just intercepted the ball and, in essence, dashed all hopes the Seahawks had in tying the game. Blaine offered a wry smile that stood in stark contrast to the boisterous cheers from everyone else in the room. His smile had nothing to do with the fortunate outcome for the Eagles. He could care less about football. Blaine was happy the game clock would now imitate the real clock because the Seahawks were out of timeouts. The crowd would disperse soon, and his prey would come into full display.

His smile widened.

chapter5

This time I was wide awake when I heard the knock on my front door. For about ten seconds, I wondered who it could be before it dawned on me. Although he promised he would be at my place in five hours, Matt had actually shown up eight hours later which was fine by me because it gave me enough time to catch up on forfeited sleep due to series of unforeseen events.

"Wuddup Matt!" I said, opening the door.

"Yo! EC!" he responded as he walked in.

Matt was one of the few friends I acquired after my celebrity status. Our friendship began when he represented a group of black teenagers in a class-action lawsuit against a co-op natural food store in Brooklyn. Even though the judge did not rule in his favor, I appreciated his courage. I befriended him and soon realized he genuinely believed in his decision to represent those youths, and he was not doing it for the attention. I would often tell him, "You're a cool white boy. You're definitely invited to the cookout!"

"I thought you said you'd be here in five?" I teased.

He sucked his teeth, "Man, traffic was crazy!"

"As a lawyer, you really suck at this lying thing," I said, tongue-in-cheek.

"Hey," he raised his right hand in mock surrender, "sue me, ok!"

Matt tossed his backpack on my couch and walked to the closet to hang the vinyl suit bag he carried over his shoulder.

"Are you hungry?" I asked, as I walked to retrieve the TV remote control on the couch.

"Come on man," he said casually, "you know I'm always hungry! Why do you always ask that?"

I shook my head, "Well, this is not Queens or Brooklyn, so let me know what you want because everything will close in about an hour."

"It's only 6pm!"

"Yea but it's also Rehoboth on a Sunday during the off season!"

"Well, what about that seafood joint we went to the last time? Are they open?"

"No, they closed at 5 today."

"Well, pizza or Chinese will do then."

I reached for my phone and ordered two large pizzas and an assortment of Chinese delicacies.

"Are you expecting anyone?" Matt asked.

"No, why do you ask?"

"All that damn food," he exclaimed. "Who's gonna eat it all?"

"You!" I said.

He chuckled and continued towards the bathroom.

By the time he came out, I was already glued to the television watching the news about Senator Gibson's daughter. For the umpteenth time, the newscaster on CNN regurgitated everything they knew about the story thus far. They highlighted its eerie resemblance to the *Tilted Grin* Killer from ten years ago, and how the looming anniversary of the killer's death could be the inspiration for this copycat effort. Experts on psychopathic behaviors were asked of their opinions and each spewed words and terminologies to accentuate the impressive reach of their intellect. One expert hypothesized on the killer's inability to express emotions such as fear or distress. He gave an example of when you clap your hands behind a person's back, a normal reaction would be to startle, but with a psychopath, responses are typically flattened. They barely startled and their palms stayed dry. Another expert delved deeper into the role empathy, or lack thereof, displayed in this ordeal. Hurting others would leave a psychopath numb and it would seem as trivial as eating with your mouth full. I felt a surge of pride knowing that my fictional character had partly inspired a social phenomenon of this magnitude. This sensation, however, was short-lived when the third expert was asked of the direct impact my book had on the offender. Rather than answering the question directly, she embarked on a soliloquy, questioning the literary integrity of my work. She deemed it marginal at best and was a bit saddened with the nation's love affair with it.

"Damn!! Burn!!" Matt said.

I did not remember Matt was standing close, so his outburst startled me. I flinched, which caused him to burst out laughing. I joined him in the laughter if for nothing else, to avoid listening to the blistering review of my book. Although, I did find comfort in knowing that Matt's sudden appearance made me startle. It meant, according to one of the experts, that I was not a psychopath.

"Well, everybody can't like your shit," I said, in an attempt to dismiss her words.

"She's hating because she didn't think of it first," Matt said.

I didn't know if he was serious or not, but I appreciated his attempt to make me feel better.

I heard a knock on the front door.

"The food is here!" I said excitedly.

"Yea!" Matt let out.

Over dinner, we finalized the plan to meet with the FBI. I called Agent Taylor afterward and confirmed our meeting for 3 p.m. the following day.

chapter6

Matt was dressed in a blue Armani suit and brown Oxford wingtip dress shoes. In the five years that I have known him, his sense of style was one thing he never allowed to suffer.

"Even when I lose, I'm winning," he would say.

For me, my ensemble was simple. I wore a pair of blue straight-fit jeans and a white collared tee shirt beneath a brown jacket. My shoes were a flat low-top sneaker that allowed me to step effortlessly with each stride. Even before my fame, I had never understood the thrill people derived from stylish dressing. I respected it but hated the need to participate in it. Now with my raised status, the pressure to conform was not as strong. I controlled most of the situations I found myself in and I could dress as I pleased. The last time I was in a designer suit was seven years ago when I was a runner-up for the Edgar Awards held in New York City, and my girlfriend at the time, Joseena, urged me to look presentable.

"You ready?" I asked Matt.

"Yes sir!" he responded sprightly. "I look good; I feel good, of course I'm ready!"

I smiled as we walked towards my black 2019 Nissan Maxima. Another quirky detail about me: I'm not into cars. The Maxima was a purchase I made after my 2008 Honda Accord failed, for the fourth time, to take me from Brooklyn to Rehoboth.

We drove north, past Cape Henlopen State Park and onto Coastal Highway. We stayed due north for about forty-five minutes before exiting on the left onto US 13N. Being that it was December, the roads were void of beachgoers which made for a very smooth ride. Matt and I did not talk much. Whenever he was preparing for an official quest, he only spoke when necessary, and that was not the case for the duration of this ride. I didn't care. My mind was already churning through the plot twists for my next book. My only goal at the moment was for a productive meeting and a chance to siphon unique FBI knowledge.

We reached our destination in about an hour and the sight before us was demonstrably sad. The house sat at the end of a weed-infested gravel driveway. The flowers, which I imagine had once given it an air of coziness, had gone wild. A few patches of paint remained in the places protected from the weather, and the yellow sunflower was now more of a nauseating white substance. The foundation having subsided, the entire house drooped a bit to one side which gave the impression that the house had simply given up any hope of ever being a home again.

"What the fuck is this place?" Matt uttered as he got out of the car reluctantly. "Are you sure we're at the right address?"

We both stood there, unwilling to proceed without any encouraging signs that the house was safe to inhabit. We stood for an uneasy minute, before noticing the front door open.

"Ebenezer Cosmen!" A wimpish voice called out.

It was Earl Tomkievich, the other agent that accompanied Agent Taylor the previous morning.

"Yes," I responded, then added, "I was unsure if we were at the right place."

"Yea we get that a lot," Agent Tomkievich snickered, and ushered us along.

Matt and I walked across the unkempt front yard. I could hear him muttering under his breath for having to subject his modish Armani and wing-tipped shoes to such atrocity. I found it comical, but I knew this was neither the place nor the time to laugh. Fashion was serious business for him.

"You alright, man?" I asked.

"Yup." He said, curtly.

I introduced Matt to Earl before we all walked into the space.

I noticed the way Matt examined him, and it dawned on me that I should've warned him of his odd shape.

"The team is upstairs," Agent Tomkievich said. "We will be down in a minute."

He disappeared to a room upstairs, leaving Matt and I alone in the shabby-looking space. The area was populated with barstools and basic office supplies like phones, fax machines, printers, and copiers. The wooden serrated floors glinted from sunlight spilling through the thin orange curtains. The opening a few steps ahead of us resembled a makeshift kitchen with a tall white refrigerator, and next to it were three midsized stools each carrying a microwave. This was not the image I had in mind when I thought about working with the FBI. I was not expecting the sensationalized version like I saw on television, but I also wasn't expecting this level of despair.

"Mr. Cosmen," a voice called out behind me, "I'm Special Agent Frank Gordy, and I run this operation."

He was about my height, 6'3, and at least thirty years older than I was. His gray hair was cropped in a buzz cut giving him an air of military presence. He was clearly

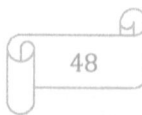

serious about his fitness regimen, and he made this fact known by the undersized blue short-sleeve shirt he wore that barely covered his bulging biceps.

"Nice to meet you, Sir," I said, extending my right hand to meet his waiting palm. "And this is my lawyer, Matt Palmer."

"Nice to meet you," Matt added.

"Do you mind if we go somewhere private to talk?" Agent Gordy asked.

"Sure," I said, "after you."

The floor creaked in protest as we three walked across the room. I saw more agents coming down the steps and I wanted to pause to take a good look at them, but I had to keep up with the deceptively fast Agent Gordy before I lost him. We entered a small room, furnished with four chairs and a round table. A black trashcan stood idly in the corner next to a gray fan.

"Have a seat," he motioned to the chairs in the room.

Matt and I took our seats across from him and waited.

"Okay, here's the deal," he began almost immediately, "I'm not gonna bullshit you. I'll let you know right now, your presence here is not welcomed. You're only here because Senator Gibson thinks it would

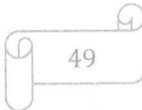

help the investigation. For some weird reason, he thinks your involvement with the case from ten years ago helped with apprehending the suspect. I can't blame him. The rest of the country is of the same belief as well. And I know you've done well for yourself because of it. I understand why he wants you, but me personally, I don't care. I've been around long enough to know how these things work. As long as you stay away from the investigation and make sure nothing gets leaked out to the press, you're alright with me. However, with the agents out there, I can't speak for them. They're young and ambitious. They've put in a lot of work, so I'm sure you can understand their frustration when someone like you shows up just because you wrote a book. They will not make this experience easy for you. I promise when I'm around, I will make sure things are under control, but I won't always be here."

"So, are you saying my client will just watch all day and say nothing?" Matt asked.

I was glad he found the courage to speak. I was completely floored by the agent's unguarded candor, and I wanted to run as far away from this godforsaken building.

"No, I'm not saying that." Agent Gordy explained, "He can ask questions. He can offer opinions, but I'm just letting you know that your analysis will not be respected.

Like I said, if I'm around, you won't have anything to worry about. I can set them straight, but that will not always be the case."

"So, in your view, or the senator's, what's the need for my client to be here then?"

"I can't speak for the senator," Agent Gordy said forcefully, "you'll have to ask him that if you—"

"I find it difficult to believe that you would take on someone new in your operation and not question it," Matt interrupted the FBI agent. "And just moments ago, you said you understood why the senator wants my client. What was that understanding?"

I thought Matt was brave for doing this.

"Mr. Palmer correct?" Agent Gordy confirmed.

"You can call me Matt."

"Mr. Palmer," Agent Gordy neatly ignored his request, "I answered that already. I said for some weird reason, he thinks your client's involvement with the case from ten years ago helped with apprehending the suspect. And not that it's any of your business, but I've established with the senator that your client will be tolerated mainly as an observer. His opinions and questions will be endured in small doses and that's it. Any move by him to jeopardize this investigation will result in his immediate termination, and maybe more, depending on if any laws are broken."

"Is that a threat?" Matt asked.

Agent Gordy let out a mild laugh. "I don't make threats."

Due to no contribution from me, the atmosphere in the room was thick with ego and testosterone. I had seen this fearlessness from Matt in the past, but I felt like Agent Gordy would be a foe to wisely avoid.

"Can you give us some time alone?" Matt asked.

Agent Gordy looked at his watch, "Okay I have a flight to Washington in about an hour, so please make it quick."

When we were alone, Matt turned to me and asked in a whisper, "What do you think? Do you think you can handle it?"

Despite of all the conflicting voices in my head, I answered yes.

"Are you sure?" Matt continued, "You can easily—"

"Yes, I'll do it." I repeated, resolutely.

"Okay, then."

When Agent Gordy came back in the room, he had some papers for me to sign after Matt was done perusing its contents.

"So, do you have any questions or concerns?" he directed the question at me.

"Yes," I said, "just one question. I know you said I won't be able to say much, but how much access do I get? Will I be in the room when decisions are being made about profiling and when thoughts and theories are being assembled?"

Agent Gordy looked me in the eye, "You will be pretty much present during the day-to-day operations, and when you're not physically at a location, we will try to organize video conference calls twice a week to keep everyone abreast on what's happening. Of course, in case of dangerous field missions, you'll have to sit it out due to your lack of training. No one will lose sight of the fact that you're a civilian, so don't worry about being in the line of fire. But just remember, nothing gets leaked out to the press unless we want it to."

I nodded.

"Any more questions?"

I shook my head and Matt did too.

"Great! Come on, let's go out there and I'll introduce you to the team."

He began by introducing me to the odd-looking pair, "I believe you've met Agent Taylor and Tomkievich."

"Nice to meet you again," I said politely.

"This is Agent James Brady, Todd Gabbert, and Nikkyta Hunter," Agent Gordy continued, then quickly added, "Two more agents just left for the airport. They are flying with me to Washington, so I guess you'll meet them next time. When we reconvene on Thursday, we can talk at length of everyone's expertise. Right now, I have to head out before I miss my flight."

After exchanging compulsory parting words with Agent Gordy, I turned and shook hands with my new colleagues offering each of them a practiced smile. Agent Brady was short with blonde hair. The color of his eyes looked unnatural, so I safely concluded he wore contact lens. Agent Gabbert was about my height and he was the only one without a suit or dress pants. I felt a little connection with him on the strength of our relaxed attitude towards fashion. His long bushy eyebrows, mustache, and sideburns occupied almost his entire face.

Then there was Agent Nikkyta Hunter. With Agent Gordy gone and Agent Taylor in the improvised kitchen pushing some buttons on the microwave, we were the only two African-Americans left in the room. The first thing I noticed when I shook her hands were her eyes. All the doubts I had due to that small testosterone-filled room with Agent Gordy were instantly melted away when I peered into her eyes. She was so beautiful, so... seductive. She was so different from anyone I had ever seen that I could not understand why no one in the room was as disturbed as I was. Why was no one else's heart wild like the breeze when stirred by the sighs of her smile? Why did everyone not go mad with the movements of her jaw when she uttered, "Nice to meet you." From the flight of her hands, the gilt of her grin, the gentle movements of her facial expression—I did not miss a single one of her gestures. I had never believed in love at first sight, but damn, this was close.

The ride back to my beach-house was not as quiet. Matt had a lot to say about the entire process, but the testy exchange with Agent Gordy dominated our time for a while.

"You just got to let him know you're not intimidated because of his position," he said, smiling. "Honestly, I like the guy."

"Whatever bro," I said, "you were about to get your ass kicked."

"Na, I'm a lawyer. He wouldn't dare."

I chuckled and left it at that.

Matt continued by emphasizing the need to be vigilant with everything that was happening, and to take heed of Agent Gordy's warning.

"I know, I know," I said.

"And one more thing," he said, with seriousness in his tone, "don't do anything with Agent Hunter, at least while you're on this case. I saw the way you looked at her. They might not notice, but I know you, and I know how you get around beautiful women."

"What are you talking about?" I offered a flimsy defense, "I wasn't even looking at her like that."

"Whatever man," Matt said unimpressed by my guard, "I know you. Please don't do anything stupid. At least wait till the case is over."

"Whatever," I said, unwilling to admit anything.

We rode in silence the rest of the way. Before I made it home, we stopped at the seafood joint he requested the day before for shrimp, crabs, and beer.

"So, what's the damage for this service you just rendered?" I asked.

"It's pro bono," he said, between mouthfuls.

"Why?" I protested, "You drove all the way from Queens to check—"

"Consider this payment," he said, pointing to the mess of broken crab shells on the newspaper. "Plus, I'm sure you and Ray are planning something big after this mission. You can pay me then."

I nodded as I sucked out the shrimp from its skin. The FBI committed to paying me $4,300 a month until the killer was in custody or killed. It was a nice payday for doing nothing. But I was not doing it for the money. I would have worked for free. I needed the unique knowledge to use for my next book. At least this is what I tried to tell myself. The truth now, however, lay somewhere between that and the unforgettable image of Agent Nikkyta Hunter.

chapter7

Matt headed back up to New York shortly after we left the seafood joint that evening. I tried to convince him to stay until the morning, but he had to appear in court early on Tuesday. And even though I had to get back to the city by Tuesday night to prepare for my TV show, it felt like my weekend in Rehoboth had not been as productive as I would have liked it to be. So, I decided to scrutinize a few pages of my manuscript instead. It would make up for the spontaneous night out with Tim, his girlfriend, Jasmine, and her friend, Cassandra, the other day. It felt like a lifetime ago, considering all that had transpired. A part of me wanted to call him and share some of the interesting developments of the past two days, but the thought was quickly erased from my mind. Even though I considered Tim a good friend, like Ray, our friendship began before my success. But unlike Ray, I didn't have the same level of trust, and with the FBI as my new employer, the need to have trusted friends was paramount now more than ever.

I managed to edit about five pages before drifting off into a deep sleep. I felt like I owed my body that much, considering the task ahead. I didn't know for sure what to expect, but I wanted to be fresh and attentive when interacting with my new colleagues from the FBI.

Agent Gordy's dire warning had tugged me deeply in a variety of different directions. First, was fear and an unwillingness to immerse myself in such hostility. Then, after trading stares with Agent Nikkyta Hunter, I felt an outpouring of courage course through me. I wanted to impress her. I had to prove to her that I was much more than just a writer of fiction. That, in spite of my lack of training, I had the mettle and determination to keep an erect posture in the face of a deranged killer.

Now, as I drifted through the remaining minutes of the day, the truth began to set in. I knew certain things to be accurate beyond a reasonable doubt. One was the eagerness to work with the FBI regardless of how the agents felt about me. Senator Gibson, a man who I never met, demanded my presence and I still hadn't a clue as to why. Agent Gordy insinuated it had something to do with the bogus belief that I helped solve the case from ten years ago, but I have no idea why he, or anyone, would believe that when I had mentioned, on multiple interviews, my lack of involvement with the case.

I went to bed with these facts seared into my brain.

The sound of my phone buzzing on my nightstand woke me up the following morning. It was 5:42 a.m. I was a bit disoriented when I reached for it to see who was calling.

I sat upright after realizing the caller.

"Hello."

"Ebenezer," Agent Gordy's undeniable voice sounded on the other end of the phone.

For the first time I realized I hadn't considered how to address him.

"Eh ... yes ... Commander?" I managed to spit out, recalling something I might've heard in a movie.

"I didn't mean to call so early," he said, alertly. "I know we agreed that you would start on Thursday, but there's been a slight change to that plan. Senator Gibson is giving a press conference at 9 a.m. today and has requested your presence there. A plane is waiting for you at the Dover Airforce Base as we speak. Agent Brady will be there to receive you. You're expected within the hour."

"Expected at the press conference or at the airport within the hour?"

"At the airport," he responded firmly.

"Ok, umm, I ...," trying to organize my thoughts. "Do you, sir? ... I mean Commander, do you know why my presence is needed? And why I would need to take a plane to get there? Where am I going?"

"I don't know why the Senator requested your presence," Agent Gordy said calmly. "You need a plane because it's the fastest way to get to Washington."

"D.C.?!" I blurted out. I didn't mean for my words to escape my lips with such alarm.

"Yes, D.C.," Agent Gordy reiterated. "I recommend you get going immediately. The plane is waiting."

"Oh, right! Ok, sir ... I mean, Commander ... I'll be there."

"Good," he said.

I felt a rush of adrenaline blast through my blood as I darted towards the shower. I really didn't know the source of my excitement, but it felt good to be requested. It felt like I was really part of the team. The notion that Senator Gibson explicitly demanded my presence gave me a thrill I had never felt before. For a fleeting moment, I thought about my show with the ID Network. I was needed in New York no later than Wednesday morning for the taping. If this press conference with Senator Gibson ran past schedule, this would become a foreseeable issue. The producers of the show strongly expressed the need to be on set by the start of filming. The proper equipment, custom backdrops and graphics were all there; and although it was possible to record remotely, we were sternly warned to reserve such times for true emergencies. My new development with the FBI, I thought, definitely constituted an emergency. I decided I would call when I was on the plane to D.C.

Within less than 25 minutes, my Maxima was snaking through the narrow streets leading out of my neighborhood and travelling northbound on US Highway 13 towards Dover Airforce Base. My mind iterated through a myriad of reasons as to why my presence was needed, but I couldn't seem to settle on anything that made sense. I called Ray, waking him up from his sleep, to ask for his opinion.

"I know yo' dumbass didn't impress them that fast," he teased. "I really don't know, bro."

"Whatever, bro," I said, contemptuously. I was not in the mood for Ray's indiscreet honesty. I didn't think I had impressed anyone either, but to be told so imprudently fouled my mood a little. "I gotta go," I said rashly.

"Alright man, keep me updated," he said, oblivious to how his words made me feel.

I thought about calling Matt for a second opinion, but he was another one with an incautious delivery. I wasn't ready to listen to his successive disregard of my abilities. I settled my frame into the seat of my car and rode the rest of the way in silence as my mind drifted, wondering what lied ahead.

I entered Dover Airforce Base through its main entrance, along the west side, and was instructed by a lanky security guard to park my car next to a blue and gray van with government tags. The base was massive and spread widely in all directions with indistinct buildings dotting the distance. The last time I was there was two years before when I brought my father, an airplane enthusiast, for their annual air show. The show included static displays of military aircrafts and equipment, and flight parades of the Thunderbird and Blue Angels demonstration team. It was a sight to behold.

I took a moment to draw in the cool breeze of the season and caught a glimpse of colorful leaves gyrating on nearby trees in the crystal blue sky when my thought was suddenly interrupted by the sound of my name. I looked over my shoulder and saw two figures walking towards me. It took a few seconds to recall their names before they stood within an arm's reach.

"Good morning Agent Gabbert, Agent Brady," I said, nodding my head politely as I stretched out my right hand.

I noticed Agent Gabbert grabbed my hand willingly, but not Agent Brady. And when he did, he barely made eye contact. In my mind, I quickly listed him as one of the unhappy few who Agent Gordy warned me about. I was glad Agent Gabbert seemed accessible so far because our shared attitude towards fashion was a topic I hoped we could bond over later. He was dressed in an ill-fitting khaki pants and a blue checkered collared shirt. His shaggy hair matched the unpredictability of his clothing choice and for a moment, I wondered if he was dressed as an undercover. Agent Brady, on the other hand, was sharply dressed in a tailored brown suit and a dark blue overcoat with the FBI's logo boldly printed in yellow on the left breast pocket.

"All set?" Agent Gabbert asked.

"Umm, yea ... I guess," I responded unsurely.

"I know," added Agent Gabbert, "this has to be new for you, but you'll get used to it. Just remember to always pack light."

I smiled as I got in the blue and gray van with my metal gray Samsonite luggage. The men situated themselves in the front seats as the van coughed to life. Minutes of serpentine maneuvers around the base brought us to a medium-sized charter jet sitting idly in an open airfield. From my vantage point, I could see the pilots in the cockpit acknowledging our arrival.

"Alright," Agent Gabbert said, "it's go time. We have to be in D.C. in less than an hour."

The insistence in their steps prompted me to match their haste although I wanted to pause and relish in this moment, soaking in the drastic turn of events my life had taken. Just two days ago, I was a somewhat successful writer. Now, I worked for the FBI, albeit just as a consultant, but it included boarding flights in the middle of an airfield to meet senators in D.C., like distinguished men of great importance.

Agent Brady led the way with a small briefcase and a backpack. I followed dutifully, rolling my luggage and Agent Gabbert brought in the rear with a book bag he had thrown messily across his back. The airplane was white with two broad red stripes extending across its body. On the tail, was the lettering CH-800 written boldly in italics. I didn't know what it meant, but of all the things I was unsure of, this mattered the least. I made a mental note to revisit it later. The air-stairs were narrower than anticipated, so I held my luggage in front of me as I carefully trudged up the steps. Due to his height, Agent Brady was able to walk through the door, but Agent Gabbert and I needed to bend a little to pass through. At the entrance, one of the pilots shook our hands and welcomed us on board. He held my hand a little longer and eagerly informed me he was a fan of my work. I was taken aback by his words. Thus far, I had only interacted with people who either knew nothing of my work or were irked that my work was the only reason for me being there.

"Thanks," I said graciously.

"So, when are we expecting another thriller from you?" he asked.

As I was just about to form my lips to answer, I heard agent Brady warn sternly that we had no time for informal chatter. Although I agreed with him, my preconceived notion of him made it difficult to appraise his words without an ulterior motive.

"We'll talk later," I said to the pilot and turned towards the cabin.

It was an eight-seater medium-size jetliner with two full-service lavatories at the front and rear of the plane. The space was divided into three sections for increased privacy. Agent Brady had already assumed a seat in the first section. I wanted to be nowhere near him, so I continued towards the rear. I wished I was last in line, so I could sit close to Agent Gabbert and build more rapport with him during the flight. Now I had to pick a section and hoped Agent Gabbert would follow suit. I went to the last row in the aircraft, close to the other lavatory. I wasn't sure why, but Agent Gabbert struck me as the type to sit in the back, next to a toilet.

I was wrong.

He found a seat in the front next to Agent Brady. I couldn't imagine them having anything in common, other than being white, but I guess I was wrong. From where I stood, I could see the two were already chatting light-heartedly and it made me wonder if they were talking about me. Why did I even trust him to begin with? I asked myself. Because he can't dress like you? What the hell is wrong with you? Thankfully a sound in the lavatory ended my wayward thinking. It was the sound of a toilet flushing and moments later the rattling of the washroom's doorknob. This meant there was a fourth passenger on board that I was unaware of, but I didn't recall seeing any other luggage.

I hastily opened my laptop and stared intently at the screen to appear busy. I smelled her perfume before I saw her and my heart immediately skipped a beat. Standing before me was the striking image of Agent Nikkyta Hunter. I didn't think it was possible, but she looked more radiant today than our first encounter. Her gray pantsuit hugged her curvy physique with a perfection that suggested she was carved by one of the great fifteenth century artists. I was happy to be sitting down, because I could not imagine how my unreliable legs could have withstood the weight of my body.

She occupied the seat across from me and simply asked, "How're you doing?"

I realized I needed to get over the feeling immediately if I were to get anything meaningful from this experience. With my mild celebrity, I had interacted with Keke Palmer and Janelle Monae—two women I also found breathtakingly attractive, and I was able to preserve my composure around them. We met when we were all in discussion to adapt Tilted Grin into a television series on Hulu. They were cast for the leading roles and I was taken on as the series' executive producer. There had been a slight delay with the project but continued reassurance from the executives at Hulu that the show would happen gave me hope.

"I'm well, and you?" I said, summoning my inner calm.

"Eh, besides the norm, I guess I'm fine," she said, flashing her beaming smile.

I didn't know what she meant by the norm. I wanted to ask her, but a voice in my head thought that it might be too forward to ask.

"Nice morning to fly," I offered instead.

What the fuck?! Are you a meteorologist now?

"I guess," she offered with a sigh, "but I'll never get used to this flying thing."

I interpreted her words as one who was scared of flying. I enjoyed learning this fact about her. Nikkyta had unknowingly dissipated my ability to think and comprehend effectively both times I had been around her, so I loved the notion of seeing her helpless to a phobia. In my head it put her at a disadvantage and put me in a position to rescue her.

"You know it's the safest form of transportation," offering a fact I read in an article.

"Yea, yea, yea," she said dismissively. "I've heard that nonsense plenty of times, but that does nothing to explain how I really feel. It's not natural for humans to fly. Our role is to roam the earth either by foot, car, train, boat ... anything that doesn't defy gravity."

I let out a hearty laughter.

"You sound just like my agent," I said, then quickly realized how pompous that made me sound. "I mean he's my childhood friend. He shares the same feelings about flying. Every time we go somewhere, he's constantly complaining about flying and how unnatural it is for something that heavy to tear through the sky with such blinding speed."

"Is that what you think I'm doing ... complaining?"

Oh shit! I thought to myself. ""Eh ... no, no, no, not like that. I mean he-"

"Calm down," she laughed, revealing her dazzling white teeth that shined as a beautiful contrast to her dark chocolate skin, "I'm just messing with you. These guys tease me about it all the time, but I don't care. Your agent is a smart guy for thinking that way."

I laughed, hoping to give off the impression that I knew her words had been in jest. I wished she had not noticed Ray's description as an agent. I wanted the conversation to flow between two ordinary people, not one that needed an agent.

"So, how do you manage the spontaneity of the job?" I asked, hoping to change the topic.

As she was about to respond, the captain's voice crackled on the speaker above us.

"This is Captain Stephenson. Welcome aboard. We will be in the air in about five minutes. There's a system going across east to west along our path, so this will cause for slight turbulence during our ascent. But once we reach our flying altitude of 15,000 feet, we're expecting a smooth ride and an on-time arrival in Washington D.C. The weather in Washington is currently 32 degrees Fahrenheit with mild winds. Please secure your seatbelts in preparation for takeoff, and we hope you enjoy the flight."

"See?" Nikkyta said, almost immediately. "Turbulence already. This is what I'm talking about."

"It's only mild turbulence," I said, hoping to provide comfort. "Trust me. You won't even feel it."

"Oh yes I will," she retorted. "I feel everything when I fly."

I was about to continue with the chatter when I heard the revving of the twin-jet engine. It would've required me to raise my voice, close to the point of shouting, in order to be heard. I decided I didn't want her to hear me screaming. I would wait to reach our cruising altitude before I spoke. In the meantime, my thoughts transported back to when I was a kid listening to Ray go on incessantly about the peculiar experience of flying. I chalked it up to his need to always find something to talk about. I had never once considered the experience as unique as he claimed, especially being the son of an airplane enthusiast. Even before my fame, my father had taken me onboard everything from small propeller jets to massive Boeing and Airbus planes. Now, sitting next to this black beauty, and hearing Ray's voice in my head, made me pause to relish in everything that was happening. The airplane thundered across the wide stretch for about fifteen seconds, with the trees and houses dashing by with dizzying swiftness, and then I felt it tilt, causing a sensation of weightlessness. The plane wobbled as it climbed through higher altitudes, and in about two minutes, I felt it levelling off. The deafening roar of the engine drowned the dissonance noises coming from different areas of the plane. I stole a glance at Nikkyta, and noticed she was stock-still. Her face was expressionless as she gripped onto the armrest as if her life depended on it. I wanted to laugh, but I didn't feel like I had built enough bonds with her to do so just yet.

"Are you okay?" I asked.

She nodded, despite the conflicting expression on her face.

I didn't question the accuracy of her response. Instead, I opened my laptop and stared at my manuscript while waiting for her body to appear relaxed before continuing our conversation. Thankfully, the captain's voice materialized on the speaker to inform us we were in the clear and it was a smooth ride to DC.

In an instant I noticed the tension in her face settle, and her grip on the armrest was released.

"Are you okay?" I asked again.

"Yea, I'm fine," she said, forcing a smile. "I don't like take-offs and landings. And also, turbulence."

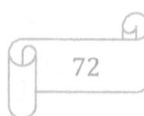

I wanted to spew another fact, but I decided against it. It was useless. I offered a supportive nod instead.

"So, you never answered my question earlier," I said.

"What question is that?"

"I asked how you dealt with the spontaneity of the job."

"Oh, I'm sorry," she said, "I mean, it's not that bad. I've been with the Bureau for seven years now, so I guess I'm used to it. It's not a big deal anymore. In the beginning I missed my friends and family a lot, but I quickly learned, in this profession, to be anything worth a damn, availability is one thing you must have."

"Where's your family from?" I asked.

"Charm City baby!" She almost yelled with shameless pride in her voice.

"Really!" So, is this fear of flying a Baltimore thing?"

"No," she chuckled. "Why do you ask?"

"My childhood friend is also from Baltimore."

"You mean your agent?" she clarified.

I felt she was being cheeky by continually referring to Ray as my agent in spite of my description.

"Yes," I said.

"So, does that mean you're also from Baltimore since y'all were childhood friends?" she asked.

"No, I was born and raised in Philly. Ray, that's my friend's name, and I grew up together 'till his parents divorced when we were in the eighth-grade. He moved with his dad's family to Baltimore, but we maintained our friendship the entire time."

"Cool," she said. "I didn't really grow up in Baltimore myself. I'm a military brat, so I've lived everywhere. San Diego, Kansas City, Fort Worth, Tulane for college, and for the past five years, D.C."

"Hold up," I said, raising my hand in protest. "You lived in all these places and you're still scared of flying?"

"Yup," she said, without a hint of shame or regret, "and I will always be like this no matter where I live."

I chuckled.

I loved the ease with which our conversation now flowed. She smiled easily at my words, and I no longer had to overanalyze everything I said. It settled me. I felt comfortable putting her in the column of agents that tolerated my presence and in turn, were allies, which, by my count, was two-and-half. I knew for sure Agent Gordy tolerated my presence. He told me that much, just as long as I remained within the confines of his guidelines. Agent Hunter, so far, had proven to be a dependable ally. I knew I was being too quick reaching these conclusions, but it felt right. Agent Gabbert was on the favorable track until he decided to sit with Agent Brady, and with that act, earned him the half point. Agents Taylor and Tomkievich were a bit of an enigma; I was still a bit confused on where they stood. Agent Brady was not liked. He gets nothing. Zilch. Nada.

Now with my new ally, I decided it was time to test the sturdiness of our relationship. I began to ask questions to clear up the haziness in some of the things I had dealt with so far.

"I began with something light, "So, what's with that house in Dover? It looks really rundown!"

She snickered.

"Yea, I know," she said, rolling her eyes. "The Bureau acquired that property about a year ago when local police brought us in. It was foreclosed about three years ago, so we got a deal for it. Agent Tomkievich actually suggested it. He figured it would keep us close to the action, but at the same time, maintain our cover. As you know, these killings have been going on for at least a year now. It started in Bridgeville, then Seaford, and so on. We don't spend the night there; it's just a staging area for official business. We go to nearby hotels to lodge for the night."

"These killings began a year ago?" I blurted out, unable to mask my shock. "Why did you guys wait until now for my services?"

"No offense, but we don't need you," she said flatly. "We have this under control."

I was stung a little bit by her words, but I didn't show it.

"So, tell me something then," I said, leaning closer so I would not be loud and risk being heard by the two agents in the front. "If everything was so under control, why am I a consultant then? Why am I needed for this emergency press conference?"

Her reaction was unexpected. She broke out in an uncontrollable laughter leaving me clueless as to how to act.

"I'm sorry," she finally said after almost a full minute of laughing. "I didn't mean to laugh like that. You were serious, too!"

"Serious about what?" I asked.

The direction of the conversation was beginning to upset me, and out of petulant spite, I was considering rescinding the full point I had given her moments ago and placing her in the same half-point category as

Agent Gabbert, leaving Frank Gordy as the only agent in my corner.

"Are you serious about not knowing your role here?" she clarified, no longer laughing. "You really don't know why the Senator wants you?"

"No," I said, a little embarrassed for not being able to make the logical leap she seemingly expected out of me. "I wouldn't ask if I knew."

"Ebenezer," she said, and I realized it was the first I've heard her call my name. It sounded so sweet, so lovely, so heavenly...

Focus!

"You are a celebrity. You wrote a book that's somewhat connected to this case. He's a politician and your involvement commands some votes, no matter how small. You motivate a fraction of his constituents," she continued, "that's it. It's all politics, baby! What's that Jay-Z song again? Politics as Usual."

"But ... but ... his daughter died from this," I said, trying to find a rationale. "How can ... could he do that?"

"Oh, he is saddened by her death," she said with a straight face, "but you can't deny the uniqueness of this opportunity. He may never get a chance like this in his life. He is a white, 48-year-old, charismatic, good-looking Democrat with a viral video of him rescuing a black woman being attacked by her white boyfriend. Now couple that with the death of his daughter at the hands of a murderer, possibly riding the unenviable coattails of a notorious killer from 10 years ago, and you, the famous writer that seems to inspire-albeit innocently-all this to begin with. If that's not a path to presidency, I don't know what is. God Bless America," she finished sarcastically.

I was speechless and a little uncomfortable for not being able to make the rational jump myself. My presence for Senator Gibson's press conference was just to encourage a small corner of the electorate.

"Am I the only one who doesn't know this?" I finally asked.

"As far as the group, yes."

"How come Agent Gordy kept telling me he knew nothing of my involvement?" I asked, not caring if I had broken a code of discretion by letting her know the boss was being stingy with information.

"It's not his job to tell you," she said flatly. "You would've figured it out anyway."

"Why did you tell me?"

"I don't see the big deal in telling," She said, "Agent Tomkievich and I are the only two behavioral scientists in this group, so it's our job to unfurl that level of details from a situation. Agent Gordy might not have been able to break it down to you with the same level of simplicity I just did, so rather than confusing you, it was safer to have you figure it out on your own. He, just like the rest of these guys, is a hardcore street agent. They thrive in the field, knocking on doors and chasing down bad guys. They have minimal ability to sort through the thin nuances of human behavior. Agent Gordy understands the politics of it all, the balancing act required to keep the political brass happy and simultaneously live up to the oath he took. That's why he's able to tolerate your presence. Most of these guys haven't been around long enough to acquire that skill, and some of them never will. That's why your presence here was a huge point of contention in our morning meetings. It took some time, but Agent Tomkievich and I were able to convince them of your innocence. He made it a point to visit you with Agent Taylor two days ago just to explain in detail if you had any uneasy questions."

I sat quietly for the duration of the flight. The haste at which our conversation crossed the simplicity of Charm City to the profound nuances of human behavior frightened me. I needed time to process the avalanche of information that was just dumped upon me. I needed time to reflect, to understand and fully maximize my time here. If I were to believe her, I have three agents to focus on—Gordy, Hunter and Tomkievich. Gordy, because he was my boss, but Agents Hunter and Tomkievich's minds were all I really needed for my book. They possessed the depths I would need. As behavioral scientists, they could take me down the different layers of a killer's mind and share exclusive content that would forcefully announce my arrival as a formidable author in the genre. As I imagined this life for myself, another thought barged into my head. One inspired by ethics and principles. I questioned the difference between Senator Gibson and me. In our own unique ways, we were both trying to benefit from the death of his daughter. He was trying to transform the emotions of a nation into votes, and I wanted to ride the unexpected connection of her unhinged killer towards literary greatness. I knew the voice I'd end up listening to. I'm not proud of it. I wished I owned a higher principled stance.

chapter8

BLAINE GRUBBER did not expect to be at the bar for this long. He was on his fourth bottle of Guinness and his prey had yet to move. Five bottles were his limit upon which his trademark caution and strong attention to small details would suffer. He felt an intense urge to use the bathroom, but he worried his prey might decide to leave.

Damn it! I should've gone after my second bottle, he thought.

A few minutes later, while listening to the boisterous guffaw from his prey, Blaine decided it was safe to use the bathroom. *She's not going anywhere,* he thought, hoping to reason with the opposing voice in his head. He quickly walked towards the secluded corner where the bathroom was located, and made a right. Thankfully, there were no lines. Most of the patrons had since left the establishment following the Eagles' victory to continue the celebration in the streets. The space appeared hygienic, considering the belligerent state of the fans bursting in and out. Inside the bathroom were two stalls and four urinals. One of the stalls seemed occupied and the other was wide open. If he could help it, Blaine preferred to use the stalls regardless of his intent. He was the type to go to the bathroom, sit down, and pee.

He didn't care. He loosened his belt, and his oversized pants immediately dropped down to his ankles. Seconds later, he let out a sigh of relief. He exited the bathroom without washing his hands and rushed back to his seat to resume watch of his prey. When he returned, his heart dropped. His prey was nowhere to be found. Frantically, his eyes swept about the poorly lit space, but there was no one of significance. Just a few stragglers at the bar and an interracial couple in a dark isolated corner pressing their lips passionately against each other. The televisions had been muted, and in their place was the grungy sounds of heavy metal music.

Blaine panicked.

He aggressively demanded the bartender's attention who at the time was taking the order of a drunken couple.

"Wait your turn asshole," one of the couples slurred, reacting to Blaine's impatience.

Blaine ignored her. This was not a fight he needed at the moment. Locating his prey dominated every other inclination. He rapidly instructed the bartender to close out his tab and marched towards the exit, leaving his half-full sweaty bottle of Guinness stout on the bar top. As he was about to walk out, he heard the bartender call out that he forgot his card. Frustrated, and a bit embarrassed, Blaine walked back to retrieve his card. He pushed through the double doors and stepped onto the street. The poor lighting inside the pub now matched the gray gloomy sky outside. Binged before him were the usual hustle and bustle of this part of West Philadelphia. The 30th Street train station stood boldly in front of him. To his right were tall buildings that lit up the Philadelphia night sky and in all other directions were uneven buildings of Drexel University, Amtrak, and other small establishments. The people walked decisively to and from the train station. Some of them ran in order to make their trains, and the drivers sped through yellow lights narrowly avoiding pedestrians that walked sluggishly. The city was a little more active this evening because of the Eagles' victory, and a few young men, all dressed in jeans and different jersey numbers screamed, "E-A-G-L-E-S, EAGLES!!!"

Blaine found everything about football revolting, and he hated that he had to travel this far, to this football-crazed city, for his prey. A prey that appeared to have evaded him. It was not as if his prey had a distinct physique. Not too tall, or too short. Not too fat or skinny. His prey had proportional body parts that seemed to mesh well with the characters that paced determinedly all around him. It was 6:43 p.m. Early for his prey, Blaine thought, but he also remembered the big announcement tomorrow. It was paramount that his prey was present for this announcement. This would mean his prey needed to go back to Delaware soon. Go to sleep maybe. *Too bad it would be the last thing she ever did.*

This realization prompted a slight smile.

The smile was quickly stifled when he recalled he had work to do. He joined the masses and raced across the street towards the train station's entrance. He pushed through the doors and immediately made a left. Blaine paced with the determination of someone that frequented this space. He moved impatiently yet sure. He adeptly avoided the construction workers, slow movers, and panhandlers. He was hopeful her movements had not changed from the information he gleaned a few weeks ago. After few turns and after trudging up a mild ramp, Blaine ended up at the gate for the trains to Wilmington, Delaware. He struggled to maintain stable breathing, and this made him very angry. He blamed the bottles of Guinness for his feebleness. He was not drunk but felt the alcohol surging around in his head, making him woozy and unsteady on his feet. He canvassed his surroundings for his prey, and then he permitted a huge smile. His efforts rewarded.

chapter9

I had been to D.C. many times in the past. First was with Ray when I visited him in Baltimore, and later, as a famed author for one event or another, but never as an invited guest of a U.S. Senator. It offered a privileged view of the most powerful city in the world. A black Lincoln town car was waiting at the bottom of the single runway at Hyde Field when we landed. With swift efficiency, we all deplaned and walked towards the idling vehicle. I had a lot of questions, but I held back. I thought it would be wise to follow blindly until I was alone again with Nikkyta. The driver of the town car was a burly-looking man dressed in a black and yellow uniform and a hat that managed to cover his head. I heard Agent Brady refer to him as Moses when we got closer to the car. With the FBI's knack for packing light, the trunk of the car sufficiently held our luggage. Agent Brady sat in front and Nikkyta and I got into the backseat, and almost immediately, the car peeled off leaving the aircraft in the distance.

"Is Agent Gabbert not coming with us?" I asked Nikkyta.

She shook her head.

"Why not?" I asked.

"Agent Gabbert is on a different mission for the day. He will be rejoining the team on Thursday."

Suddenly, her mood was all business. It was as if I had imagined the aviophobe beauty next to me who was proud to call Charm City her own. Nikkyta stared closely at her phone and Agent Brady leafed through the morning's Washington Post that was on the front seat. They all acted as if riding through the nation's capital and not having to deal with the demands of traffic was standard. We meandered through private roads often reserved for the president or other world leaders. I wanted to play along, to act as nonchalantly as they were, but I couldn't. It all felt like an extravagant dream. A dream which began with a visit from the odd-looking pair of FBI agents at 4:32 a.m., meeting at Dover Air Force Base, to the early morning call at 5:42 a.m. to be in Washington D.C., to now maneuvering effortlessly through one of the busiest and most heavily guarded cities in the world to meet with a US senator that explicitly demanded my presence for his emergency press conference... Putting it all together this way now made me question everything. I was now considering the possibility of all this being part of an elaborate hoax for a television show I was unaware of. It suddenly sounded like Ray's handiwork as an attempt to keep me relevant in pop-culture. Perhaps to make me go viral.

I've been so stupid! Come on! Ray's from Baltimore! So is Nikkyta. They probably knew each other, and they decided to plan this. He knows I'm a sucker for dark-skinned women. She's probably not even an FBI agent. There's no way they could have all this access, yet they stay in that shabby-looking house in Dover. This is the government! They have the money. They are known for wasting money! How could I be so stupid?!

"Are you okay?" Nikkyta asked.

"Yea," I flinched, then quickly added, "Why do you ask?"

"Umm... we're here." She said matter-of-factly, "It's time to go."

I looked around my surroundings and realized we were no longer on the road. We were in a neighborhood that looked far removed from the gigantic D.C. architectures.

"Where are we?" I asked.

"We're in Georgetown," Nikkyta said, as she exited the vehicle. "Senator Gibson lives here."

I stepped out of the car and was immediately enthralled by the sight around me. It was the perfect intersection of historic charm and upscale freshness. The stone sidewalks, grand buildings, and the tree-lined neighborhood introduced me to a side of D.C. I had never seen before. And for the second time in this exploit, a beauty that came close to love at first sight struck me. The Senator's home was on Wisconsin Avenue. It was a Victorian-style edifice with an intentional rustic look and feel on the exterior giving it an added touch of class and elegance. It was early so the waterfront dining and cobblestone streets were empty. A few runners and cyclists raced past us in their wireless earbuds and cellphones wrapped around their biceps. I caught a whiff of the scent of one runner, and I thought it smelled of the privilege and class often reserved for the one percent.

"Is this where he's having the news conference?" I asked.

"You ask way too many questions," Agent Brady blurted out. "Why don't you just be quiet and follow us?"

His words felt like being blindsided by a swinging door. He had been quiet since he discouraged the informal chatter with the pilot, so I thought his plan was to leave me alone, and only speak when necessary. That was my plan. Considering what Nikkyta shared on the flight, I determined to only interact with Agent Hunter and Agent Tomkievich, the behavioral scientists. And of course, Agent Gordy because he would be my boss.

Agents Gabbert, Brady, and Taylor were only to be interacted with when necessary. My question had not been to him, so I was unsure why he felt compelled to answer. I entertained no delusion that I could take him in a fight. In spite of his height, the man was built like an ox, and I was certain he packed the strength of a few oxen, but I knew I needed to say something, if for nothing else, to set a precedence that I was not to be talked to that way.

As I was about to talk, I heard, "James, chill out. The man was just asking a question."

It was Nikkyta.

I was grateful for her protection, but the primitive part of my brain struggled with the idea of a woman coming to my rescue. Over the years, I'd been in countless symposiums championing women's rights. These events spoke chiefly from a vantage point of the women as victims, and in such roles, men like me put forth a fervent defense against those cowardly men. Now as a victim, and a woman as my liberator, I felt strange. It was a role society had not prepared me for, yes, but it was also a role I didn't want to be in.

"No, the press conference will not be here," Nikkyta said, "it will be at the capitol steps."

I wanted to ask a follow-up question, but Brady's issue and Nikkyta's rescue made me think better of it. I decided to remain quiet and follow them blindly; however, in my mind, I made a vow to react swiftly, with words of course, the next time Agent Brady said anything rude to me. I desperately needed another opportunity to let him—and maybe Nikkyta— know I was not afraid.

Agent Brady pushed the doorbell when we reached the massive beechwood door. I heard some movements inside, and moments later, the door yawned open to reveal a middle-aged Hispanic woman standing before us. She held on firmly to the remains of her youthful good-looks in her black form-fitting dress and bright yellow high-heeled shoes. Her chest was adorned with a thin gold chain that held the letters J.G. which I later learned the letter stood for her deceased stepdaughter, Jennifer Gibson.

"Hi," she said, offering a beautiful smile. "You must be the FBI agents. I am Marcella Gibson, but you can call me Marcy. Please come in. My husband will be down shortly."

As we all walked into the plush living space, my mind instantly went to the conversation I had with Nikkyta on the flight here. I recalled her listing the reasons why this was the most opportune time for Senator Gibson to run for presidency, and I realized she missed one: a white man with a gorgeous Hispanic wife. That type of coalition would no doubt, command a healthy chunk of the constituent.

We all sat on a wide three-seater couch and awaited the Senator's arrival. Agent Brady kept his attention on the newspaper he was reading in the car. Agent Hunter stared insipidly at a painting on the orange wall in front of us, and I tried to keep my composure. I wanted to take in everything but still give off the impression that it was not my first day on the job. We waited for about six minutes before hearing the clattering of footsteps down the spiral staircase. I refrained from looking, but only because the two agents beside me did not. They continued with whatever they were doing as if they visited senators daily...or maybe they did. They finally looked up when the footsteps were almost within an arm's reach from us. Agent Brady was the first on his feet to grab the senator's waiting palm.

"Agent Brady," the Senator's booming voice filled the room. "Nice to see you again. How was the flight here?"

"Not bad, Senator," Agent Brady said, smiling.

Seeing the muscles on Agent Brady's face contort into a smile was weird. He seemed innocent, like a harmless boy incapable of upsetting anyone.

As if it was a campaign event, Senator Gibson effortlessly transitioned to the next smiling face. "Agent Hunter," he said, holding her eyes a little longer, "How're you doing this morning? Sorry for having to wake you up so early."

"Eh," Nikkyta brushed it off, "that's part of the job. Just wished I didn't have to fly here."

"Hahahaha," Senator Gibson let out a hearty laugh. "Are you still scared of flying?"

"What do you mean still?" Nikkyta said, tilting her head to the side. "That'll never go away."

Their repartee informed me that they'd been in quite a few casual settings before. I didn't know why, but this realization was unsettling. It ruffled me internally. Nikkyta was not my girlfriend, and quite frankly, I shared no belief that she would ever be, yet her chummy deportment with the senator disturbed me. I wanted to barge out of the elegantly-designed space and return to the life I was used to. A life where I could make characters disappear with just a few keystrokes on my IBM computer. A life where I was not disrespected by short FBI agents, and where a drop-dead beauty, like Nikkyta, willingly submitted to my needs.

"E-be-ne-zer," the senator said, taking great care to sound out each syllable in my name. "I've heard a lot of good things about you. It's a shame we have to meet under these circumstances, but life happens you know! Oh, and congratulations on the success of your book. Although, I must confess, I haven't read it. I'm sure you understand life in Washington does not allow for much leisurely reading."

"That's quite alright," I said, struggling to maintain my smile.

The scene felt awkward. Here I was, shaking the hand of a man whose daughter had just been brutally murdered by a psychopath that seemingly drew inspiration from a book that I wrote. And he didn't seem to be down or gloomy about it. He was more upbeat than everyone in the room. *Is this the makings of a great leader,* I thought, *or a greedy politician that stopped at nothing for a political edge?*

"Perhaps when I retire," the senator continued, "I will find time for such leisure. Nice to meet you!"

Then he quickly turned to his wife and said, "Honey are we all set?"

"Umm," she sounded unsure. "We were until they walked in."

I felt her eyes settle on me and it made me nervous. I feared that she was about to react the way a normal family dealing with grief would. I thought she was about to express her deep disregard for my literary efforts and me and demand that I stay as far away from their family as possible. That would make sense. It would be the only reaction that would normalize this scene.

I was wrong.

Instead, she said, "You can't wear that in front of the cameras. The optics need to reveal something a little more subdued and less flashy."

I was wearing a pair of black jeans and a lightning blue Express shirt under my Levi's jacket. I thought I looked presentable, but apparently not. Of all my choices, this was the best I could offer. Everything else in my luggage was too casual.

"This is the best I have," I said, and then quickly defended my position further. "I was not anticipating any of this, so I didn't pack much. I've been at my beach house in Delaware, and I live in Brooklyn."

"Delaware, huh," Senator Gibson sounded excited. "What part?"

"Honey we can continue that conversation later," Marcy interrupted, "We only have ten minutes; we gotta get going."

She took a couple of steps back and eyed me from head to toe a few times.

"Give me one second," she said, and hurried upstairs.

Everyone in the room was clueless on what was going to happen next. The senator raised both hands and walked away smiling. "She's the boss."

Marcy didn't leave us in suspense for long. She came down, holding a dark blue sports coat.

"Try this on," she said, tossing the article of clothing in my direction.

Just when I thought this day would not steer any further into the bizarre, here I was trying on a sports coat that belonged to a United States senator, and perhaps, a future president. *Somebody please, wake me up from this nightmare!* The senator and I were about the same height, but I was at least fifteen pounds heavier and it showed. The coat sleeves were a little too short because my mid-section consumed most of it. I was embarrassed.

"Thank you," I managed as they all stared at me like an art exhibit.

As we were about to walk out, Marcy walked up next to me and adjusted a few things on my new look. The scent of her perfume rushed through my nose. It was delightful.

"Thank you," I said again.

"You're welcome," Marcy said, as we all walked out.

Standing outside, was the imposing posture of Moses. He was now standing in front of a limousine. A few paces ahead, was the Lincoln town car we rode in earlier. The confusion on which car to ride in was quickly answered when I saw Agent Brady and Agent Hunter walk towards the car. Agent Brady got in the driver's seat and adjusted the seat to compensate for his height, and Agent Hunter sat in the passenger's side. Naturally, I sat in the back. I looked behind, just in time to see Marcy enter the rear of the limo with her husband soon after. Moses controlled the vehicle, and soon, the two-car motorcade was on its way to the capitol steps.

chapter10

Before we walked down the steps, we were given a strict set of instructions on what to do. On multiple occasions, a short stubby-looking man reiterated the need to suppress the urge to smile at any point during the press conference.

"This is a somber event," he said, in a voice much more imposing than his posture suggested. "We just lost Jenny. We miss Jenny. We are doing this for Jenny."

This was the first time Jenny Gibson was mentioned—the first time it felt like the mournful event it was meant to be. Even though it was rehearsed, it gave me a little sense of relief in seeing the subdued reaction from the senator and his wife.

We all nodded. The team consisted of the Senator and his wife, Agent Hunter and Agent Gordy who joined us when we arrived at the Capitol building, and me. Agent Brady did not make the team. In my mind I joked that he didn't meet the height requirement. It was stupid and petty I know, but I was comforted telling such jokes at his expense. At the base of the steps were a ton of reporters each gripping either a microphone or a smartphone. Behind them, were their respective camera people angling for the perfect position that would capture all of the Senator's expressions. A podium stood at the bottom of the steps, and I figured that was where we would be. It took about two minutes to make it to the bottom step, and we all assumed our positions that had been meticulously decided by the senator's team. Senator Gibson stood in front of the podium, and to his left, was his wife, Marcy. She was dressed in all black and their facial expressions had morphed to exactly what to expect from a grieving parent. Nikkyta stood behind Marcy with a stoic expression on her face. Her gray pantsuit hugged every lovely curve on her body. To the senator's right I stood in my black jeans and borrowed coat. There was no need to instruct me not to smile because I have not found any part of this ordeal comical. Behind me was Agent Gordy. His biceps were noticeable in his dark gray suit.

"Good morning," Senator Gibson began somberly, "sorry to have you guys out here so early on this brisk Tuesday morning. I will make this brief. I wish I didn't have to do this. I wish no parent would ever have to do this. No parents should be pre-deceased by their sons or daughters. We, unfortunately, have had that experience."

The senator paused and held Marcy's gloved hands a little tighter.

"A week ago," the senator soon continued, "we received a phone call from the Delaware State Police that will forever change us and will certainly change everything I do in my life from this point on. Our beloved Jenny was brutally taken away from us by the hands of a deranged killer. The dreams and aspirations of our bright little girl were snatched cruelly by this unhinged murderer. I will miss my daughter. We will miss our Jenny. Even as a devout man of God, I cannot pretend to understand why He deemed this fate suitable for us. I want to ask God why. Why does He think we deserve this? What had my Jenny done to earn such a gruesome end?"

He paused again, this time reaching in his coat pocket to fetch his handkerchief.

Our immediate surrounding was silent like the early hours at a graveyard. The only discernible sound was the blaring horns of the D.C. traffic that we effortlessly avoided on our way here. I was amazed with the senator's performance and the ease at which he summoned the tears and assumed the role of a grief-stricken father following his enthusiastic demeanor at his Victorian home in Georgetown. It was remarkable. It made me wonder if he ever loved Jenny as he currently proclaimed. I was not naïve to the notion of politicians as liars. As a matter of fact, I had led charges against them in the past, especially during election seasons, embarking on ardent verbal skirmishes with my friends about their deceitful ways. Aside from President Barack

Obama, I had placed a high level of distrust against every politician that I'd ever talked about regardless of their political party or professed stance on issues I cared for. As a result, Senator Gibson's act should not have come as a surprise to me. But it did. Perhaps it was because I thought issues like death was an agreed topic to reveal decent and genuine human qualities.

"But I have been doing a lot of reflection over the past week," the senator's commanding voice snatched back my attention. "I have prayed a lot. I've asked for forgiveness for thinking this way, and I know with His infinite mercies, I will be absolved of my sins. I trust God. I know there's a reason for this, but it's not within our comprehension as humans to understand it immediately. I might not know His intentions, but I know it's never to mislead us, and with this, I am at peace. My family is at peace. We thank the American people for their continuous support and prayer, and we know that we will come out of this stronger with the memories of Jenny fueling us to achieve our goals. Thank you. God bless you, and *God Bless America*."

As soon as the senator uttered the last word on the prepared speech, a disharmony of voices emerged from the reporters below each screaming for the senator's attention. He surveyed the reporters for a bloated second before pointing to a red-haired woman in green fitted pants and a black coat with the letters CNN in red and white.

"Good morning, Senator," the voice of the reporter sounded. "I'm Brianna Segall from CNN, and first we would like to extend our condolences to you and your family."

"Thank you very much Brianna."

"Senator, are there any viable leads to who might have committed this murder?"

"Thank you," the senator said politely, "Right now we have the law enforcement working diligently on this, and I think it would be unwise to reveal any findings. Those you see behind me are Special Agent Gordy and Special Agent Hunter. They are part of the team working this case, and I am certain that they will bring this killer to justice. I have my full faith in the FBI, and I know they will deliver just like they have always done."

"But are there any leads? You alluded just now that there might be some findings but just unwise to reveal it. Does that mean—"

"Brianna," the senator barged in, a little forcefully to relay his message, "I don't want to say anything that might jeopardize the progress made by the fine men and women of our law enforcement. As you know, Jenny was not the only victim of this killer, so it would be unfair to the other grieving mothers and fathers, brothers and sisters, and uncles and aunts to say something carelessly and end up threatening a conclusive resolve to this matter."

His answer seemed to quiet the reporter from CNN and he effortlessly pointed to the next reporter.

"Good morning, Senator," the reporter said, "Patrick Davis from Fox News. First, we at Fox would like to offer our heartfelt condolences for your loss."

The senator responded with a nodding gesture to show his words were appreciated.

"We know the original killer from ten years ago drew his inspiration from the fictional novel, *Tilted Grin*. We also know that the 10th anniversary of the killer's death is in a few weeks. Any concerns that this might be the motive for these fresh killings? And is that why Ebenezer Cosmen is here? How concerned are you that his books inspired these killings?"

My heart skipped. I felt a knot in my stomach, and at that moment, I was glad I had not eaten anything. There was a strong chance it would've surged back up and stolen the show. Despite my invitation, I never thought I would factor much in this press conference. I was expecting to only be there for the viewers watching at home. I imagined at least one person might recognize me, but not from the pool of reporters. Being a mildly successful author, unlike musicians or movies stars, we, for the most part, could walk through airports, malls, and other public places without being noticed. I loved the anonymity of it.

"Ebenezer is here as a consultant for the FBI. This young man," he turned to look at me and placed his hand on my shoulder, gently patting the smooth texture of his sports coat, "due to no fault of his own, is placed in an unenviable situation by this mad man. Ebenezer should not be castigated because of the perverse choices of this deranged killer. He is a good author and even a better person, and I refuse to live in an America where creative minds are bottled-up out of fear trumped up by an unhinged murderer. We will not allow it. We stand firmly with Ebenezer as he continues to polish his craft and entertain readers for decades to come."

My reaction was that of surprise, shock, disbelief, amazement, wonderment, awe, stupefaction, bewilderment... I was unable to heed to the warnings of the stubby-looking man. My facial muscles relaxed, and my lips curved upwards into a smile. I stole a glance at Nikkyta and noticed that she too was smiling. The senator's unflinching endorsement of my work gave me a sensation I hadn't felt in a long time. I stood there like a proud son, after a radiant endorsement from a father, and the feeling was euphoric. I could only imagine what Ray must have been feeling at that moment. I'm sure his mind was working on ways to exploit this development. He would probably prompt the host of my next show appearance to play the clip as my introduction. The rest of the press conference returned to the tragic event they all came for, but I was no longer listening. The glowing recommendation put me on a natural high, and I was unsure if I ever wanted to come down to earth. The press conference ended about twenty minutes later after four more TV networks were able to ask a question or two.

We rode back in silence to the senator's home in Georgetown. This time, the cobblestone sidewalks and waterfront dining spots were populated by the locals and tourists. These groups were differentiated by the ones that stopped to take pictures, no matter how mundane, and the ones that appeared to take their privileged space for granted. The senator's limo pulled up to the sidewalk and the Lincoln town car followed closely behind. A third vehicle accompanied us on our return trip. It was a van filled with close advisors and campaign officials. Even though the senator had yet to formally announce his intention to run for the presidency, it was the chatter all over the news. A little over a week ago had been the rumored date for his announcement, but the news of his daughter's death happened first. However, despite the tragedy, the pundits still believed his intention remained the same, and the death of his daughter would only delay the inevitable. When we all walked through the door, the first thing I noticed was an elegantly arranged feast of an assortment of breakfast sandwiches and pancakes.

"Tea, coffee, and juice are over there," Marcy announced, pointing to a spacious corner in the room.

The senator grabbed the remote control and turned on the television. He switched the channel to CNN, and some of his staff sat while others remained standing. Everything around me was happening too fast, and I struggled to keep up. I managed to find an untenanted corner and claimed it as my own. I looked about the room and noticed everyone engaging in their own little conversations. The senator was talking to his campaign manager, the short stubby-looking man that I thought would admonish me for smiling at the press conference after his stern warning not to do so. I noticed Nikkyta across the room talking to Agent Brady. I wanted to join them as they were the only familiar people in the room, but I thought better of it. I was not in the right mindset for Agent Brady's mood, so I remained in my corner and observed. Soon, I saw the campaign manager urging everyone in the room to be quiet as he raised the volume on the television. Seeing myself on the screen and the ill-fitting sports coat embarrassed me a little, and nothing felt of greater importance at that moment than to remove the coat. I wondered if Nikkyta had noticed how hideous I looked in the coat. I doubt if she would say anything, especially since we deplaned at Hyde Field. She had gone from an approachable colleague to all business. It made me wonder if that's what I would continue to get in the field. I wished she were a little relaxed; I would need that in order to converse at length for information needed for my book.

Almost everyone in the room offered their attention to the CNN reporter on the screen. The consensus was that the senator did well, and his press conference struck the proper tone. "He looked presidential," was the phrase the experts used incessantly throughout the segment. When it was done, everybody returned to their micro-chatter, and the room became impersonal again. I stood for about two minutes alone. I was beginning to enjoy my isolation when I noticed Nikkyta walking towards me. She wore a bright smile on her face as she approached. I felt my body tense and I prayed she wasn't appraising the unflattering coat I had on.

"Hey there, Mr. Author," she said in a playful voice, "congrats on the roaring endorsement. How do you feel? Has your agent called you yet? I'm sure your phone must be blowing up!"

"That was wild," I said, neatly avoiding her questions. "Did you know that was going to happen?"

"Know what was gonna happen?" Nikkyta asked.

"That he was going to endorse me the way he did."

"Ha!" she chortled. "Remind me to talk to you about all this when we're alone."

The prospect of us being alone was all I heard. It sounded delightful. I wanted to discard this political event and make that happen immediately.

"Okay," I said instead, "I need to find Marcy and give back this coat. My phone is also in my jacket."

"She's over there," she said, pointing to one of the many small groups in the room.

At that exact moment, Marcy looked and saw Nikkyta pointing in her direction, so she did us a favor and came to us.

"You guys did well today," she said, holding a glass of orange juice.

I did not recall doing anything worth commending. If anything, we disobeyed the instructions not to smile.

"Thank you," I said anyway, then quickly added, "I can get my coat now and give you back this."

"Hahaha," Marcy laughed. "You can keep it. Let me grab your coat."

She walked away, leaving no room to decline her offer. I looked at Nikkyta for answers and she returned my stare with a shrug. Moments later, I was wearing my Levi's coat while holding a new sports coat on my arm.

"How long are we staying here?" I asked Nikkyta who was still standing next to me.

"I'm waiting for Frank to let us know if we'll be flying back to Delaware today or Thursday."

"I still have my car at the air force base in Dover. Can I leave it there overnight?"

"I believe so," she said, "you're one of us, at least for now, so the same privileges are extended to you. But aren't you going back to Brooklyn tonight for your show tomorrow?"

"I was thinking about staying—"

I paused, wondering how she knew this when I haven't shared this information with her.

"How did you know that?" I asked. "We never talked about it."

"Come on Ebenezer," she said unconcernedly, "we're the FBI. We know these things. Why do you think Agents Taylor and Tomkievich came to your place that early? We thought you were heading back to Brooklyn early that morning, so we were trying to get you before you left."

I was unsure if I should be outraged over the apparent invasion of my privacy. I wondered if my constitutional rights were being violated, but considering the casual tone in her voice, my guess was such invasive breach of my confidentiality could be supported by formulating an elaborate legal jargon and attaching it to the widely flung issue of National Security.

"Well," I said, hesitantly, "I was thinking about staying in D.C. for the night to record the show remotely. All I need is a plain background and a laptop with a camera. I have the laptop and I'm sure hotel walls are plain."

"Interesting," she sounded impressed. "When is the filming?"

"Tomorrow morning, which reminds me, I have to call the producer of the show. I meant to call on the flight here, but I was busy consoling you and your fear of flying."

This made her smile.

"Whatever," she said tapping me lightly on my arm. "Go and make your phone call. I'll check with Frank on what's next."

I was alone again as she blended with the political operatives in the room. I placed a phone call to Todd Granger, the producer of the show on the ID Network.

"Hello?" a groggy voice sounded on the other end of the line.

"Hey Todd, it's Ebenezer," I said, a little more energetic than I intended.

"Who's this?" He almost yelled. I could sense the irritation in his voice.

"Hey Todd. Ebenezer Cosmen," I said, much louder than the first time. "Did I wake you? Can you hear me?"

"Eb?" he said now fully awake, "What the fuck man? Filming is not till tomorrow. I got a headache!"

"I'm sorry man," I said, lowering my voice now that he was alert, "I'm calling to let you know that I won't be there for filming. I have an emergency—"

"Bullshit," he said. "Come on man. Why are you really doing this? You know how much it cost the net—"

"Look," I said forcefully, regaining control of the conversation, "I won't be able to make it tomorrow alright! I'm with the FBI for the foreseeable future, and I—"

"Wait! What! What the fuck are you talking about?" He blurted out. "What the fuck did you do? FBI! Damn! Is it for tax evasion"?

"No, I didn't do anything wrong," I halted his thoughts before it began a rumor, "I'm consulting on their investigation of the *Tilted Grin* killer, so I don't really know when I'll be free. My guess would be till they apprehend the killer, and who the hell knows when that would be."

"Yea, yea, yea, I understand," he said. "Thanks for letting me know man. And good luck with everything."

I was not expecting to change his mood as quickly as I did.

"Thanks, man," I said, "so, for the filming tomorrow, is a blank wall and my laptop camera still enough."

"Em... absolutely..." he uttered. He said it in a tone that indicated he had more to say.

"What is it?" I asked. "You sound like you wanna say something."

"Ehhh I mean I probably shouldn't say." He sounded unsure.

"Come on man. Let it out."

"Do you think it's.... um... I mean, is it possible to feed the show some exclusive information from this case? I mean that's if it's not jeopardizing anything..."

"No, no, no," I said, derailing his train of thought immediately, "I was specifically warned not to leak anything. The slightest whiff of suspicion and I'm out."

I stopped short of telling him my hidden plan of using the details of this experience to write my next book. My response was enough to halt his ambitions.

"Alright, alright," he surrendered, "I won't be good at my job if I didn't try."

"Alright man, I gotta go," I said, "I'll reach out later to set everything up."

"Good luck man! Please be safe."

When the call ended, I checked to see my phone which seemed to be buzzing every three minutes. The message on the screen said I had twenty-seven unread messages. Even for someone of my status, that was a lot by 10:30 a.m. The only time I recalled having more was when the original *Tilted Grin* killer was connected to my book. I remembered having to turn my phone off in order to preserve my sanity. As I was about to check my messages, I felt a slight tap on my shoulder. I saw Nikkyta's beautiful face when I turned around.

"What's up?" I said.

"Frank said, barring any new development, we're all set till Thursday. He will keep up with the local police and update us as needed. Do you have any idea where you wanna stay?"

"I'm not well-versed with the area," I said. "Where would you recommend?"

"Umm... it depends on how much you want to spend?" She said, then jokingly added, "not to say that's an issue for you."

"I just want somewhere nice and walking distance from everything. I don't think I can get the same VIP treatment with the traffic that I've been getting all morning, and I don't feel like driving."

"For the right price, you can," she said. "It's all about money."

"Yea, I'd rather not waste that kind of money."

"Well," she said, looking away as if in a deep thought, "the Donovan is nice, and I don't think it's that expensive."

"Is it close to everything?" I asked.

"Yup. We can drop you off when we leave."

"Sounds good," I said, "when are we leaving?"

"As soon as I find James," she said, as her eyes scanned the room. "Oh! There he is! Hey, James!"

Before James made it to us, I slyly asked, "So, what do you have planned for the rest of the day?"

"Eh.." she began, unsurely, "I think I just want to enjoy my place for a while. I haven't been home in about four days. I might just look at the files from this case and relax."

I wanted to ask more, but James was already within an earshot range from us.

"Are you ready?" He asked.

Nikkyta nodded.

I noticed he didn't even bother to check if I was ready. It vexed me, but I maintained my composure. We said our compulsory goodbyes to the relevant people in the room. Senator Gibson shook my hand tightly and thanked me for everything. He made it a point to let me know he meant every word in his press conference. I thanked him for his kindness and joined my colleagues, who were waiting for me by the massive beechwood door.

The Lincoln town car moved slowly on Wisconsin Avenue and then made a slight right onto M Street. The shops and restaurants were now in full operational mode, and the streets were packed with a demographic that was comprised mainly of Caucasians. They all walked in different directions, on the phone, each laughing at their conversation. I wondered how many of them had read my book. Did they like it, or did they share a similar opinion as the expert on CNN?

I snapped out of my thought when we arrived at the Kimpton Donovan Hotel. The chic-looking building was situated on Thomas Circle right at the foot of the desirable 14th Street stretch with its line of shops, galleries, bars, and restaurants. When I checked-in, after a lackluster goodbye from Nikkyta and none from James, the attractive employee at the front desk informed me of the close proximity to the metro station and the White House. I was glad to be close to everything even though I had no desire to be anywhere near the White House or any politically themed space. With the euphoria now faded, the experience with the senator had drained the leniency I had for that world. As I walked towards the elevator, I realized Nikkyta and I never exchanged phone numbers. This awareness made me upset. I would've loved to reach out to her later for a bite and drinks.

The disappointment was evident in my steps as I walked out of the elevator. I moved lethargically wondering how I would spend the rest of the day without her. It was as if I've never known life away from her. I made a right onto a cozy carpeted hallway that led to one of their seventeen spacious suites. I opted for the suite because the price difference between that and the standard rooms was less than two-hundred dollars. It was close to one of the communal spaces with a rooftop lounge and swimming pool, but that meant very little around this time of the year considering the forecast for rain and a plummet in temperature later that night. My room, however, came as advertised. The palatial expanse offered over a thousand square feet of space. I relished in its dreamy details of marble bathrooms with unique spiral cocoon walk-in showers and floor-to-ceiling windows that peered out onto the urban action below. My view included the statue of George Henry Thomas perched boldly on a horse on Thomas Circle and an artery of roads connecting M Street, Massachusetts Avenue, and Vermont Avenue. The imposing structure of John Russell Pope's National City Christian Church stood northwest of the circle, and smaller buildings and neighborhoods gorged across the landscape. I immediately went through my routine whenever I checked in a hotel. First, I looked in the closet for the suitcase-stand and then placed my luggage on top. I fetched my toiletries and took them to the bathroom where I quickly assessed the space.

It was very impressive.

Next, I continued by taking off my shoes and plugging in my electronics. I started with my laptop. Making sure I had everything ready for the remote filming, then I connected my Alexa smart speaker on the nightstand away from me, and lastly, my phone. I only had fourteen percent of battery power left, and as I connected the charger to it, I realized I had yet to read any of my now 37 messages. Most of the messages were old friends and acquaintances letting me know they just saw me on TV with the senator. I smiled and moved on to the messages from Ray. His thoughts were strung along in ten consecutive messages with each new message escalating the contents of the previous. He was ready for the next marketing strategy. In the first eight messages, he laid out a rough-and-ready plan on how to merge the press conference in with the 10th anniversary release of *Tilted Grin*. His thoughts were unclear, and I was not in the mood to make sense of it, so I skipped the last two messages and moved on to the next one. My father and baby sister, Caroline, both acknowledged they saw me on television. My father's message read like that of a proud parent, while my sister's stayed true to form—an annoying little sister. She urged me to try and smile a little, that it was the only hope I had to end the curse of bachelorhood. I smiled at the message, but it seemed to prepare me for the last message in the queue. It was from my ex-girlfriend,

Joseena, whom I was engaged to for three years. The message simply read: "Looking chunky and uncomfortable in that coat E-bibs!"

On the face of it, the message appeared simple and unassuming, but for me, it packed much more significance. I cherished the fact that she noticed the coat. That she noticed my physique and the discomfort during the brief clip of me on CNN. At that moment, all thoughts of Nikkyta were disintegrated. Only Joseena occupied my mind. I wanted to see her, hold her, and tell her I wanted nothing more than to be around her. She was the only person I've really entertained the idea of spending the rest of my life with, but I did not have the maturity and wherewithal to validate my position. Cowardly, I used the excuse of her lack of spontaneity as a reason to end the engagement. Joseena had a nine-year-old daughter, Zora, from a previous relationship, so her movements were not as impulsive as mine. There was a great deal of planning before we did anything, and although this was a little bit of an issue, it was not as much of a deal-breaker as I had made it seem. Zora was smart, funny, and incredibly audacious. We connected well, and she even gave me the original nickname E-bibble which later condensed to E-bibs. I missed them both, but I knew that I was not ready. I was—and still am—unprepared for that level of commitment, and up to today, I live in regret knowing that I strung her along for as long as I did. We had since reconciled, but I was no longer allowed to see Zora. Such emotional ebbs and flows were unsuitable for a nine-year-old, and I agreed. Joseena and I texted during special occasions like birthdays, Christmas, whenever I was recognized for a literary feat, or when I appeared on television. I tried to keep up with her life on Instagram, and I guess, although I was not certain, she did the same. Now, alone in this magnificent room, I wanted her badly. In that exact moment, as if not wanting to be outdone, I felt my phone buzz to life. I imagined it was another acquaintance, reaching out to inform me of my appearance with the senator. I cursed at the phone for intruding in my delightful thought of Joseena. When I stared at the phone, however, I smiled, because it was a D.C area code and I desperately wanted it to be Agent Nikkyta.

chapter11

Agent Nikkyta reached out to know how I made out with the hotel booking and I was glad she did. Her interest allowed for a warm feeling within me. It appeared she cared. At least that was how I chose to translate her gesture. I wanted to ask how she got my number, but I quickly thought better of it. She had proven thus far that my efforts at shielding my personal information were as porous and ineffective as pouring water into a basket.

"So, how are the case files going?" I asked instead hoping to extend the conversation. "Did you find anything new?"

"I never even started," she said, "I got home and started doing other things."

"Yea, I know that feeling," I said. "Well, at this point, do you feel like there's something you might be missing?"

"Of course," she said confidently, "there's always something new to discover when perusing through case files. I'm just not in the mood for it right now."

Really, so what are you in the mood for? I thought.

"I understand," I said timidly, "I don't feel like doing much either. I just have to figure out where and what to eat."

"The last time I stayed there, I remember going to the restaurant downstairs. I think it's called Zentan. Good food from what I recall."

"Oh yea, the girl at the front desk told me it was closed for renovation." I said, then boldly added, "Do you recommend anything else?"

"Not really," she said discouragingly, "I'm not much of an eat-out person, so my guess would be just as good—or useless—as yours."

"Really," I uttered, excited to explore the topic she laid before me. "With your travelling, I would've thought that you ate out a lot."

"Oh, I do," she corrected, "but not because I enjoy it. It's just something I have to do. When I can control it, I definitely stay home."

"Hmm, interesting," I said. "So, what are you doing today to control it?"

"What do you mean?" she asked.

"What are you cooking?"

"I'm making burgers, fries, and baked beans," she said proudly. "A little comfort food to battle this weather."

I wanted to invite myself or say something that would prompt her to invite me, but the words eluded me. I could neither find the proper words nor the courage to express my intention. I hated this fact about myself. I must have written well over a million words since I began writing ten years ago, but I could never seem to find the right things to say in situations like this. Even Joseena had accused me of this debility. Over time, she had learned to recognize my non-verbal cues, and everything worked out, but with Nikkyta, she did not know me that well yet. Or maybe she did! Well, I hope she did. She's a behavioral scientist after all.

"Wow that sounds hearty," I said, gutlessly.

"You're free to join me," she said.

Her words were unexpected. It sounded like the best thing I've ever heard in my life. I felt my heart somersault with joy and excitement.

"I'll take you up on that," I said, calmly.

"Good," she said, then quickly asked, "Do you have any food allergies?"

"Not that I know of," I said. It wouldn't have mattered even if I did. Barring any life-threatening condition, I was willing to subject myself to anything if it meant being next to her.

The conversation continued for about ten minutes, but I was incapable of comprehending anything. The idea of being alone with Nikkyta was the only thought on my mind. For a brief second, I thought about Matt Palmer and his strong warnings not to allow my carnal feelings for her influence my mind. It made sense. I knew I should heed his advice, but the intense imagery of being next to her had robbed me of all ability to think. I quickly dismissed Matt from my thoughts by concocting a cockamamie justification for my action. I planned to be there in two hours, which was an hour later than the earliest time she gave me. With my newfound purpose, I marched towards the bathroom for a quick shower. The lightning blue shirt that was disregarded by Marcy happened to be the best article of clothing I had with me, and for the first time in a very long time, I wished I had better choices. My fashion sense suddenly became a source of concern. I strongly considered visiting one of the shops on 14th Street to augment my appearance, but I thought better of it. I calmed the mental tussle going on in my head by convincing it that it was just a casual meeting between colleagues to look over case files and eat burgers. I killed some time by watching an episode of Law and Order on TNT. Obviously it was an episode I'd seen before, but I kept the channel and followed along with the storyline in hopes of picking up a term or two that might impress Nikkyta.

My UBER arrived five minutes after it was ordered, and I made it to her building in about seven minutes. I was a little surprised to learn she lived in close proximity to the hotel. She lived in Columbia Heights in northwest D.C. From my panoramic vantage point, I immediately noticed a social convergence borne of a myriad of races and culture. Major retailers and thriving restaurant scenes lined up the strip and further added to my confusion as to why she was not the eating-out type. The temperature was now in the south 20s and it was beginning to drizzle as forecasted, so the street was not up to its full potential. The multitude all walked with a purpose to escape the approaching storm.

The phone rang twice before she picked up.

"I'm outside," I said, as evenly as I could, hoping I was able to suppress my excitement.

"Alright, be down in a sec."

She soon materialized in a gray Hoyas basketball t-shirt and black tights. Even in her casual getup, she looked every bit as stunning as her professional outfit.

"Did you walk here?" she asked.

"No," I said, "I would've if I knew you lived so close."

"Oh," she chuckled, as she led the way. "Yea I keep forgetting you're not from around here; it's actually faster to walk, with all the traffic."

We walked through the lobby of her apartment building and made a left down a long carpeted hallway. There were sitting areas to the left and right of us as well as what appeared to be a library. The space had about five shelves fed with books erecting almost to the ceiling. A red-top pool table sat in the room next to it with the cue sticks deliberately laid on the surface to form an X.

"I barely use these rooms," Nikkyta said, "because I'm never here, but it's meant for socializing."

I nodded like a prospective renter as I kept up with her quick pace. The entertainment space reminded me of my Spring Garden apartment when I lived in Philadelphia. I, too, rarely used the space, but it was not for the same reason as Nikkyta's. I preferred being in rented cabins for my work, and when I felt the urge to shoot pool, I visited Lucky Strikes in downtown Philadelphia.

Our walk ended at the entrance to the elevator. The cramped space was the closest we'd been, and it made me nervous. I was suddenly concerned about my breath even though I recalled brushing my teeth before leaving the hotel. This anxiety banned every desire to talk although I had nothing to say. I was relieved to be in an open space again when the elevator opened onto the seventh floor. We walked about half of the hallway before stopping at apartment 716. Her apartment was warm, inviting, and comfortable. It spoke in distinction from what I had imagined. As an FBI agent that was always on the go, I was expecting a sparsely abstract concept, with furniture and decorations sporadically situated about the room without much thought or effort. What I witnessed, however, impressed me. The smell of pumpkin and orange vied tirelessly for the domineering scent in the room. At different coordinates on the flower-patterned wall were framed pictures of revered African-American women like Mae C. Jemison, Katherine Johnson, Bessie Coleman, and Madam C.J. Walker. Her entire apartment was smaller than my suite at the Donovan, but she was able to make the most of the area. A brown two-piece sectional was to my right, and a green accent chair across from it. In the middle of the furniture was a multi-colored soft Moroccan rug covering part of the wooden floor. I noticed, besides the pictures of the respected figures on the wall, there were no pictures of her or her family. I wondered if they were in the bedroom. How I wished I could see her bedroom.

"Make yourself at home," she said as she walked towards a partitioned space which I assumed to be the kitchen. "Do you want anything to drink?"

"Water is fine," I said, as I sat on the green accent chair.

"Are you sure," she called out from the kitchen, "I have beer and wine if you'd prefer?"

"Umm... maybe when the food is ready."

"Well, the food is ready," she re-appeared from the kitchen, "so what will it be?"

"I'll do wine then," I said, "but not a lot. I still have to film the show for the network."

"Oh, yea that's right," she said, as she disappeared back to the partitioned area. "What time is the filming?"

"Typically, between nine and noon if I was in New York," I said, "but remotely might be earlier."

"Yea, you definitely don't need to be drinking much then," she said. "I'll make sure you only consume a glass."

"Deal."

I heard sounds of plates and utensils from the kitchen, and she soon showed up with a tray.

"Are you sure you wanna sit there?" she asked. "The couch is more comfortable, and you can rest the tray on your lap better."

I'd rather you rest your ass on my lap, I thought.

"Okay," I obeyed, and moved towards the two-piece sectional.

It was very comfortable. My muscles relaxed in a manner that suggested it was made specifically for my body.

"Wow," I exclaimed, "this feels so good."

"Yea I spent a couple dollars on it." She said with a tinge of pride in her voice, "I'm sure it's not as expensive as yours though, but it's pretty good quality."

I wished she didn't insinuate about my wealth as much as she did. I felt uncomfortable. I wanted us to be on equal footing. I would hate to think her unguarded display of hospitality was a ploy to get to my riches. First, was the insistence to refer to Ray as my agent, after I edited his role in my life as my childhood friend. Then, at the senator's, when I asked for a place to stay, she made a comment about the hotel cost not being an issue. Now, she discounted her couch when comparing it to what she imagined I paid for mine.

"No," I said, "mine is not this comfortable. Trust me. Where did you buy it from?"

"Some furniture store in Virginia," she said, and before I could respond, she added, "How do you like your meat?"

I was glad she left it at that.

How do you like YOUR meat? I thought, lewdly.

"Medium well," I said.

"Cool, I'll be right back."

She showed up with two orange plates festooned with burgers and potato wedges. She returned to the kitchen and came back with another medium-sized bowl filled with baked beans. The aroma from the feast gave the impression that I was in for a one-of-a-kind dining experience.

"Sorry I don't have cable," she said as she sat next to me with the remote in her hand. "I have Netflix, Hulu, and HBO-Now. Do you have any preference?"

I wanted to tell her that the *Tilted Grin* series would soon debut on Hulu with Keke Palmer and Janelle Monáe, but quickly disregarded it. I figured it would only add to my concern of not wanting to come off as a celebrity in her presence.

"No, not really," I said. "I'll watch whatever you watch."

"What do you watch when you are home?" she asked, as she scooped a liberal serving of baked beans onto her plate.

"Not much really," I said, "prior to this *Tilted Grin* killer copycat, I rarely watched TV. Now, I might catch a news report or two."

She didn't say anything with her mouthful. She just nodded her head.

The meal fitted every imagination suggested by its aroma. Each bite stirred a celebration of seasoning and flavor in my mouth that was rarely experienced even at eminent five-star restaurants. I was not quite sure if it was due to my hunger, but the meal was the best I'd had in a long time. In Brooklyn, I experienced very little home-cooked meals mainly due to my impulsive movements. I once hired a cook to prepare a meal twice a week, but that experiment was quickly dissolved due to my unreliable appetite.

"Do you like it?" She asked, when she was done chewing.

I had a mouthful, so I did the nodding. Enthusiastically. I made sure there was no ambiguity in my response.

She smiled, and I could tell she was pleased. Her reaction reeled me back to a conversation I had with my late mother.

"Son," she had said, "There aren't many things better than passionately letting your woman know you enjoy her cooking."

Although Nikkyta was not MY woman, I was able to impart the same message. Thinking of my mother placed me in a somber mood. I wished she was alive to enjoy my success as a novelist. When I was younger, she had been my biggest supporter when it came to sharpening my craft. She was an English teacher, so she alerted me on some of the pitfalls to avoid as a writer. During my freshman year in college, her life was taken by a drunk driver in Atlantic City where she and my dad were celebrating their twenty-second year of marriage.

"Do you want more?" Nikkyta's voice sounded, ameliorating the mood again.

"Eh...I really want to," I said, "but I don't think I have room for it."

"Are you sure?" She asked.

I nodded.

She smiled and cleared the area. I stole glances at her as she walked away, and it was as if she intentionally added more twitch in her movement. I knew even if that was the case, I did not pack enough courage to act on it, especially with only one glass of wine. I wished I didn't have the recording with the network the next day that way I could justify emptying the bottle and build enough nerve to act on my wild thoughts.

"Do you want to look over the case files?" she called out from the kitchen.

I looked at the time, and it was 5:54 p.m.

"Sure," I responded.

Although, I was not ready to revert to being an FBI consultant just yet, I did want to bask more in our informal setting at least for the rest of the evening. I cursed at myself for not refusing the offer.

I saw her walk across to where I assumed was her bedroom to retrieve her laptop. I noticed the same twitch as she walked back towards me. I realized my once revered tolerance for alcohol was now weakening. With just one glass of wine, I thought I was seeing things. The fact that she asked to review the case files meant she was not in the mood for whatever my alcoholic mind was hoping for. But as she continued to narrow the gap between us, I saw no disproof of my understanding. She was certainly switching in slow, wide seductive motions that swept swimmingly from left to right. She got within inches from my face and gently placed the laptop on a side stool. Was this really happening or was the wine messing with me? She turned to me and softly placed her succulent lips against mine. I sat stock-still, vindicated, but also incredibly confused on how to react. My mind raced disobediently, struggling to discern between reality and the bogus promises of alcohol. It took a few seconds, although it felt like a lifetime, for me to join the real time with my surrounding. Tiny jolts of electricity pulsated throughout my body as our lips pressed passionately against each other. My inquiring hands quickly reached around the curves of her butt that was now sitting on my lap. I grabbed and squeezed each cheek with much delight sending her into wild convulsive movements. She let out a soothing sigh as she pressed her body deeper onto mine. My hands traced its way up her back, beneath her Hoya t-shirt, until I encountered the devilish boundary created by her bra straps. With one proficient motion, I squeezed and released two of the three hooks that held it in place. With my ex Joseena, her breasts were smaller, so her bra straps only came with one hook. Finally, the last hook was unfastened with ease, and I felt the bra's tension relax. My hands immediately wandered to the front and cupped the voluptuous delight that waited for me. After a few moments of fondling, I decided it was time to watch what I eat. I lifted the t-shirt over her head and mindlessly tossed the bra aside, exposing her bare chest. I plunged my head on her left breast and she let out a gentle, "Ahhhh."

It was as if every sound that fled her lips enriched me with a hidden courage I never knew I had. I flipped her over until her back landed safely on her comfortable couch. I was efficient like a sharp knife, cutting straight to the chase by pulling down her tights and buried my face in between her thighs. The slippery landscape that awaited me gave me strength. It fueled me. I was no longer confused. I might have problems getting started, but at this advanced stage my animalistic instincts had taken over. I moved with the grace and elegance of a big cat. Nikkyta's hips gyrated in all directions as I nibbled passionately.

She finally paused and summoned a distinguishable voice amidst the frenzy to ask, "Do you have protection?"

Oh shit!

"No," I said. I wanted to explain that I didn't want to assume anything by bringing one, but I realized that would further kill the mood.

"It's cool," she said. "I do."

Whew!

She escaped from my captivity and walked towards her bedroom. This time, the twitch was evident. Perhaps it was before too, but I noticed it now. Without waiting to be invited, I followed her, my erect penis leading the way. We were completely naked. I used the time it took to retrieve the condom to marvel at her body. A collection of perfectly placed arcs and bends that drove me crazy that one body could amass so much beauty. As soon as she returned with the protection, I gently nudged her onto her queen-size bed and resumed the feasting. I used one hand to caress her breast, while my tongue licked between her legs and my other hand secured the condom. It was a skill I had been commended for in the past. When I rose from between her thighs, she was staring at me, biting her lower lip. My lips glistened like a well-fed man. She begged for me to enter, and I complied. With one swift forceful motion, I slid into her.

chapter12

BLAINE GRUBBER felt his head pounding from all the noises around him. The decision to drink almost four bottles of Guinness stout was shaping up to be one of the dumbest things he had ever done. He was not one prone to doing dumb things. His exhaustive approaches to everything have been a source of pride for him. Standing just a little over 5'2 and weighing about 112 pounds, Blaine had learned a long time ago that in order to be efficient, he had to enrich his mind because his gaunt physique would mostly put him at a disadvantage. This realization had caused him to embrace the mind-over-matter philosophy. He meditated, visualized, focused, talked to himself, changed toxic habits, removed temptations, read obsessively, and employed short-term memory when it came to past failures. This set of rules was perfected over the years, and now he felt confident with its application. The first few killings happened without many qualms from the Delaware State Police. Their skillset was an inferior match for his eidetic mind. He was able to carry out his deeds while the course of the investigation pointed in the opposite direction. He needed more challenge. He began killing at a much faster pace, knowing that would pique the interest of the FBI, an organization he referred to as a *formidable foe*. He knew the behavioral scientists for the bureau would interpret the sudden spike in his killings as that of one no longer able to control his urges. They would panic and act swiftly, thus making way for his true prey: The first high-profile case in a career he hoped would produce a lot of high-profile cases.

Jennifer Gibson had unwillingly stumbled onto his line of sight on an unsuspecting July day. It was a little over a week after Independence Day, and the charismatic senator from Delaware, Terry Gibson, was giving a speech in Wilmington on domestic violence against women. The talk was inspired after he quickly became a leading voice on the subject following the rescue of a black woman from her abusive white lover. The entire incident was captured on an iPhone camera and it went viral. The senator bellowed in an authoritative tone across a field of people that gathered at Rodney Square to listen to his opinions. Blaine was in the crowd that day. He was there recruiting his next victim when he saw Jennifer Gibson. She stood next to her father as his balled-up fist punched the air with enthusiasm and unrestrained belief that domestic violence would soon be a thing of the past. Blaine noticed how apathetic Jenny looked. It was obvious she did not want to be there. To the other side of the senator, was a Hispanic woman in great shape. She wore a loose flowery dress and the look on her face matched the fervor in the senator's voice. Blaine quickly decided. Jennifer, not the Hispanic woman, would be the high-profile case he sought. The woman in the flowery dress was, for one, too old for his liking. She also gave off the impression that the highs and lows of life might have hardened her, and she possessed a physical presence that his elfin body might not be able to withstand. Jennifer, on the other hand, was a privileged kid that would most likely elect flight over fight when confronted with the choices.

Over the next few months, Blaine began monitoring her movements. He learned she was twenty-four years old and a graduate student at Drexel University. She was studying Early Childhood Education and worked at a daycare in West Philadelphia. She disliked her father and especially her step-mother, the Hispanic beauty. Jennifer was an avid Eagles fan and she enjoyed the bar scenes immensely. Through social engineering, Blaine was able to befriend her, in one of his many disguises, and obtained her login information during one of her many drunken stupors. He read through her emails and online diary where she spewed, in great details, her vitriol for the woman that took her mother's place. Blaine garnered some important information during this period, and he decided the perfect day to execute his plan would be the day before the senator scheduled a news conference to announce his run for presidency. Blaine felt this would make Jennifer a true high-profile case. Outside of her all-American-girl persona, her father's meteoric ascent in politics would bring the wild media squall that had been missing from his previous killings.

As he tried to steady his gaze on his prey, Blaine felt a sudden urge to vomit. He looked up at the train statuses and noticed that the train to Wilmington was not due to arrive for another ten minutes. It would be enough time to empty his stomach and return to his alert self without the fear of his prey disappearing again. He ran to the nearest bathroom and emptied the contents in his stomach. When he returned, his prey was still there, engrossed in something on her phone. Blaine flirted with the idea of sitting next to her but thought better of it. It would be too risky, he thought, even though he had thoroughly changed his look from the time they met a month ago. Blaine had adopted a method he read in a novel titled *Tilted Grin*. He was able to create vastly different disguises where even the most observant detective would miss the resemblance.

Following a three-minute delay, the train to Wilmington gently glided through track number three. Blaine monitored his prey as she entered the third car. Moments later, he entered the same car and sat five seats behind her. She was still absorbed by the contents on her phone, and for a brief second, Blaine wished he could enjoy in her entertainment. He guessed she was probably on Instagram, reacting to her 11.2K followers' comments and reactions to her pictures from Sláinte Pub and Grill. While he waited, Blaine had observed the unending picture-taking and laughter with her friends. He was a little surprised and incredibly pleased, that none of them were accompanying her to Delaware for her dad's big day. It would have meant more bodies and a bit of distraction from the main target. She was perfect at about 5'4, slim, with natural blonde hair that she occasionally dyed black or red. She loved her independence and was determined to thrive without the imposing shadow of her father's influence. She lived with two other roommates in a four-bedroom house on 39th and Baltimore Avenue in West Philadelphia. Besides people with foreknowledge about her past, Jennifer Gibson had hidden her father's identity extremely well. The idea that she would even ponder to be there for this announcement was a reality Blaine had not considered. He only gained knowledge of this fact when he hacked into her email account and saw the correspondence between her and the senator. The dialogue carried on for two weeks, with both sides ardently defending their position in their rift. A resolution was finally reached, and Jennifer promised she would be in Delaware the night before the announcement. The senator offered to have his driver pick her up, but she declined. She informed him she would be watching the Eagles' game at Sláinte Pub and Grill and would take the train to Wilmington afterwards, where she planned to stay in a hotel and not at the family home in Claymont.

chapter13

We laid wordlessly on the bed for about a minute, with both parties trying to control their breathing. I was expecting to be snatched from a dream in my luxurious space at the Donovan and curse at the cruelty of what had just happened. The ticking of the gold-plated square-shaped clock on the wall seemed to reassure me that this was real. The room was now pitch black as a result of the gray sky outside and the thick curtains inside.

"That was nice," I broke the silence.

"Mmhmm," she said reassuringly.

"I've never done anything like that before," I continued.

"What," she said, "have sex?"

I chuckled, "No, not that." I paused to pace my breathing before continuing, "I've never gone down on anyone the first time."

"Is that right," she said. I felt the confidence building in her voice, "So what made you?"

"I'm not sure," I said truthfully, "it just felt like the right thing to do."

"Well, it felt great."

"You felt great, too," I said, naturally.

I was teeming with pride, hearing her laud my sexual prowess. I wanted to turn over and pull her closer to me for the rest of the night, but my courage had been depleted. I had no idea what we were. Was this a one-time thing or the beginning of something lasting? Would my gesture be received willingly, grudgingly, or be blatantly refused? These questions hindered my ability to do anything else besides lay there, control my breathing, and hope for the best.

"Thanks," she said, and immediately sprang up.

She reached for the light switch, and in an instant, the dark room was flooded with light, as she continued towards the bathroom. I suddenly realized I was still naked with the condom covering my limp phallus. Slightly embarrassed, I too leapt to my feet and walked towards the living room to retrieve my clothes. I flushed the condom in the bathroom after she came out.

"Are you hungry?" she asked, when I came out of the bathroom.

Yea, hungry for you! I thought.

"No, I'm still full," I said, "I should be fine."

She was wearing another Hoya t-shirt. This one was burgundy, and it hugged her body a little more

intimately than the gray one she had earlier. And for her bottom, she wore a green men's boxer shorts.

"Did you go to Georgetown," I asked, "you seem to have a lot of their shirts."

"No, I did not," she smiled, "it's just Hoya country around here. You can't escape not seeing a few of their merchandises in stores. I only wear them when I'm indoors."

"I have a friend that only wears Harvard and MIT shirts even though he went to a community college in Colorado."

"See, I don't do that," her smile widened. "I'm proud of my alma mater, and I rock them often."

"Tulane, right?" I asked.

"Yessir!" She proclaimed.

Her facial expression took me back to our second meeting on the plane, when she proudly claimed Charm City as her own. That moment felt so long ago. A lifetime of favorable events seemed to have transpired since then.

"Did you live on campus?" I asked.

"Yes, I did," she said, then added, "nothing beats going to school in New Orleans. It's the most exciting city I've ever been to."

"Oh yea, why's that?"

"Have you ever been?" she asked.

"No," I said.

"Well, it's gonna be difficult to explain," she said. "You just have to go and experience it."

"Maybe we can go after this case," I ventured boldly.

Her response to my audacious statement took a few seconds, but I regretted it almost immediately.

"Hmm, maybe. So, do you wanna look through some case files?"

The swift change in topic instantly decimated my accruing courage. I wanted nothing but to leave her space and return to my suite to sulk at my foolish attempt of bravery. She had cleanly disregarded my offer, and now we were on her bed about to look at the case files. The light in the room was now emanating from the two nightstands that stood at opposite sides of the bed. On the wall, were more pictures of accomplished African American women: Condoleezza Rice, Shirley Chisolm, Gwendolyn Brooks, and Loretta Lynch. I found it odd that there were no pictures of herself or close family members in her house. I wanted to ask her about this, but my blunder had mugged me of my nerve. I sat upright and reviewed the particulars of the case instead.

chapter14

CASE NUMBER: 998B011518

Offense: Suspicious Death.

Victim (s): Beverly Morgan

Race: White/Caucasian

Location: 115 S King St, Georgetown, DE 19947 (Post office parking lot)

Reporting Officer (s): Detective John Dykstra and Detective Adam Baxter.

Date: 15th day of January 2017

Narrative/Summary: This unit and unit 5836 (forensic team) were requested to respond to the above address to process the scene of a suspicious death. Upon our arrival there were two clean knives and a bloody knife at the scene of the crime. Next to these weapons was the body of a nineteen-year old Caucasian female, Beverly Morgan. The coroner's office had the time of death between 0200hrs and 0500hrs. This information had since been endorsed by the Chief Medical Examiner of Sussex County. Beverly was about 5'3" and weighed approximately 123lbs. At the time of death, Beverly was missing her right ear and her nose had been severely mangled. A UV source was used at the scene to check *for any foreign materials on or around the body with negative results. Although tire impressions were observed at the scene, these tire marks were smaller then a car. Early conclusion is a motorcycle. A few feet away from the body, Detective Baxter and I discovered some doodling. It was the drawing of a smiley face sloped slightly to the left, with the words "you make me smile," scribbled under the face. The chalk we believed was used for the sketch was left at the scene, along with an eraser (see AC#99004535).*

Status: Open/Active.

Of all the things to worry about, my first cringe worthy moment after reading the first case file was the officer's use of "then" instead of "than" when describing the tire marks at the scene. It's stupid, I know, but I could hear echoes of my mother's voice highlighting this *catastrophe.*

I was saved from this irrelevant thought when Nikkyta said, "So, what do you think?"

"Ummmm," I said, timidly, "I'm really not sure. I mean I feel like there should to be more information on the report. I don't know if I have enough to—"

"There is," she said, "there was more information when we asked for the actual case file hard copy, but it was just useless information to fill out all the void spaces in the lengthy paperwork. What you see here, along with the crime-scene photos that I haven't shown you yet, are all you need."

I nodded confidently, hoping to appear like I knew what I was doing. In reality, this was my first time ever seeing a case file, and in spite of what I knew, I recoiled when I read the use of the tilted grin faces, just like I described in my novel. The committer in my work of fiction was also obsessed with leaving body parts and unusable evidence at the scene to misdirect the investigators. The unused knives at the scene, from my deduction, was his attempt to lead the investigation astray.

"Do you have the photos on your laptop?" I asked, hoping to glean more.

"No, I have actual copies of that," she said, as she reached for a manila folder on the side of her bed. "That was my next step."

She was right. The crime scene photos gave me everything I needed to know. Overall photos of the scene were taken to display the approach to the area including street signs, street light locations, possible public cameras, and any usable objects at the scene. Photographs of the body and its immediate vicinity were also taken. It was the most gruesome sight I had ever seen. A wave of nausea raced through my body, and I felt a strong urge to rush to the bathroom and empty the burgers and baked beans in my stomach. I realized this was only the first of nine crime scene photos, and I didn't have enough in me to empty. I decided to stay strong and face the gore. The body of the victim was twisted in a sadistic manner, exposing her missing ear and distorted nose. The tilted smiley face was noticeable in one of the photos and I found myself staring at it longer than I should. The weight of the moment seemed to overwhelm me. To imagine that an idea conjured up in my mind was now the source of a real-life homicide scared the shit out of me.

"Wow," I said, "you're right. There's definitely more to see from the crime scene photos."

"Yup," she said nonchalantly. "And just so you know, it gets worse. This was the very first killing that started it all. We didn't join the case until after the fifth, and Jenny ended up becoming the ninth."

"And, no clues yet?" I asked. "Anything, height, weight, race?"

"In the fourth killing, he was caught on camera with a mask on." She said, "At the time, we thought that was great. We were able to match a physique to the guy. Unlike the character in your novel, the guy is small. Only about 5'2" and perhaps 110 lbs, and that's being generous. We manufactured some theories and began amassing a profile. We believe this particular killer gets his high from being able to dodge the mighty FBI because he was probably teased a lot in school due to his miniature physique. He did not fit well with the average American's definition of power. His lack of muscle and height probably made him unpopular with the females. So, this is his revenge. Although, his victims so far had been young skinny women, and children. It was not quite the demographic to prove that he was a badass, but that was probably the physique of women that constantly turned him down."

"So, why the need to use my book?" I asked, "My character was not turned down by women as a kid. He only chose that demographic because they were easy and would not fight back as aggressively."

"I think that's more of his misdirection," Nikkyta jumped in. "If you watched the news, even before Jenny became a victim, it was partly about the murders and the other, partly about your book. I believe he's only doing that to continue the distraction and affect the investigation. We want him to think that, that's why we too continue to play along. Don't get me wrong, your presence here was definitely ordered by the Senator, but as you had already observed, that was a self-serving move on his part. Remember when we were at the senator's house and I told you to remind me to tell you something later when we were alone?"

I nodded.

"Well, this was part of it. The senator planned all this out, even the part with the questions. Those reporters agreed to let the senator review their questions before they asked. The high praises for you was part of a prepared speech. I'm not quite sure what you can offer to this case. Hope I haven't offended you."

"Oh no," I said, truthfully, "I'm definitely not offended, and I can't say I'm overly shocked with the planted news reporters either."

I was glad she checked to see if I was offended. It gave me hope that she now cared a little bit about my feelings.

"That's the theory anyway, as it pertains to the killer," she said, "But it's not concrete yet. It's just one of the many areas we're considering. The more case files we review, you will notice his first three killings happened almost exactly two weeks apart. It took him a total of six weeks to execute the killings. Then he began killing at a much faster pace. Two in one week. That was when the Delaware State Police brought us in. We interpreted this spike as a person no longer able to control his urges and was now killing with the slightest impulse. But this theory became problematic between the last victim and Jenny. The period took close to six months, which was the longest he'd waited since he began. We're not really back to square one, but most of our theories, besides the profile we've assembled, have been debunked or at least highly questionable."

"How did you even get into this?" I asked abruptly hoping to get a recess from the mind of this deranged killer.

"What do you mean?"

"Like, how does one become a behavioral scientist for the FBI? I'm sure you don't go on a job recruiting website and fill out mundane information about yourself."

"Oh," she chuckled. "Well, you're right, it's not a website you go to. The job is not listed on Indeed or Zip Recruiter. I was approached during my senior year at Tulane. As a psychology major, we were told to listen and analyze the Ted Bundy tapes on one of our projects. Apparently, my analysis blew the minds of some of our faculty members. It prompted them to pass my paper to the Behavioral Science Department in Quantico. Yadda, yadda, yadda, they came knocking. Two large government officials came to my dorm room and pretty much offered me a job. Of course, they didn't give me the details of what I'll be doing, but they assured me it would mirror my research on Ted Bundy. After seeing what I would be making my first year, I was pretty much sold. With guidance from my parents, I signed an agreement, and the rest, as they say, is history. I've been with the department for seven years now, and I still enjoy what I do."

"Wow," I said, "do you still have that paper?"

"The one on Bundy?"

"Yes."

"Absolutely," she said, "I still refer back to it sometimes when I'm working a case. Especially copycat ones. Because Bundy, just like Elvis, has been impersonated a lot, but impersonators always lack the man's intellect and confidence."

"It sounds like you admire the guy?" I asked.

"I admire his mind," she said, unflinchingly, "I just don't care for what he chose to do with it."

"You said you go back to the paper once in a while for copycat cases, did you do so for this one?"

"No," she said bluntly. "Both methods are vastly different. It would only cause more confusion. I don't think this killer matched Bundy's wit."

I didn't know why, but I felt a little disappointed that the *Tilted Grin* killer was not on par with Ted Bundy. I suddenly wanted to be involved in the narrative of creating the greatest serial killer of all time. It was an asinine thought and I hated that it gripped me the way it did.

"Well," I said, exhaling, "let's continue with the case files."

CASE NUMBER: 28QRC012918

Offense: Homicide.

Victim (s): Peggy Greene and Dianne Greene.

Race: White/Caucasian.

Location: 23420 Sussex Highway, Seaford, DE 19973 (Comfort Inn and Suites).

Reporting Officer (s): Detective Carl Firko.

Date: 29th day of January, 2017.

Narrative/Summary: I was dispatched to the above address for a double homicide of a mother and daughter. Dianne Greene (26), and her daughter, Peggy Greene (9), who were guests at the Comfort Inn and Suites, were found beaten to death in their standard, two twin-size room. The daughter was bludgeoned with a baseball bat found at the scene, and the mother was stabbed repeatedly on the neck and died after a massive blood loss. There are no signs of forced entry, so we're still unsure how the killer made it in. Neighboring guests in nearby rooms did not hear any sounds of struggle.

Additional Information: Killer was believed to sketch an image of a smiling face, and beneath it were the words, "all you gotta do is smile."

Status: Open/Active.

The detective's use of strong language like 'bludgeoned' made the already gruesome scene even more so. I asked very little questions as we flipped through the pages of the remaining case files. Each case spoke of a different method of killing, but the reoccurring theme continued to be the tilted grin smiley face at every scene. The killer's writing was initially determined to be that of a lefty due to some known quirks of left-handed writers, but the very next killing disproved this thought process and the web of confusion lingered.

I wanted it all to end. I wondered how people could look at such images daily and still function normally in society. It made no sense to me. With nine cases, I was fed-up with the process. I needed time away from the frightening images. I wanted something normal. Something spontaneous, but enjoyable. Something that did not involve death and the horrors that came with it. I pushed the case files to the side and grabbed Nikkyta's arm. I pulled her forcefully towards me and kissed her lips with the passion of a thousand waterfalls. I wasn't sure if it was my vigor or a twisted strength she derived from the grisly pictures, but she too matched my animalistic potency. This time, we did not have to adjust to the newness of our bodies. I approached her as if every curve, crevice, and contour belonged to me. I maneuvered with the familiarity of a seasoned lover that had committed every part of her form to memory. She matched my efforts and we fucked. Hard! And it was glorious.

Loss of breath, we both stared aimlessly at the ceiling with our naked bodies surrounded by the ghastly images of murdered victims.

chapter15

The sound of the phone brought us back to the present.

"Who da hell is calling," Nikkyta said, as she reached for her phone on the nightstand. "Oh, shit! it's Frank!" She declared loudly and was instantly on her feet. She placed her right index finger on her lips, a gesture warning me to be quiet, before she spoke.

"Hey," she opened casually, "what's up?"

She nodded unquestioningly for a few minutes, then added, "Yes we dropped him off at the Donovan earlier."

A bit more nodding ensued before they said their goodbyes.

She turned to me with a blasé expression and said, "He wants us back in Delaware. He said it's important, but he's not telling me anything. We're heading back early tomorrow morning instead of Thursday. We would've gone tonight, but the weather outside is not conducive for flying. I think you need to go; he just asked of you. I'm not sure what his plans are, but I think it'll be safer for everybody if you're at your hotel just in case he calls or stops by your hotel."

I agreed with her assessment, but I felt cheapened with the haste at which she was getting rid of me. It was as if the careless passion and desire had only been my vivid imagination that was never executed. It was as if she did not feel anything. *Or maybe she didn't? Man, get a hold of yourself!*

I packed up my things as instructed, and as I was about to walk out the door, she pulled me towards her, and our lips touched. Just as quickly as my grievances rose, it melted away. I was reassured again.

"Do you want me to make you a plate?" She asked, when we came up for air.

I shook my head and returned to the kiss.

"Your UBER will leave," she finally said, pulling herself away from me.

"Ok, ok, just one more," I pleaded.

"Nooo," she said playfully, as she pushed me away. "Goooo."

"Please just one."

She pulled me closer and gave me one long kiss.

As I turned to walk away, she called out my name. I turned expectantly, and she said, "Next time you come over, make sure you bring condom. We can't do this again. Don't worry I'm on the pill, but let's not make that a habit."

Edmund Okocha

I nodded and walked away feeling fulfilled.

chapter16

WITH TWO more stops to go, Blaine Grubber was beginning to feel a rush of adrenaline, in anticipation of what was about to happen. He tried to suppress the excitement, but couldn't. The killing was going to be his best work. He could feel it. What better way to announce his presence on the big stage than performing an eccentric show for the experts, copycats, and future killers.

The stage had been set.

Blaine was able to access Jennifer's Hilton Honors account from her email and obtained her reservation information. As a diamond member, Jennifer was able to select her own room when she checked-in electronically. She chose room 484, a standard non-smoking room with a king-size bed. Blaine was able to reserve the room across from hers, with equal amenities. He had already checked-in earlier in the day before taking the train to Sláinte Pub and Grill to meet with his prey. The room was modestly furnished, although, he didn't care about that. Most of his time would be spent in her room. The killing, he imagined, would be a work of art. He planned to take his time. To make sure the FBI agents marveled at his acute attention to small details. He knew the thrilling niceties would never make it to the news, but he wanted it to remain in the hearts and minds of the agents on the scene. He wanted to be studied for decades to come, the way Ted Bundy and Charles Manson were.

As the train departed Marcus Hook station with Wilmington next, Blaine could feel a smile forming on his face and he quickly blocked it. He knew there would be plenty of time to smile and perhaps even laugh, but now was the time to focus. His prey had since given up on the contents on her phone and was now staring pointlessly out the window as the train sped through the graffiti-burdened walls and improvised dumpsters that appeared to line its path. It took about fifteen minutes for the train to pull up at the final stop. The crackled voice of the conductor announced that this was the final stop and all bags and belongings were to exit the train at this time. Jennifer walked determinedly through the station. Luckily for Blaine, the Wilmington train station paled in size and grandeur to the 30th street station in Philadelphia, so he was able to keep up easily with his prey. She stopped at a food stand and bought a hotdog, which she dolloped with ketchup and mustard.

Last meal, Blaine thought, as he permitted a sardonic smile.

Jennifer spent a few minutes walking around a bookstore but came out empty-handed. Blaine sat patiently through her lollygagging. He had come this far. What's a few more hours before the show? Jenny finally realized the train station had nothing to offer, and she walked out onto the brisk night to hail a taxi. She didn't have to do too much because lined up to her left were a row of taxis to pick from. She stated her destination, and the vehicle soon meandered its way out of the station. Blaine followed with the next taxi in line. He didn't need to rush because he knew the destination, but he wanted to be there when she checked in, just to make sure there were no last-minute changes to her room selection. Thankfully, there was a small line when Blaine arrived at the hotel lobby, so Jenny had yet to check-in. There were three people in front of her, so rather than straggling around and raising doubts, Blaine walked to the pantry, which was within an earshot of the front-desk attendant and acted as if he was buying something to quiet his stomach rumblings.

"Hi! May I help you?" the front-desk attendant asked Jenny with a practiced smile.

"Hi, I have a reservation for Jennifer Gibson," she said a little fatigued.

The front-desk attendant seemed to have trouble locating her reservation. The development gripped Blaine with fear. He tried not to look in their direction, but this sudden turn of event would surely thwart everything he had worked so diligently for.

"I e-checked-in," Jennifer offered, "I'm not sure if that would help."

"Oh!" the attendant exclaimed, allowing for a real smile, "I'm sorry about that. Yes! That will definitely help."

She reached for a pack of small envelopes on her right and sorted through its contents. In just a few seconds, she emerged with Jennifer's reservation information.

"Thanks for being a loyal diamond member Miss Gibson," she said. "And also, thanks for using our E-check-in system. Is it okay to use the Amex card on file?"

"Yes, please."

"Awesome! Would you like a snack, and your choice of soda?"

"Eh...just a bottle of water," Jenny responded.

"Oh, there should be two bottles waiting in your room," the attendant said sprightly, "and if you need more, just let us know."

"Nice. Thanks."

"Sure! No problem," the attendant said, then continued with her memorized spiel. "You'll be in room 484. Elevators are to your right. Breakfast is served on the sixth floor, from 6am to 10am. These are your room keys and the premium Wi-Fi password is in your envelope. Please feel free to call us here at the front desk if you have any questions."

"Thanks," Jennifer said politely.

"My pleasure."

As she was about to walk away, she suddenly remembered a question she forgot to ask, "Excuse me, where's the gym?"

"Oh, at the end of this hallway," the attendant said, pointing towards a well-lit path, "make a left, and it's the second door to the right. It's a 24-hour full-service gym, and it's accessible with your room keys."

"Thank you so much."

"You're welcome. Have a nice stay."

Blaine quickly abandoned his time at the pantry and followed his prey towards the direction of the elevator. To his right was an American Airlines poster, advertising a low fare round trip to Paris, and for reasons unbeknownst to him, Blaine allowed his mind to wander. He pondered if he should reward himself with a trip after his masterpiece with Jennifer. He wondered if it would be enjoyable to introduce a heart, which had only known darkness, to the city of lights.

chapter17

I was up and ready to go by the time my phone chimed to life.

Nikkyta was back to her professional demeanor when the call was answered. I informed her I would be down in a minute. The next few seconds were spent making sure nothing was left behind. It hadn't been difficult because most of my time was spent at Nikkyta's apartment, and balance of the night, recounting every intimate maneuver. If Commander Gordy hadn't called, I wondered how many rounds we could had managed before reaching a truce. It was fruitless harboring this thought; I needed to switch to my new role as an FBI consultant and leave the intimate memories for later.

James was in the driver's seat and Nikkyta sat next to him. The trunk of the Lincoln town car popped open and I stowed my luggage carefully. A Louis Vuitton bag and an Under Armour tote bag were already there and I mentally assigned them to Nikkyta and James respectively.

"How're you doing?" James asked.

I was shocked to hear him speak to me. The warmth in his voice carried no traces of deceit or dishonesty.

"I'm well, and you?" I said, cautiously.

"Not bad," he continued, "just another early morning, nothing new. Are you a hoop fan?"

"Yes, I am," I said, still unsure of myself, and Nikkyta gave off the impression that this was normal. She sat, unconcerned, looking at her phone.

"Catch any games last night?" He asked.

From my vantage point, I thought I caught a glimpse of Nikkyta cracking a smile, ever so slightly, and it made me wonder if images of us last night was flashing through her mind the way it was through mine. Our fused bodies convulsing in unbridled ecstasy and passion like a perfectly executed porn scene with the horrifying images of mutilated bodies strewn haphazardly around us. I was lost in this memory and I forgot to answer his question.

"Well, did you?" Nikkyta said, turning around, and snatching me away from my thoughts.

"Huh," I reacted sharply. "Ummm, yea. I mean, no. No, I didn't watch any games last night. I was knocked out early, I mean—yeah. Why, any good games?"

"Are you okay man?" James asked continuing to stifle me with kindness. "You sound like you're somewhere else."

"Yea I'm fine," I said, looking away from Nikkyta, so I could focus, "just getting mentally prepared for the day that's all."

"Don't stress too much man," he said, "You'll be fine."

Who's this guy?? I thought.

"Thanks, man," I said.

"No worries," he said, then quickly returned to the hoops topic, "you missed a great game last night! Sixers and Thunders! I'm guessing you're a sixer's fan, right? Being from Philly and all?"

"Yes, I am," I said, uncertainly, "I think Embiid and Simmons will do great things in this league."

"Oh, for sure!" James agreed, "but not last night though. Russel Westbrook came to play! The game went into triple overtime!"

"Oh really?!" I gave off a learnt display of excitement, "I missed a good one."

Even if I was alone the entire night in my suite, chances were I would not have been watching the game. Professional sports were something, I realized, I preferred to enjoy live, and with my comfortable financial situation, I did that often. I enjoyed the ambiance and the people. Seeing a sea of fans from different backgrounds all resting their allegiance, at least for three hours, on a group of tall men with unique athletic prowess made me hopeful for mankind. Over the years, I'd picked up a few facts to keep me relevant in conversations, and with Brady's surprising interest in this topic, I decided to use more of these facts, and hopefully create an unanticipated coalition with him.

"So," I began, expectantly, "are you a wizards fan?"

"Oh, hell no!" he blurted out, as if I had just insulted him. "I'm from Tulsa Oklahoma. Thunders, baby!"

"Oh, nice," I said, then quickly spewed some of the facts I knew about his team, "Yea, Westbrook and his triple double run have been impressive."

"True, true," he said. "But Paul George is really the guy to watch on that team, trust me. He's not getting enough credit."

"Yea, I think ever since Durant left, it's been tough to fill in that second spot." I continued, hoping I was impressing him. "He'll definitely get his due. He was not exposed enough when he was in Indiana."

He nodded, and it felt weird how much I enjoyed it. I appreciated his endorsement. It was not quite at the level of the senator's bold statements the day before, but it felt good. Although, one thing I didn't lose sight of the entire time, was Nikkyta's silence. Besides the brief moment she turned around to wrench my attention back from last night, she had been quiet. I wanted to know what kept her consumed, but keeping up with Brady seemed to take precedence at the moment. We continued around the league, and by the time we arrived at Hyde Field, we were laughing staggeringly about LaVar Ball and his antics. We all walked to the trunk of the car for our luggage. I had been right with the Under Armour and Louis Vuitton owners.

I noticed it was the same plane as before, or at least an exact replica of it. Agent Brady led the way, followed by Nikkyta, and then me. She was still quiet, although no longer on her phone, but it was beginning to bother me. A strange thought crossed my mind. *Is she jealous that I'm now friends with Agent Brady?* I incinerated the thought from my mind almost immediately. I decided I needed to break the silence, and I saw the perfect opening to do so. The lettering CH-800 on the tail of the plane had been something I noticed two days ago but didn't care much for the meaning. Now that I had more information, I had time for some mundane facts.

"What does that stand for?" I asked, pointing to the tail of the plane.

"What," she asked.

"That CH-800 on the tail of the plane."

"I'm not sure," she said, politely.

James overheard our conversation, "It's to determine the number of seats on the plane. The CH-800 means it's an 8-seater. CH-1500 would mean a 15-seater and so on."

"The man is filled with useless knowledge," Nikkyta teased.

"Be quiet," he retorted, smiling, "you're just mad you didn't know it."

"Hahaha," she laughed out loudly, "trust me. I am not that."

I was a little taken aback with their comfort level. Their carefree banter continued till we arrived at the plane's entrance. The same pilot that avowed his fandom at the Dover Air Force Base was there to greet us as we boarded. His exchange with Nikkyta and James was tame—professional, but when he got to me, his demeanor changed. He grabbed my palm enthusiastically and reiterated his admiration for my work. He asked the same question he did the last time.

"When should we expect another thriller from you?"

I wanted to respond, but I feared Agent Brady might barge in like before to kill the dialogue. I didn't want to decimate the rapport we seemed to have formed over basketball.

"We can definitely talk about this later," I treaded lightly, not trying to offend a true fan of my work.

Outside of planned events, I seldom bumped into fans, so having to abandon this rare opportunity, was tough. I wanted to suspend all else and talk freely with the pilot. To really show him my personality and with a bit of luck, leave him with the impression that I was a really good person, just like the imprint left on me upon meeting Jada Pinkett-Smith.

"Ok sure, no problem," he said, letting go of my hand.

He kept smiling, which gave me hope that I might not have offended him as much as I thought I had. I made a right to the rest of the cabin. My initial goal was to sit next to Nikkyta in the rear lavatory, but Agent Brady's sudden mood swing was beginning to make me reconsider. There were tons of basketball stories to keep us entertained for the duration of the flight. The reality when I faced the cabin, however, was nothing close to what I expected. The space was packed with the entire team. Beginning from Commander Gordy, then Agents Gabbert, Brady, Hunter, Taylor, and two faces I was seeing for the first time. The only absent face was Agent Tomkievich, the oddly-shaped, short, fat man. I took a hesitant step, perusing the space for a vacant seat. Sitting next to Nikkyta was out of the question because she was sitting next to Commander Gordy. They seemed to be reviewing a document together. I wondered if it was the gory case files that encircled us after our visceral lovemaking the night before. Agents Brady and Gabbert were on the same seats as the last time we were coming from the air force base. I recalled wondering if they were talking about me with the way they were smiling. My chances were dwindling for an 8-seater. The third pair of seats were occupied by Agent Taylor and one of the unfamiliar faces, leaving only the seat next to the other unfamiliar face as my only choice.

I sat next to her after securing my luggage in the overhead compartment and offered a practiced smile.

"Hi," she said, extending her hand, "I'm Vaishali Kumar, I'm in-charge of anything computer-related for this group. My strength is systems programming, but I've dabbled in enough applications programming to be relevant in it."

I nodded impressively as she spilled her credentials without preamble. Vaishali was of Indian descent and this fact was evident in her mildly-accented English. She was beautiful in a platonic sort of way. Her bushy eyebrows inclined slightly as she spoke. Her emerald green eyes appeared eager to validate her place on the team. She had a round button nose that seemed to fit with her high cheekbones. Her thin lips speculated a timid attempt at coral lipstick, and when she smiled, a set of dazzling angel-white teeth gleamed beneath. Her wavy coal-black hair plunged over her broad shoulders and routed its way down her left arm. Vaishali was heavyset, but she exuded the poise of a woman unbothered by society's misplaced perception of her kind. She had on a pair of tight blue pants and a free-flowing green blouse, which sagged to the left, exposing the thin strap of her beige bra. She sat with her legs crossed as she spoke.

"Nice to meet you," I said, grabbing her waiting palm. "I'm Ebenezer Cosmen."

"Yea, I could've seen you the other day," she continued with zeal in her voice, "but we were in a rush to the airport. Well, the air force base, but you know what I mean. So you're a writer, huh?"

I nodded, although not fully comfortable with the solitary labeling of a writer. I preferred the dual description of a writer and a programmer. It nourished my ego with the illusion that I was a smart guy. The perpetual narrative, especially from people who knew me before *Tilted Grin* and both sides of my brain working, was a portrayal I wished to nurture for as long as I could.

"Yes," I said, then I added, a little combatively, "but I was also a programmer before my writing career took off."

"Yea, I saw that in your file."

I have a file? I thought.

"So, what specifically is your role with the team?" I asked.

She snickered. "How much time do we have? The thing is, I do everything computer-related for them. And that's both software and hardware, so it's really difficult to narrow it down to one thing. Or even a few things."

"Wow," I said. "So, but what are the examples of some of the things you've done so far?"

She looked up as if in a deep thought, then returned with a sigh. "Well, for starters, I designed an operating system that we use specifically for this case. No offense to Windows or Mac, or even Linux, but I just felt we needed a more streamlined application to help with the haste at which information was going in and out. Although, it's still in its beta stage, and the rest of the Bureau know very little about it, Frank approved it for this mission. I demonstrated it for him about two years ago, and he promised he would make good use of it if the opportunity presented itself. I also help out with menial communication stuff like the switches and routers, fiber optics... I even wrote a messaging app that we use for everything from—"

The pilot's voice crackled through the speakers above, interrupting her patter and I was glad it did. I should have never revealed that I was a programmer as smugly as I did. It was obvious Vaishali was infinitely better with computers than I ever was or would be. The level of skill needed to create an operating system was something I couldn't even begin to fathom. To know that I was sitting next to a person that had moved through the rigors of that task suddenly made me feel small. I should've stuck to being called a writer, at least that way I could stand as a leading figure in that task.

When the pilot was done, Vaishali smoothly continued with her remarkable list of abilities. By the time she finished, I wasn't too sure if I was even the foremost go-to writer as I had originally thought.

"Wow," I exclaimed, "is there anything you can't do?"

She let out a nervous laugh. I noticed she was blushing, and I saw a different side of her beauty. Her eyes relaxed on the excitement, and the flawless symmetry at which her features laid on her round face added a little more to her allure. Her cheekbones turned red and she simply said, "Oh yea, there's a lot I can't do."

I admired her attempt at humility, but was convinced she could do it all. A strange feeling of insecurity overcame me. At first, I had entertained the idea of being one of the smartest in the room, especially with my dual skills, but after spending time with Nikkyta, and now Vaishali, my confidence was beginning to wane. I wondered where my intellect stood amongst these people. This question occupied my train of thought for the duration of the flight.

Next to me, was the voice of Vaishali revived and jabbering about something.

chapter18

The temperature at the Dover Air Force base was slightly colder than Washington DC, so I delayed Vaishali's exit by a few minutes to unzip my luggage and get my Levi's jacket. It was the only article of clothing I had to combat the cold. I did not anticipate being here for so long. The plan was to work on my manuscripts in my beach house and then return to New York for the show. Becoming an FBI consultant and jet-setting back and forth from Dover to D.C. was never part of the plan. The story of the "Tilted Grin Killer," especially since its first high-profile prey, was now the leading news report on all the major networks. The unending buzzing of my cellphone was becoming unbearable and Frank Gordy promised to get me a temporary phone when we arrived at the safe house.

As we exited the plane, a blue and gray van with government tags waited idly by the end of the runway.

"Is it possible to get my car?" I asked Frank Gordy.

"Yes," he said, without breaking his stride, "Agent Hunter will ride with you and you guys will meet us at the building."

I tried to hide my excitement. "Okay."

We walked the remaining yards to the van, and got in. This time, I sat next to the other unfamiliar face on the plane.

"How're you doing man," he said, in a smooth deep voice, "I'm Antoine."

"Hi," I said, grabbing his hand, "I'm Ebenezer. Nice to meet you."

Even though he was sitting, I could tell Antoine was a man of considerable height, and I immediately pigeonholed him as someone with substantial knowledge about basketball. I imagined him, Agent Brady, and myself at a bar, watching a game after a stressful day. The imagery brought a false sense of camaraderie I desperately needed with the group. Even though I was close with Nikkyta, and Vaishali and I seemed to connect on our shared love for computers— although I paled in comparison, I wanted to accrue allegiance with a male colleague. I believed that sort of work environment would provide the balanced information I needed for my next project. Agent Gordy was my Commander, so I didn't anticipate him being much of an ally. He seemed tough. And I mean tough in every sense of the word. His protruding muscles and uninterrupted scowl on his face, his clipped responses and determined strides, his seeming un-readiness for small talk and ordered posture all confirmed my assessment. I only wanted his attention as the last resort. As for Agent Gabbert, he seemed approachable, but the more I learned about him, the more I saw our only parallel was our stress-free attitude towards fashion. I realized I hadn't seen or heard enough of him to restfully state where we stood. Agent Brady and his opposing personalities made it impossible to understand him. Agents Taylor and Tomkievich, the odd couple, appeared to be FBI lifers. They came off as the type that only talked about the job, even at an invented bar setting with basketball on the screen.

"All set?" Nikkyta's voice jarred me away from my daydream.

"Yes," I sprang up.

I reiterated to Antoine that it was nice to meet him, to which he nodded in reply.

As the van pulled off, I heard Vaishali's voice call out, "See you later!"

This made Nikkyta chuckle.

"She's a piece of work isn't she?" she said.

"Yea," I agreed, eagerly, "is she always like that?"

"You mean, like, talks a lot?" She asked.

I nodded, as we continued our stride toward my Nissan.

"Oh yea," she said, "didn't you notice the only vacant seat on the plane was the one next to her. You're the rookie, so you get to endure it. You're lucky it was just an hour flight."

"She is smart though," I said, as if to defend her.

"No doubt about that," she agreed. "She just doesn't know when to be quiet and reflect."

"How long has she been with the FBI?" I asked, as I pressed the button on the key and watched the trunk of my car pop up obediently.

"About four years now," she said, "She came straight from MIT with a lot of rave and fanfare, and I must say, she has exceeded all expectations. At just twenty-four years old, she has influenced so much in the agency. Her future is very bright."

"Do you think there are people jealous of her rise in the bureau?"

"Oh absolutely," she said as she sat on the passenger seat after stowing her Louis Vuitton bag in the trunk. "Especially men overpowered by their pre-historic notion on the role of a woman. But she's in the right spot. She came up under the tutelage of Agent Frank

Gordy. As a matter of fact, we all did, except Agents Taylor, Tomkievich, and Jackson."

"Jackson?" I darted her a confused stare.

"Antoine," she clarified. "His full name is Antoine Jackson. They are a little older. They've been with the Bureau for a while."

"Why do you think Frank prefers younger agents?" I asked.

"I don't know if he necessarily prefers younger agents," she said, "I just think there's a certain 'it' he looks for. And it can exist in anyone, regardless of their ages. But of the young group, Agent Gabbert is the oldest. He's 33. Agent Brady is 32, I'm 29, and of course, Vaishali, 24."

"What's Agent Jackson's specialty?" I asked.

"He's a field guy as well. He used to be a D.C. officer for twelve years before switching sides. He also used to be married to Agent Gordy's daughter before her death."

"Oh wow," I exclaimed, "I didn't know that."

"How would you?" she retorted, "It's not like it made national news. This happened about thirteen years ago. I was still in high-school then."

"How did she die?"

"Armed robbery gone wrong."

We rode in silence for a while, after the drab topic of Agent Gordy's daughter. Within that time, I began revising my strayed judgment of Agent Gordy. The brief lesson I just garnered about him was enough to extend an invitation to the imaginary bar for a basketball game.

We arrived at the hideous FBI hideout in about twenty minutes, and Nikkyta instructed me to pull-up about twenty yards to the cul-de-sac at the end of the street. Nikkyta and I walked in, avoiding as much of the unkempt grass in the front-yard as we could. The house was already bustling with activities. I could hear Agent Brady and Agent Gabbert upstairs chortling about something. They seemed to be genuine friends even though, outwardly, they shared nothing in common beyond the color of their skin. In a corner to my right were Agents Jackson and Frank Gordy. They were discussing something in a voice just above a whisper. They talked with subtle hand gestures and the look on their faces took on one burdened with anxiety. I observed the pair differently now with a tinge of empathy upon knowing the unenviable grief they shared. Despite Commander's Gordy's leveled approach with his team, I couldn't help but regard his relationship with Antoine stronger than the rest. Losing my mother had been my nearest confrontation with losing a loved one, and I recalled how it strengthened the bond between my father, Caroline, and I.

I saw Agent Tomkievich and Taylor in the provisional kitchen heating up a snack in the microwave. The title of being an odd couple was beginning to agree with the way they moved. They seemed to do everything together. I could hear rattling noises coming from the room next to us, and I safely assumed it was Agent Kumar. I wondered what she was up to. In my brief time with her, she awakened the long-forgotten pleasure I derived from software developing. In spite of the extreme disparity in our skillsets, I enjoyed talking to her. Her superior knowledge of computers was humbling. It was the chastening I needed to put things into a proper perspective. We could both speak with an unbending consistency methodically unfurling the body of a computer program down to its skeletal beginnings of ones and zeros. This surprising commune provided an avenue for me to insert myself in the team beyond, in my view, the inadequate title of "consultant." I wanted to mean more. Before Vaishali, I struggled to find a place within the team. Agent Hunter and Tomkievich's abilities as behavioral scientists were something much beyond my scope of comprehension. My transitory knowledge about the human brain and its complexities made me far from being a contributing force to the team. And unlike the field agents, I have never shot a gun in my life. I do not even own one. I have been a fervent proponent against civilians owning guns. I felt that privilege should be reserved only for the professionals, and in spite of my role, I'm certainly not one.

"What's Agent Kumar doing in there?" I asked.

I did not expect Nikkyta to quench my curiosity. I merely asked as a license to end our time together and go work with my new ally. She had shown willingness to interact with me without much reservation. Although, Nikkyta had also granted me access, in all manner of speaking, I was not mentally armed to grasp the delicate tones of behavioral science. It was a topic too complex for me, and I only intended on taking it in small doses to fill in the gaps as needed in my next book.

"Who knows," Nikkyta said, allowing for a slight chuckle. "You wanna go check it out?"

I nodded like an eager son granted permission to go play outside.

"Enjoy," she said, and climbed upstairs to join Agents Gabbert and Brady.

The floor squeaked as I walked towards Agent Vaishali. The odd couple offered a polite nod and a smile as I walked past them. They were consuming, in timid bites, chicken melt dinner pastries, and I thought about stopping for a quick chit-chat, but Vaishali's task appeared more promising.

She was in the same testosterone-filled room where Commander Gordy had frankly laid out my job description. The room was no longer what I recalled. The round desk and four chairs from the last time had been substituted with a long round-edged rectangular table with a phone and a speaker at the center. Two comfortable-looking chairs were positioned at each end of the table, and a pair of four identical chairs were lined up both sides. There were three laptops on the table along with two smart phones and swirls of blue ethernet cords. Vaishali was balancing on one of the chairs, with a screwdriver, appearing to secure a camera on the opposite side of the entrance door.

"What're you doing?" I asked. I did not intend to, but the sound of my voice startled her a little, and I immediately felt bad about it.

"You scared me," she said, losing control of the screwdriver and placing her hand on her generous breasts.

"I'm so sorry," I pleaded, as I hurried to retrieve the dropped tool, "I didn't mean to scare you."

"No worries," she was laughing, as she gently descended from her elevated position, "you'll learn that

I startle easily. I'm sure you'll hear the guys call me jumpy once or twice before all this is done. I'm doing multiple things at once. First, I'm trying to setup this video conference call with Jeff Cumberland. I don't think you've met him. He is the eighth person on the team. Well, with you, ninth. But you get what I mean. He's currently in Texas, following up on a lead, so we need to keep him updated with what's going on here. I'm running a patch through the Operating System to fix a vulnerability I observed two days ago. I wrote an algorithm for it, and I'm pretty sure it's fixed, but Commander Gordy would need more than "pretty sure." I'm also setting up your new phone, along with your laptop, that will have my OS. So, yea, it's a lot!"

"Do you mean like another physical phone or just the OS?" I asked.

"An entirely new phone with my OS." She clarified proudly.

I nodded slowly.

I had a mild idea about the tasks she was attempting, and with a little guidance, I knew I could be of help, so I offered.

"Do you mind if I help?" I asked.

"Well of course I don't mind," she said sprightly, "you're tall too, so you can help with this camera."

She pointed at the device, barely latching on to the wall. With the few inches afforded by standing on my tiptoes, I was able to reach the camera. I drove the screws in place and gave it a forceful nudge to ensure its safety.

"All done!" I said eagerly, "What's next?"

She smiled, "Wow, you're really trying to impress the FBI, huh?! Well, in that case, we can get the wires going. We'll connect the ethernet cord to the camera input and the other end onto this PC. The IP address to use is on that piece of paper. We're doing static IP. Just make sure you change the network and sharing center. And mind you, we use IPv6."

"Really!" I exclaimed. "Is that an FBI thing? I've only used IPv4 when I was with the tech company in Philly."

"Eh, not really," she said, "I won't say it's an FBI thing. I've seen several departments in the agency that still use IPv4. I guess it's just a personal preference. To me, I find IPv6 more secure, especially with the 128-bit addressing system and the hexadecimals. It also reduces the size of the routing table, making it more efficient and hierarchical. But the real reason for me is IPv4 is running out of addresses. With smartphones, tablets, gaming systems, the 4.3 billion addresses would not be enough. With IPv6, it uses 128-bit addresses and is capable of creating addresses in the undecillions."

"Interesting," I said, not knowing what else to say. She was reaching the realms of things I knew very little about, but unlike behavioral science, I felt like with some effort, I could comprehend the vital points.

"Is IPv6 faster?" I asked.

"Not really," she offered. "They've actually done some testing on it and discovered that IPv4 might be a little faster, but there are some disputes with the testing. I just think that with all the testing, the human mind wouldn't even notice the—"

"All set?" Agent Gordy's voice interrupted.

He was standing by the door with his left shoulder leaning against the wall. On his face, I thought I noticed a hint of a smile, but I was unwilling to explore it. Even with all the favorable descriptions of him and his unquestioned affiliation with honesty, he still made me nervous. His daunting presence still made me conscious of everything I did around him. I obediently connected to IPv6 as instructed and typed the IP address and the subnet mask populated upon clicking on the text field below. I walked up to the camera, all the while avoiding eye contact with him, and turned it on. A gentle beep sounded, over the voice of Vaishali talking to Gordy, followed by three blinking red lights that subsequently turned green indicating their connection. The three-way handshake, a term used to acknowledge communication between the client and the server, was established.

"You still recall all this stuff?" Commander Gordy asked.

It took a few seconds to realize the question was directed at me.

"Ahhh... yes," I said, nervously, "This is pretty basic stuff. But Agent Kumar is light years ahead of me with this stuff."

"Whatever," Vaishali said, rolling her eyes but unable to conceal her red cheeks. "He's just saying that."

"Vaishali," Agent Gordy called, "take a compliment for once. The man genuinely respects your intellect."

"I refuse to be complimented for something so easy and rudimentary," Vaishali said in a mocking voice.

"Oh boy," Frank Gordy said, permitting a huge smile, and then turned to me, "you see what I have to deal with?"

I, too, allowed a smile.

"Well," Agent Gordy said, keeping his smile, "what's the time frame?"

"Give us thirty minutes," Vaishali said. "We'll be all set."

"Alright," he said, "I'll alert the rest."

Before he walked away, he turned to me and said, "Are you doing okay?"

"Yes, yes I'm fine," I responded quickly. "No worries so far."

"Good," he said. "We're about to have a meeting to update everyone on what's going on. Jeff Cumberland, I'm not sure if I've told—"

"I did your job for you," Vaishali interrupted playfully, "I told him about Jeff. You're welcome."

Frank laughed.

The ease at which they all talked to him, and the auspicious rapport he seemed to share with them made me realize my assessment of him might have been rooted in false logic. There was nothing about this man that revealed the authoritarian label my mind had prematurely given to him. He was nice. He was approachable. Besides the pissing contest with Matt in what seemed like years ago, he was friendly. Yet, I still felt rigid in his presence. My posture remained erect and my attention span settled unwaveringly on his expression in order not to miss an important signal from him.

"Why thank you," he said to Vaishali. Then returned his attention to me he added, "We will be meeting with Jeff today. I'll introduce you two. There's a possibility senator Gibson might be in the meeting. It's against protocol, but I'm allowing it this time. There will be no exchange of ultra-sensitive information, but just like I expressed to you the other day, no leaking to the media. Regardless of how unimportant the information is, we get to dictate what they get."

"No worries," I said, "nothing is leaking from me."

"Good," he said. "Vaishali, you got anything?"

"Yes, go away so we can finish our work."

Commander Gordy threw up both hands in mock surrender as he left the space, laughing.

chapter19

"**C**an everybody hear me clearly?"

We were looking at a split-screen image of the senator and a man I learned was Jeff Cumberland. From his sitting position, he looked a bit obese, especially in comparison with everyone besides Agent Tomkievich, but unlike Tomkievich, his weight seemed to be evenly distributed judging only from the top-half available on the screen. He had dark eyes, a puffy nose, and average-sized dark lips. His cheeks were round, and on all these distinct features lay a full head of white hair.

Both men nodded their response and Commander Gordy continued.

"Good. First, I'd like to welcome Ebenezer Cosmen to the team." He waited for a few seconds before continuing. "He will be taking on a consultant/advisory role. I'm sure we all know by now he wrote the book that seemed to have inspired this deranged killer."

"Oh my God! Are you serious?" Vaishali let out in gasped horror.

It took me a few seconds to realize it was a joke. Her humor appeared to lighten the mood in the room a little and everyone seemed a little relaxed afterwards.

"Agents Tomkievich and Hunter are leading the mental and behavioral aspects of this case," Agent Gordy continued with remnants of a smile still evident on his face, "along with reading the book, there's been an extensive effort on their part to gather a workable profile to work with. I will yield to them for a professional assessment of the case from a behavioral stance. Most of you have already heard this before. This is mainly for Ebenezer and Senator Gibson. Jeff, there might be a thing or two that are new from the last time we spoke. Gentleman, lady, the floor is yours."

He made a sweeping gesture for the two behavioral scientists to take over.

I wish I had better control of my reactions. My immediate temper, when I heard Nikkyta had read my book, was to dart a disbelieving stare in her direction. The look on my face did very little to conceal my discomfort. I thought our time together meant, at least, sharing small details like that. I did not know her reasoning for holding on to that piece of information, but whatever it was, it made me upset. My sulking made me miss the first few minutes of their summary. Agent Tomkievich's voice finally reeled me back in.

"So, as you can see," Agent Tomkievich pointed to an image on the screen, which was now showing on everyone's laptop. "The ear was found a few feet away from the body, and the killer had to walk to the other side to sketch his trademark. This level of comfort implies that he was not in a hurry. The killer must have been planning this for..."

His timid voice trailed off aimlessly in my head, in large part due to my unwillingness to revisit the gory images from the previous night. I'd seen all I needed from those images, and until I heard something new to excite my interest, I chose to focus on the dishonesty that seemed to have occurred. Why had Nikkyta read my entire book and not mentioned a word of it? Was it because it was not a good work of fiction? We've had . time—right from the hasty flight to D.C., to the steamy night at her place. I felt there was ample time to share such information. I wondered if I was being irrational. If I was making this a bigger deal than it actually deserved.

"Ebenezer?" The sound of my name pulled me away from my thought.

"Huh," I uttered blankly, "I'm sorry I didn't get that."

"Are you okay?" Commander Gordy asked. "You seem like you're elsewhere. Wanna take five?"

"No, no, no, no," I said, hastily. "I'm sorry. I'm back. Can you please repeat that?"

Reluctantly, Commander Gordy said, "I was asking if you had any questions with Agent Tomkievich's analysis, but now I'm not sure if you even heard anything he said."

Admitting I didn't hear him would mean I wasn't listening. It was not an impression I felt like leaving, especially not on the first day, and definitely not with my fervent advocate on the split screen. I had seen the pictures a day earlier, and I had been briefed by a scantily-clad Nikkyta on the behavioral aspects of the case. I felt that would guide me if Agent Gordy had a follow-up question to test my honesty.

"No, no questions," I tried to muster as much seriousness as I could. "I am definitely following so far."

I yearned to read the faces of everyone in the room to see if I was believed, but that would be too much. I concentrated on the few faces in front of me, and they all seemed to buy my story. Senator Gibson offered a satisfied smile, and so did Agent Cumberland. Agent Gordy's features gathered into something that resembled a smile, but I was not too sure.

"Good," Agent Gordy finally said. "So, Agent Hunter will brief us on the profile we have so far."

This time, I was laser focused on her. I made sure all foreign thoughts were kept far away from the borders of my mind.

"This killer," Nikkyta began, "is definitely using methods from *Tilted Grin*. I think we all know that. Right from the mutilated bodies to the slanted smiley face at the scene of each crime, each move has been strikingly identical to the book. That's until the last one: Jennifer."

I watched her pause for a second to gather herself. I shot a glance at the senator to observe the effect the sound of his daughter would have on him. His expression rarely changed. At this point I was beginning to expect less in terms of empathy from the senator. Right from our time at his Victorian-styled home in Georgetown, to the incredibly rehearsed press conference, Senator Gibson seemed to only use this tragedy for political expediency.

"With Jennifer," Nikkyta began slowly, "the killer was only consistent with one thing, and that is the smiley face trademark. Every other aspect of this killing deviated greatly from the first eight. Jennifer appeared to be a killing he needed to demand attention on a national stage. Of course, the media doesn't have all the details. And we believe holding it back from them will mitigate the risk of over-sensationalizing the horror and perhaps reduce rabid copycats that might obscure the case. The killer needs attention, and we believe it will be his downfall. Unfortunately, a few people might have to die, but a pattern is certainly in the works, and a few more killings would solidify our position, and hopefully, our apprehension of him."

Nikkyta took her seat after her grim assessment. The room seemed to be okay with the idea of a few people dying before we fully understood the killer. This was a fact that would never make it to the media—the callousness of it all. The brashness. In spite of its veracity, the media would exploit the lack of empathy attached to that sentiment and make the FBI chart a more humane course. Although the end result would most likely amount to more deaths as originally forecasted, concealing it in a web of compassion would help cope with it.

Agent Gordy took back the helm of the presentation, "Getting back to Jennifer," he said, "this killer was methodical. We believe there could be a drug component to this ordeal. Jennifer was athletic and markedly taller than the image we saw on the camera from the fourth killing, so to consider sheer strength and athletic prowess as the only source of overpowering Jennifer would be a stretch. Toxicology report is expected soon to settle on this line of thought. In the meantime, we've been able to identify the body with the help of the senator. We don't see a need to confirm with

DNA and dental records. The senator's word, along with Jennifer's wallet we found at the crime scene was enough to confirm the match. There would be no need straining the already backlogged DNA testing. Are there any questions?"

Agent Gordy continued following moments of no response.

"Good. Senator, I know you have to go, so feel free to do so. We're all caught up here. We will talk some personnel stuff, then close down for the day."

"Sounds good," the senator's voice materialized, "I want to thank you so much for letting me in on this session. I know it's not protocol, but I really appreciate the gesture."

"Not a problem, sir," Agent Gordy said. His lips gathered in what could only be loosely translated as a smile.

In an instant, the senator's screen faded to black.

Agent Gordy turned to Vaishali to confirm that the connection was truly gone with the senator. Vaishali offered a nod.

"Good," Agent Gordy began in a voice hardly above a whisper. It was as if he was speaking to himself. I had to lean in to hear what he was saying. "Okay now with the senator gone, there's been an interesting development in this case, that's the main reason for this emergency meeting. What we've talked about thus far was just an update for the senator, but developments such as these are reserved for us, and until I deem it safe for public consumption, it remains with us. Is that understood?"

I felt like his question was directed at me although he was not looking at me. It was something that had to be innately understood by the team after all. I doubted if he would see the need to say it if I wasn't in the room. I nodded like the rest of the team. For me, the idea of being privy to a sensitive development was gratifying enough. I was a freaking FBI agent! Alright, alright... consultant!

"Earlier when I said something about the senator identifying Jenny's body," Agent Gordy began, "that was not entirely true. Although we took the senator's identification, we did not bypass the DNA analysis. It was delayed, but not completely discarded. Two days ago, I received a phone call from the Delaware State Police about the victim, thought to be Jenny, being someone else. DNA and dental records were analyzed, and the result was not a match. I received the definitive result last night. Now, we are not sure if the senator was involved in this deception in any type of way, or if this was just an honest mistake because the victim looked exactly like Jennifer Gibson. I'm expecting more information on who Jane Doe is. In the wake of this mismatch, the body was examined closer and we found out it had been prepped—most likely professionally— by a makeup artist. The detail was incredible, down to the fake tattoo of a heart on her wrist to match the one Jennifer has. With the exception of Agents Hunter, Jackson, and Tomkievich, everyone is hearing this for the first time, so feel free to stop me at any point if you have any questions. The killing of this unsub was definitely done by the same killer. The usual—""

"Un-sub," I sounded each syllable of the word aloud carefully, "what does that mean?"

"Oh, I'm sorry," Frank said, "It means Unknown Subject. We are yet to determine the identity of the victim, so that's what we will call her for the time being. But the local authorities are working on it." He paused to guarantee comprehension on my part before continuing. "The usual signs from the previous killings were consistent with this one, but the main difference was the incredible makeup work done to shift our focus towards Jennifer Gibson. The victim also has a huge gun wound on her head. This development has birthed a plethora of unanswered questions: Is Senator Gibson a legitimate grief-stricken parent, or is he capitalizing on the political edge this would bring? In the meantime, the senator is now considered a person of interest, but this is not information to be shared with anyone outside of this room. He should not even know about this until we get something more concrete because he would surely involve the media, and it would be difficult to remain focused at that point. We will investigate all areas of this case and try to find a motive as to why this unsub was made to look like Jennifer. Any questions?"

I had plenty, but I didn't want to be the one to go first. The development vindicated my suspicions since I arrived at the senator's Georgetown residence. The lackadaisical approach after losing his daughter was unseemly. I questioned how much he truly cared about her, but it all made sense now, at least to me. I did not possess the type of analytical minds Agents Hunter and Tomkievich had, so I might not be able to see beyond the obvious, but it clearly seemed like the senator was either involved in the killing—although that appeared highly unlikely because of the high stakes involved—or he knew it was not Jenny, but realized the impact of what his daughter's death would mean for his political aspirations. And when the truth surfaced, no one would blame him, except his political foes, for not knowing the victim was not his daughter. From the gory pictures I saw with Nikkyta during our steamy encounter, I, too, thought it was Jenny. There was nothing about the image to make me question her identity. Anyone would have had similar thought. Well, maybe not anyone because according to Agent Gordy, Nikkyta knew of these doubts by the time of our escapades and she did not share any of it with me. I was not upset about this. If the roles were reversed, I wouldn't have either. I simply marveled at her knack to remain unmoved and function normally amidst such heavy objections. She was a consummate professional, and the more the particulars of the case revealed itself, the more the realization dawned on me. I needed to accept that and refrain from immature emotional outbursts over a concocted relationship that had no chance of ever coming to pass.

"I have a question," the hoarse voice of Jeff Cumberland sounded, and the room instantly granted him its attention. "When do you deem it appropriate to alert the senator that he's a person of interest, or a suspect, or even that the victim was not his daughter? I mean, what do we need to have before we make this public?"

"That's a good question," Commander Gordy said, "for now, I would like to gain more clarity in terms of motives. I know we all have our pre-conceived notions about politicians and whatnot, but as professionals, we cannot afford to act on that alone. The media circus and public opinion will dismantle the flimsy case we have right now. We would need something stronger. I don't know specifically what that would be, but I'll know once we get it. At least then we can face the media onslaught with facts and steady statements."

The room remained silent for a while. Everyone seemed content with the information thus far, but to me, there was one key question that still remained unasked. I played the question repeatedly in my head to make sure it wasn't stupid. I thought about forgoing it in fear that I might have overlooked a logical leap to help with the answer that they may already have, but the weight of the inquiry obliterated my ability to think clearly. I needed to know *this*. Timidly, I raised my hand.

Agent Gordy smiled. I wasn't sure, but I suspected it was because of my politeness.

"Ebenezer," he said, granting me the floor.

"Thanks," I said, then cleared my throat before continuing. "I'm sure Jennifer Gibson has seen herself plastered all over the news in the past seven days. If she's really alive, why not come forward and at least clear this up? And if she's somehow involved in this deceit, why is she not a suspect—I mean person of interest—like her father?"

"Excellent question," Agent Gordy said. I didn't have enough time to pause and scrutinize his reaction to my question to tell if it was genuine or an overreach on his part to boost my confidence. Because if it was indeed an excellent question, then I shouldn't be the one asking it in a space full of professionals.

"Right now," he began, "I have alerted a special team in Quantico to search for Jenny Gibson. It's a covert operation, and only exposed to the people who need to know. The working theory right now is that if the senator is in on this, then it's well within his capability to make sure Jenny remains missing. She is definitely a person of interest, but nothing more beyond that as it currently stands. That might change once we know more. Did that answer your question?"

I nodded. I had a few follow-ups, but I refrained from asking. I felt like I could find out the answers as the case progressed.

"Any more questions?" Agent Gordy asked the room.

There was a long silence before he spoke again.

"Good," Agent Gordy said, rising to his feet, "let's get checked in, relax, and keep your phones near. We will convene tomorrow evening if nothing else has happened before then. Ebenezer, you have a few options. You can either stay at your beach house in Rehoboth, or join us at the Sheraton. Personally, I recommend you join us so you won't have to consider the hour ride just in case we have to make a hasty departure. I'm not sure if you have enough clothing and whatnot, but just let me know. It can be expensed to our account. Also, work with Vaishali for your new phone and laptop. We have a secure network where correspondences only circulate amongst us."

"Sounds good," I said, "I think I'll join you guys. And no need for the expense. I'll handle that."

The room dispersed in seconds and the screen with Jeff went black leaving Vaishali and I alone.

"Let me see your phone," she said, reaching out her hand.

I dug in my pocket and brought out my iPhone. I turned it on and unlocked it using the retina display. Before handing it to her, I realized I had twelve new messages. When I looked at it, my heart skipped a beat. I realized I hadn't contacted Todd Granger, the producer for the TV show on the ID Network. It was now 12:36 p.m., and from my calculations, that was outside the window of recording. Although I'd seen the network make concessions in rare cases, and I'm sure they could make such exceptions for me, I knew his reaction would be explosive. He would need a detailed explanation to forgive me for this oversight.

"Can you give me like five minutes to make this call?" I asked of Vaishali. She nodded in affirmation and walked out the room. I took a deep breath and placed the call.

chapter20

THE FOUR bottles of Guinness that once subdued Blaine's movements were no longer a factor. The train ride, coupled with the excitement from lingering around Jenny's trail, had awakened his senses. He was fully alert and ready to accomplish what he hoped would be, his best work. He looked about his room, perhaps for the last time, to make sure there was no incriminating evidence left behind. Blaine had no intention of returning to his room. The spectacular murder was to happen in Jenny's room after which he would continue towards the exit. All he had was his gym bag. In it were things he would need for the act. Things such as a makeup kit, sharp X-ACTO knives, a silencer for his gun, a hammer... Blaine came prepared for his prey. This was the most he had ever packed for a victim, but he viewed it as a sign of respect for his first high-profile prey. He wanted it to be mistake-free, to linger in the minds of detectives long after today, and most importantly, to be secretly admired by law enforcements and copycats just like some of the great killings of the past.

Blaine's thought was hastily derailed by the sound of a door closing. It was so close that it had to be Jenny's door. Instinctively, he shot a glance at the iHome speaker on the nightstand. It was 8:43 p.m. Blaine was expecting his prey to be in bed in preparation for her dad's big announcement the following day. His plan was to commence the killing at 9 p.m., so this unforeseen movement caused him to worry. He gently opened his door just in time to see Jenny turn the corner towards the elevator. She was dressed in a dark-gray high-waist stretch yoga pants and a loose black top. Her bright pink sneakers were a departure from the dark theme of her outfit. Her right hand held onto her phone and dangling from the edge of the device was a pair of white ear buds. For a fleeting moment, Blaine paused to admire her dedication. He has had a front-row seat of her day, right from Sláinte Pub and Grill, to cheering on the Eagles, to the long ride on the train, and finally, checking into her hotel room. For her to remain dedicated to her workout regimen was impressive to him. She earned a point in his mind for her commitment to physical fitness. The idea of getting physically venerated had crossed Blaine's mind on multiple occasions, especially right after a killing. The physical chore often required to carry out the killings was a part of the process he hated the most. With his fragile body, it was a constant source of concern to overpower his targets before the actual killings. He had been very creative at devising plans that would place his victims in vulnerable positions before execution, and Jenny would not be an exception. From reading her emails over the past two weeks, Blaine had learned about Patricia Simon. She and Jenny were very close, and Jenny had informed her about her trip to Delaware for her father's announcement. Patricia had made a tentative promise to be there for the event but was unsure on when she would make it to Wilmington. Blaine's plan was to call Jenny's cellphone, which was the number the hotel had on file, and disguise himself as someone from the front desk. He would tell her a lady, by the name of Patricia Simon, was at the lobby asking to see her, and due to their security policy, it would be imperative that she came down to properly identify her. Blaine was certain that bit of information was wrong and extremely convoluted, but he safely assumed Jenny was not well versed with hotel protocol. She would oblige as requested, leaving an opening for the rest of the plan to proceed easily. Blaine was slightly perturbed with her last-minute decision to go to the gym, but he cleanly avoided the urge to let it rule his attitude. He used the free time to go over his plan and make sure all margins of error were eliminated. He rummaged through his gym bag to ensure everything he needed was easily accessible. During this digging, a piece of item fell out of the gym bag, but Blaine did not notice.

He estimated about an hour wait, so he turned on the television to see what the news had been saying about him. He found it amusing with how little they knew about the killings. They were working on facts and theories that had not been relevant since the second or third killing. Although he knew not to put too much stock in the reports, he was aware the FBI knew a lot more than what the news outlets were reporting, but the FBI would rather muffle the evidence in hopes to capture him without the meddling of the media. Blaine had been very careful about this fact. He took painstaking measures to reveal a part of his identity, but still maintained his inconspicuousness. He sweetly recalled a moment during the fourth killing when he deliberately revealed his masked face for the camera. He knew that that development would derail the FBI investigation for a while before they realized its futility. It was just like when he decided to use his left hand to scribble the words beneath the smiley face, knowing they would explore some known quirks of left-handed people in search of accepted labels and stereotypes to build a profile. Bringing the FBI along on this wild goose chase was exciting. It was almost as exciting as the actual killings. All he needed now was to make sure Jenny's killing lived up to the lofty expectation he had dreamt up in his mind.

As the news report switched to politics, Blaine heard footsteps in the hallway. *How apropos,* he thought, because the news report was now discussing Senator Gibson's march towards 1600 Pennsylvania Ave the next day; meanwhile, his daughter was taking her last steps towards her hotel room. Blaine stepped lightly towards the door to verify it was her. Jenny's room was right across Blaine's, so he saw her walk in. Drenched in sweat, Jenny's hair was pulled up into a tight bun as she staggered slowly into her room. Blaine felt an upsurge in his heart rate. This had not happened since his first two killings when the reality of what he was doing was still a novelty. He had since developed different techniques to handle the thrills that came along with his line of work. He quickly chalked the nerves as a result of his first high-profile case. He believed that the more prominent victims he amassed, the more regulated his heart rate would become.

In fear of linking his main phone to the killing, Blaine had bought a disposable phone for this undertaking. He expertly navigated to his contacts and arrived at a number he saved as "JG." He took a deep breath before dialing.

"Hello," a voice materialized almost immediately.

Blaine was not expecting the quick response. He wasted some split seconds arranging his thoughts. He cursed at himself for how disheveled he had been so far, especially for a killing that was meant to rival the greats.

"Hey ummm," Blaine began, in a practiced tone. "Can I speak to Jennifer Gibson?"

"This is Jennifer," she said, sprightly.

"Hi Jennifer, my name is Gabriel and I'm at the front desk. I have a Patricia Simon here at the lobby to see you. I want to—"

"Oh really! Pat is here!" Jennifer reacted excitedly, "send her up. It's okay."

"Yea ma'am," Blaine sounded reluctant, "we typically don't do that. It is hotel policy that after 9 p.m., our guests must come down and identify their visitors. We can't just allow anyone to go upstairs."

"Really?" Jennifer sounded skeptical. But it was late, and she was not in the mood to argue over something so inconsequential. She was elated Patricia had decided to provide support for this event that she had dreaded for months. She would have to paint a rehearsed smile on her face the entire time and exhibit a faux display of enthusiasm and gusto for her father's ambitions. And worst of all, she would have to interact amicably with his wife, Marcy.

"Alright, no problem. I'll be down there in a second."

Jennifer gathered a few things and pulled the hotel door open. Standing before her was the small figure of Blaine Grubber. His gym bag hung over his left shoulder, and on his right hand was a small pistol aiming directly at her. Remnants of the smile when she thought Patricia was downstairs still remained on her face, but dread and anxiety had quickly occupied most of her expression. She stood motionlessly, trying to slowdown the events of the past thirty seconds. The haste at which her mind had just travelled between opposite ends of her emotions was exhausting.

"Do not make a sound," Blaine said calmly. "Go back in the room and sit on the bed."

It took a few seconds for the words to register in her mind, but slowly and wordlessly she obliged. Her heart raced uncontrollably like the lunatics on the interstate as she sat on the king-size bed. She struggled to make sense of anything that was happening. Just moments ago, her heart rejoiced with the idea of dealing with her father's charades with a true friend; now she was trying to figure out why a pistol was pointing at her. Nothing made sense. The only place her mind went was her father and perhaps his political foes hoping to harm his cause. Jennifer had observed the increasingly toxic rhetoric in politics, but she never imagined it would reach such levels of desolation and hopelessness. She tried to control her thoughts to no avail. She was hyperventilating. Her breathing, just like her emotions earlier, bounced from sky-scraping highs to cavernous lows. She wanted to wake up from this nightmare... or at least understand what was happening. She wanted to scream, but the pistol pointing at her chest discouraged it.

"If you do as I say," Blaine was infuriatingly calm, "we won't have any problems, but if you try to be brave, then you'll have yourself to blame for what happens next. Is that understood?"

Jenny nodded trying valiantly to suppress the sounds threatening to escape her lips.

Gently, Blaine dropped the gym bag on the floor. His gun was still trained on Jenny although he was sure she wouldn't do anything stupid. The look of fright on her face was enough assurance he needed to know she would be a compliant victim. Slowly, he unzipped the bag and brought out a blue-handled X-ACTO knife. The pointed blade glistened from the rich illumination in the room as he held it up to the light. He smiled when he stole glances at her. She was terrified and it showed. Her mood excited him. On the 40-inch TV, a reporter from the E! Network continued tirelessly about Matthew McConaughey and his current movie project. Blaine enjoyed the noise, but he'd rather work in silence when she was unconscious. The voices in his head were of better substance than the garbled content emanating from the television.

"Here," Blaine said, tossing her a pair of handcuffs. "Cuff yourself to the bed."

It had been about ten minutes and Jenny was beginning to regain control of her breathing. She grabbed the handcuffs and did as instructed. Blaine was impressed she knew what to do. He walked to her and ensured that she was properly secured to the bed. Now with her mobility guaranteed to remain still, Blaine felt at ease to move around without directing the gun at her. He quickly emptied the contents of his gym bag and arranged them neatly on the dark brown table located in the corner. He scrutinized the items for a few seconds and his face contorted forming wiggly stress lines across his forehead. *It can't be,* he thought as he reached agitatedly for the gym bag and peered in it. Jenny was quiet, but her gaze rested intently on the little man before her. He was noticeably disturbed by something, but she was too discombobulated to steer the situation to her advantage. She was still trying to accept the authenticity of her current predicament.

Blaine tossed the gym bag back on the floor and turned to his victim.

"I'm about to leave for a few seconds," he said coolly, as if he was not just agitated, "I need you to remain quiet. You've been excellent thus far, and as you can see, nothing has happened to you. I will need the same attitude, especially for this minute that I'll be gone. Understood?"

Jenny nodded dutifully as tears travelled down the smooth contours of her face.

Blaine turned towards the exit. His small hands grabbed the handle and pulled the door open. He paused for a second to look at Jenny. He was satisfied with the condition she was in. She was terrified and wouldn't do anything to jeopardize the peaceful turn of events so far. As he walked out of the room and onto the hallway, Blaine heard the undeniable sound of footsteps to his left. He felt his heart skip a beat. This was not good for him. Once the investigation of Jenny's death began, he could be placed around the area leaving the venue of the spectacular murder scene. He needed to do something fast, but he was scared to make eye contact. That would only make matters worse. He already had a memorable physique, couple that with his face and the FBI would have enough information to conduct a massive hunt. The social status of his prey ensured that would happen swiftly and competently. He needed to clear this hurdle. He needed to do something fast. His mind raced. He cursed at himself for not being as prepared as he normally would. If not for his carelessness of forgetting the black piece of rag he needed to gag his victim, he would not have had to deal with this hindrance.

Blaine decided to continue his stride without making eye contact. His room was right across from Jenny's, and in spite of his short legs, he would only need about four steps to his destination. He decided to risk it. He made it to his room before the owner of the footsteps got too close. As soon as Blaine was comfortably situated in his room, he stood on his tiptoe to see the person walk by. Mere seconds later, his face was drained of color. He turned pale and his heartbeat bounced erratically like lotto balls in a lottery machine. The person with the footsteps was the front-desk attendant and her destination was Jenny's room. Balanced on her left-hand was an elegant silver tray with a pair of white plates on it. The contents were covered, and next to the plates was a cream-colored napkin, utensils, and a salt-and-pepper shaker. The lady paused as she was about to knock to announce her presence, reacting to the opened door. Reluctantly, she peered in the space and then uttered clearly, "Room service."

Blaine realized this was catastrophic. The lady would see a sobbing Jenny handcuffed to the bed; her reaction would initially be that of shock and confusion. She might translate it as a kinky exercise between her and the dainty man that was seen exiting the room. But as soon as Jenny voiced the dire nature of her condition, her reaction will hastily morph into contacting the authorities. It would only take minutes to recall seeing his unforgettable body walking away from the scene, and his dream of being a respected killer would be dashed, all because of an amateurish error on his part. He could not allow this to happen.

He needed to act.

Fast.

The prospect of creating a spectacular murder scene was no longer of great importance to him. He needed to stop the lurking calamity. Unwaveringly, he opened his hotel door, gun in hand, and walked resolutely to the room across to confront the two ladies, that were no doubt, in desperate need of answers for what was happening.

chapter21

The dialogue with Todd was intense. He screamed and hollered about what I'd done to the show.

To his job.

To the network.

He made it sound like my action was the worst thing to ever happen to a marginally popular show on television. I did not engage in the verbal skirmish. I gave him the opportunity to spill his grievances, and by the time he was done, we agreed to record the show later that evening. The episode was to air in two weeks, so my delay would only cause a few late nights for the folks in the editing room.

I went for Vaishali's attention when I ended the call with Todd so she could finish setting up my new form of communication. The conversation with Todd placed me in a sour mood, so I was a bit repellent to Vaishali's magnetic personality. She noticed my demeanor and quickly shifted her mood to accommodate mine. The exercise transpired flawlessly, and in about forty-five minutes, I was texting a few trusted contacts to alert them of my new temporary number. Ray called immediately to make sure it was really me.

"Look," Ray said, in response to me teasing him, "I just gotta make sure; it's a lotta crazy people out there. Watch the news and it's all kinda eavesdropping and monitoring and shit going on."

"Whatever," I chuckled. "Well, I'll be in Delaware for a while, until we get this guy."

"And how close are you guys?" Ray asked.

"Come on Ray," I exclaimed, "you know I can't tell you any of that. Just watch the news like the rest."

"I can't believe you're one of them," Ray said, jokingly, "what do you think I'm gonna do with the information, tell the media?"

"Yes!" I said emphatically. "That's exactly what I think you'd do."

He laughed, "Well if I did do that, it'll be to increase your account balance."

"And I appreciate that," I said, truthfully, "but this is one time when the media can actually hurt me. I can't lie, the media has helped a lot with my career, but they are not useful this time."

"Alright, alright," Ray surrendered, "I got you. Look, I gotta run to Virginia real quick. Let's talk later."

"Everything okay?"

"Yea, yea, yea," he assured me, "just business stuff that's all."

"Alright cool. Talk to you later."

My new phone had been buzzing intermittently the entire time I was talking to Ray. The device was still new to me, so I didn't bother checking it in fear that I might accidentally end the call. Navigating the phone was a bit different from the iOS, Android, or Windows operating system. It was a custom system designed by Vaishali mainly for this group. As I began to press the buttons and swipe through the screens, I realized it was intuitive just like what I was used to. I maneuvered to my text messages and saw that I had responses from my sister, Caroline, my father, my ex-girlfriend, Joseena, and my attorney, Matt—these were the people I deemed suitable to have this number. If I were ever in an emergency situation, the aforementioned all possessed fragments of pertinent information about me that would likely exonerate me, depending on the quandary, from my predicament.

"Hey, I'm going on a food run," Vaishali said, poking her head in the room. "What would you like?"

"Ummm," I hesitated, "what are my options?"

"Olive Garden, pizza, or burgers," she said.

"What are you getting?" I asked.

She smiled, "I'm not sure yet."

"Can I come with you and decide on our way?"

"Sure," she said willingly.

I closed my new laptop and placed it gently in its bag before exiting the room. The decrepit house looked empty as I walked towards the front door to meet Vaishali in the driveway.

"Where is everybody?" I asked as I walked to the passenger side of the government-issued vehicle.

As Vaishali formed her lips to answer my question, we heard the loud and angry voice of Frank Gordy materialize from inside.

"Goddammit!!! Who the fuck did this?"

We rushed back in the house the same time Commander Gordy stormed down the steps. Behind him were Agents Hunter and Jackson at a more controlled pace.

"What's going on?" Vaishali asked.

Frank Gordy blew past her ignoring her question. Agent Jackson did not waft past her with the same speed and intensity, but he too refrained from answering.

"Somebody tell me what's going on?" Vaishali repeated, with Agent Hunter in front of her.

"We have a leak," Agent Hunter said calmly. "Someone released the information about the last victim not being Jenny to the press. It's all over the news. Although, due to its explosiveness, they are cautious with the way it's been reported, but the story is out there. It's only a matter of time before they gather enough sources and boldly report everything. The senator will definitely—"

"I need you guys in here right now!" Frank Gordy bellowed.

We all rushed to the room we were just in for the video call. Frank was conspicuously irate from this new development. His breathing was audible in the small space, and it seemed as if his muscles had enlarged by a few inches threatening the survival of his undersized shirt. Frank looked around the room and noticed two of his men were missing.

"Where are Taylor and Tomkievich?" he asked.

"They just left for Seaford to check out the cosmetologist," Agent Jackson answered.

"You said they just left?" Frank confirmed.

Antoine Jackson nodded.

Frank turned to Nikkyta, "Call them and tell them to come back immediately. It's urgent!" He turned to Vaishali, "Get Jeff on the video call now!"

After barking out the orders, Frank sunk his chiseled body in the seat next to him in an attempt to control his rage. His breathing was still labored and the look on his face remained unchanged. He kept his eyes closed and elbows resting on the table. His fingers came together in a weave, creating a landing spot for his square chin. The room was eerily still aside from Nikkyta and Vaishali trying to execute their tasks. The television in the room flashed, and moments later, the image of Jeff Cumberland appeared. His hair was a bit disheveled from his earlier appearance, and he was wearing another shirt. He had a look of confusion on his face, but he didn't say anything.

"Jeff," Frank began, measurably calmer than moments earlier, "we have a major problem with the case. I'm waiting on Taylor and Tomkievich to get here so I can update the group."

He turned to Nikkyta, "What's their ETA?"

"They just got off the highway," she said, "they should be here soon."

Minutes later, the irrefutable sound of a car engine was heard in the driveway. The front door squealed open and soon footsteps got louder. The odd couple appeared with confusion written all over their expressions.

"What's going on?" Agent Tomkievich asked in his wimpish voice.

"Have a seat Earl," Frank said.

He grabbed the remote for the other television in the room and pressed the power button. He entered the channel number for CNN, and as anticipated, the report was the leading story. The room paid attention to the report for about a minute before Frank pressed the mute button. He turned to the group and calmly asked, "Who did this?"

The room was unresponsive.

Even though I knew I did nothing wrong—I'd taken exhaustive measures to ensure my communication remained within the limits Commander Gordy clearly laid out for me a couple days ago—I still felt nervous. I felt the blame would fall on me over something careless I may have done. My mind raced back to the conversation with Ray and Todd. They were the only people that attempted to gain information from my privileged position, and I recalled vehemently dismissing their efforts. I should not have been feeling this way, but Agent Gordy was too intense for me not to. In my regular life, encounters with people like him were non-existent. I functioned well in that scene. At this very moment, I realized how much I missed that life. The pressure of this one was too much for me to handle. There was too much responsibility. The notion of possessing knowledge of things that could shift the mood of an entire nation was humbling. Quite frankly, I did not enjoy being around this much power.

"Ok," Frank Gordy continued, "I don't expect anyone to speak up now, but just so you know, once I find out, and trust me I will find out, that will be it with this group. The information will go into your personnel file, and that will be problematic with future assignments. It doesn't matter how skilled you think you are; everyone is expendable if the situation calls for it. Remember that."

The room remained silent.

It was uncomfortable.

Thankfully, Commander Gordy's phone buzzed to life. He grabbed the device and scrutinized it for a few seconds before answering.

"Frank Gordy here," he said.

His cadence indicated he was not familiar with the caller. He nodded a few times and uttered a few "mmhmms" and "uhuhs." A minute into the conversation, he motioned Agent Jackson for his pen. It glided across the table and stopped within his arm's range. He reached for the pen and was soon scribbling something on a paper. He thanked the caller for the information and hung up.

He sighed heavily before speaking.

"That was the local authorities," he began, "we have an identity for our unsub. She's Tracy McGovern of New Castle, Delaware. Twenty-six years old and a sophomore at Wilmington University. She worked as a front desk attendant at the Hilton Hotel in Wilmington. We have also confirmed that she was working the night Jenny was thought to have been killed, and Jenny's Amex report shows the same hotel booking for one night. Hotel records showed she checked in around 8:23pm, but never checked-out. So, this is the new hot spot to explore. We believe the murder either happened, or at least started, at the hotel. The shopping center where the body was found was never the scene of the crime. Just a dumping site. Taylor and Tomkievich, I need you to resume your trip to the cosmetologists in Seaford. We counted three reputable cosmetology schools between Seaford and Dover. We need to know if this killer was professionally trained because the makeup and disguise are beyond the scope of an average makeup artist. Take Ebenezer with you. Hunter, Brady, and I will take a ride up to Wilmington. Gabbert, Jackson, and Kumar will remain here in case we need to deploy an agent hastily elsewhere. Jeff, keep us posted with any new developments. And guys remember, this is not the end to this issue. I still have every intention on finding out the leak, and when I do, you will be replaced. Let's all meet at the hotel tonight."

chapter22

I felt like I had the boring portion of the mission. Visiting a cosmetologist was nowhere as exciting as the hotel where the murder might have occurred. I figured they placed me on this task because it posed the least amount of threat to my life. I recalled Frank telling Matt that I would not be placed in the line of fire because of my inadequate field training. I guess it made sense, but that rationale did very little to alleviate my dislike for the current situation. The odd couple, despite their inseparability, rode inaudibly the entire time. It was as if it was their first time together and each party was trying to figure out what to say. I tried heroically to engage them in a conversation, but their one-word responses and lack of enthusiasm quickly turned me off.

The first school, in Seaford, was called Restored Beauty School. It was a mid-level operation with about four buildings swallowed in a wide expanse of unkempt grass and dirt roads. The lady we spoke to appeared unenthused to speak to us. She provided precise answers to our questions but did very little to expound on her responses. We went to two more beauty schools spaced out over a stretch of about five miles, and each new reception mirrored the first. We decided to move further north in search of favorable treatment. I noticed we ignored one name on the list as we moved up north.

"What about Delaware Learning Institute," I inquired, "I think that's the last on the list before we head north."

"Earl already covered that yesterday," Agent Taylor responded.

"Yea," Agent Tomkievich concurred in his wimpish voice, "it was my idea that we investigate these schools in the first place. I stopped by there yesterday evening while you guys were still in D.C. and they were of no help. Although, not quite as rude as the ones today, but little information to work with."

I nodded. In my mind, I tried to imagine the thrills and excitement that Nikkyta and her crew were experiencing at the moment. I wished for a miracle to end this ordeal, but I understood it was just a fantasy. This was my fate, at least for today, as a consultant. I decided I would spend time with Nikkyta tonight to catch up on all I missed from the hotel in Wilmington. With this thought, I was able to endure the rest of my time with the odd couple, and by the end of the day, we returned to the hotel with nothing but tales of rude customer service and stretches of barren lands that lined up that part of the state.

chapter23

My room was not quite as stylish as the Donovan in D.C., but it had the basic amenities to ensure a tolerable night. There was a queen-size bed plopped in the center of the room consuming over fifty percent of the space. A pair of brown nightstands stood on opposite sides of the bed like devoted guards. On one of the stands, was a bible and a lamp, and on the other stand was a speaker-radio combo with the clock visible in bold, red numbers. A forty-something inch television sat right in front of the bed, and beneath it was a dresser with four rows of two drawers. A table stood timidly on the far corner of the room, and on it was a pen, pad, and a reading lamp with its cord twisted down to an electrical socket on the bottom of the table. The room smelt of cheap cleaning supplies and mildew. A few black stains appeared at random spots on the carpeted floor, but not enough to request a different room. I tossed my luggage on the bed and fetched a few essentials I needed to get through the night. It had been a long day filled with events that tugged on opposite spectrums of my emotions. First was the hurried trip back to Delaware for an emergency meeting with the group—a group I learnt included the senator. Then, there was the news of a possible conspiracy with the senator to fabricate his daughter's death. It was too much for my inexperienced mind to handle. I needed the systematic mind of Nikkyta to simplify it in ways that would make sense to me. Unfortunately, when I returned from my uneventful voyage with the odd-couple, we headed straight to the hotel to check-in. There were no signs of the crew that went to Wilmington. When I inquired from Vaishali, she informed me that they were still in the middle of it. *Whatever that meant.* I surrendered to the room I was assigned to and searched for something to do. Vaishali had invited me to dinner earlier with the available crew, but I politely declined. I was not in the mood to manufacture a personality that would match her fiery manner. Vaishali was fun to be with, but not when it was arduous to match her charismatic demeanor. I preferred to remain alone for the evening. I felt my stomach growling, so I decided to risk the hotel's food options. I called downstairs for their culinary choices, and of all the delicacies that the raspy voice presented, the fish and chips appeared to be the safest. I placed an order for one and I was informed that it would be brought up to my room in about ten minutes.

During that time, I attempted to make the space feel a little more comfortable. I brought out my smart speaker and connected it to the Wi-Fi network in the room, and then proceeded to instruct it to play the smooth jazz station. At that precise moment, I heard a timid knock on the door. I quickly shot a glance at the speaker-radio combo and realized it had been ten minutes since I placed my order.

"Be there in a second," I hollered towards the door, as I grabbed my wallet for the tip.

The image before me was better than food. Standing there, was the delectable figure of Nikkyta Hunter. A seductive smile settled on her face as she stood there.

"Well, hello," I said, in the best sexy tone I could muster.

"I see you were expecting someone," she said.

I thought I detected a tinge of jealousy in her voice. Or maybe that was just a figment of my imagination, in an attempt to fortify my ego.

"Yes, I was," I said slowly, deliberately leaving out information to see if her display of jealousy would reveal itself fully.

"Oh," she said, "need me to come back?"

I realized my attempt at playing hard to get would cost me this rare delightful opportunity.

"No, no, no," I said forgoing all pretense, "it's only room service. I ordered fish and chips about ten minutes ago. Please come in."

"Oh," she chuckled. "Why didn't you go out with Vaishali and the crew? There's an okay bar down the road that we typically go to."

"She invited me," I said, "but I was not in the mood. I didn't want to force anything. The ride with Agents Taylor and Tomkievich drained my energy. I was so exhausted and uninspired with them."

"Really," she more said then asked. "That's too bad. Here I was, hoping you were full of energy."

She was standing in a seductive manner, daring me to act.

After seeing her naked body on two occasions, I was no longer timid in her presence. I accepted her invitation, and soon we were a tangled mess of intertwined legs, and fused bodies, and ruffled linens. We kissed passionately for a while before delving into other things. I reached in my luggage for the condom, and moments later, I was inside her. When we were done, Nikkyta laid deliciously at peace in my arms as our breaths rose and fell. I wanted to remain like that forever, but unfortunately, it was not to be. A knock on the door pugnaciously disrupted our peaceful cocoon. We sat up, wordlessly wondering who it could be. The look on our faces revealed the thoughts in our heads. It would be disastrous for any member of the team to find out about us. After moments of no response, the knock sounded again, but this time, accompanied by a raspy voice.

"Room service."

I heaved a sigh of relief. The look of wariness on my face quickly morphed to a smile. Nikkyta was smiling as well, but she was no longer in bed. She picked up her clothes and went to the bathroom. I slipped into a pair of basketball shorts and a t-shirt and walked towards the door.

I looked at the clock on the nightstand and realized it had been over thirty minutes since I placed the order. I wondered if there had been an attempt to deliver the food, but was dissuaded by Nikkyta's muffled yet audible, moans. I tipped the woman with the raspy voice liberally, and she thanked me as she walked back towards the elevator. When I returned, Nikkyta was fully clothed and sitting comfortably on the bed with no intentions of leaving. This pleased me. We scarfed down the food as if our lives depended on it. When the plate was empty, I considered calling downstairs to ask the raspy voice for another serving, but I quickly decided against it. It was close to 10 p.m. Instead, I bought four packs of Herr's potato chips and two bottles of Pepsi from the vending machine by the elevator next to the ice maker.

"So, how was your trip to Wilmington," I asked. "Did you guys find the killer yet?"

"Ha," she laughed, "I wish. It was eventful though. We now know for sure that the killing happened in the hotel room and not the parking lot where the body was found. The room still had some bloodstains in hidden corners, most likely forgotten by the killer when he was hurrying out of the room. On that night, only three rooms, including the murder scene, were occupied on the fourth floor. The room across and the one to the right. The one across was reserved by a Blaine Grubber, and the one to the right was by a Tyrone Stanton. Tyrone was a regular at the hotel. Our findings indicated he typically lodged there at least once a month. As for Blaine Grubber, that was his first time. He paid in cash, and did not leave an address or phone number. We might be heading back to Wilmington tomorrow to talk to Tyrone some more. The Commander really has a bad feeling about this Blaine Grubber guy, but I don't know how I feel about it. Honestly, I don't imagine someone involved with these killings to be that careless."

"That's pretty good progress," I said, approvingly, "I wish I could go with you guys tomorrow. It sounds more exciting than visiting cosmetology schools."

Nikkyta let out a hearty laughter.

"Was it really that bad?" she asked.

"You have no idea," I said, gesturing animatedly with my hands, "First of all, we drove for miles on some forsaken road. There was nothing in the town. Every once in a while we would speed past a gas station or a convenience store. Then at the schools, the administrators did very little to hide the fact that they didn't wanna talk to us. To make matters worse, Taylor and Tomkievich didn't even speak to each other. They didn't turn on the radio, or even listen to a podcast. Nothing. I was ready to blow my brains out."

"It's funny because I've heard that before," she said. "but it was from Vaishali. So, I just concluded she might be exaggerating. You know Vaishali. She has an unreasonably high appetite for conversation that not too many people can satisfy. I've never really worked closely with both of them together. I've worked a lot with Tomkievich. As a behavioral scientist, he's really good at his stuff. I've learnt a lot from him. But he's the type of guy that's not that interested in climbing the proverbial career ladder. He's pretty content with his post. Me, on the other hand, I wanna take this to the top, so I had to continue with other missions. I was a bit surprised when I learnt Frank had him on the team. I thought I was going to be the only behavioral scientist for the case. I found out he was a late addition. Frank told me about it the day before were supposed to leave for Delaware. As for Taylor, outside of our joint meetings, I've never really interacted with him that much. I know he's married with two boys and they all live somewhere in Northern Virginia."

"What about Tomkievich," I asked, "Where does he live?"

"Actually, he lives here in Delaware," she said. "At least that's what he told me a few years ago when we were working on a different case. Smyrna I believe."

"Really?" I considered, "I guess that makes sense."

"What makes sense?"

"We were supposed to go to one more cosmetology school, the Delaware Learning Institute," I said, "but we ended up skipping that. Taylor said Tomkievich already visited there yesterday."

"Yup, you're right," she agreed, "It definitely makes sense. He rarely travels to D.C. with us unless it's critical. He likes to stay local, and as long as he gets the details of a case electronically, his job could be done anywhere with a Wi-Fi connection. Technically, I can be like that too, but I have my sight set on bigger things, and being present in person is definitely a key ingredient to achieving that."

"How old is he?" I continued with the questions.

"I think forty-two," she said. "I'm not entirely sure. I know the bureau surprised him on his 40th, and that's about two or three years ago, but I'm not sure."

"How long has he been an FBI agent?"

"Umm," she paused to think. "I remember when I first started, he told me that was his fifth year, so this year should make it twelve years going by that."

"That's a long time," I said, and then quickly added, "How did he and Taylor get to be so close?"

"Now that is the mystery of the century," she said, flashing her beautiful smile. "No one really knows how they got to be that close. I know Tomkievich recommended he teamed up with a field agent for this case and Frank appeared to be okay with it. He put them together and they've been inseparable ever since. I know Taylor doesn't really care about being partnered with him. He's someone that would rise to the top in this agency because he's willing to obey chain of command. He plays it by the book and rarely gets involved with baseless chatter. The higher-ups would like someone like him to head a department one day because of his squeaky clean reputation around here. The main thing I know him for is his strength. He's known to bench-press ridiculous amount of weight. Legend has it that he broke Frank's record by bench-pressing 400 pounds seven times."

I nodded my head impressed at what I heard about Agent Taylor. I knew he was no stranger to the gym with the way his suits fitted his body, but unlike Frank, he wore his size, so his biceps and other protruding muscles were left to the imagination.

"Interesting," I said after moments of silence.

I wanted to ask about Agent Tomkievich's figure, but I didn't know how to phrase the question without flirting on the boundaries of tactlessness and insensitivity. Fortunately, I felt the day had been salvaged. Learning more about my co-workers gave me the sense of satisfaction I desperately needed. As I was about to ask another question, I heard Nikkyta's phone ring. She had the same device as the one given to me by Vaishali, but her color was blue and mine was gray. For an instant, I wondered if blue was her favorite color. My mind raced through gift ideas with the color blue. Tiffany's, maybe? I realized I was going mad with these thoughts, so I switched my concentration back to Nikkyta. She was finishing up with the person on the line. She focused her attention on me, but the look on her face was confusing to interpret. Whoever the caller was, they had given her an information that didn't sit too well with her.

"What's wrong?" I asked, concerned.

There was a pregnant pause, then she slowly said, "That was Frank and he's wondering where I was. He called my room a moment ago."

"What did you tell him?"

"I told him I was downstairs, enjoying the cool breeze," she said. The wariness in her voice was evident.

"What's the worst that can happen if he finds out about us" I asked, smugly. "I mean you're an adult and can be—"

"Ebenezer, please!" she interrupted with venom in her voice, "this is my career we're talking about. In my world, sleeping with a consultant is not something that's supposed to be done. Of course, I'm an adult and I would not be reprimanded as a child, but it's the slow, but damaging reputation you build over time that I'm concerned about. I don't expect you to get it. But I need to get out of here and make it downstairs without getting caught. If I use the elevator, it might open up to Frank sitting at the lobby. If I head back to my room, he might be there waiting for me."

I was a bit rattled with the stern manner in which she talked to me. My ego wanted to defend my honor, but I realized I was being naïve. I was viewing our sexual act from the world I came from. In my world, such acts would be applauded as a great feat.

"But it's almost 11 p.m.," I said. "What would he be doing in your room?"

I realized what I was insinuating with my question, but I didn't care. Possessed with an intense feeling of jealousy, I wanted to know why it was okay to be alone with Frank at that hour.

"Are you serious," she snapped, "the man is old enough to be my father! What's wrong with you?"

I didn't think my question warranted such a harsh response.

"I'm sorry," I said, "I'm just asking a question that's all. I'm not reaching any conclusions."

She shook her head and walked towards the bathroom. A moment later, I heard the sound of running water. I grabbed the remote and turned on the television. My goal was to go another round with Nikkyta, but my poor line of questioning seemed to have ruined that. A heavyset woman appeared on the screen. She had on a flowery dress and spoke in rapid Spanish. It was a game show filled with colorful graphics and an audience laughing hysterically. I moved up two channels and arrived at a documentary about Navy Seals. Then it dawned on me! I needed to call Todd and setup my recording for the show.

In that instant, Nikkyta appeared from the bathroom. The disturbed look on her face was gone, and in its place was the tantalizing appearance that disrupted all my thoughts.

"Can you do me a favor?" She asked. Her voice sounded like a damsel in distress.

And like the knight in the shining armor I imagined myself to be, I perked up and gallantly asked, "What's up?"

"Can you please go downstairs and see if Frank is at the lobby or just outside the hotel?"

"Sure, I can!" the words rushed out of my mouth.

"Oh thanks," she said, her smile widening, "text my regular number when you get down there."

"I don't have your number," I said hesitantly.

"Yes, you do," she sounded confident. "It's the number I called you from when you were at the Donovan."

"Oh, ok," I said. "Will do."

I slipped into my slippers happy to fulfill her wish. Somewhere in the bowels of my mind was an outstanding task I had yet to complete. The call to Todd was just in my head, but it was quickly erased by the revived Nikkyta.

chapter24

THE LADIES stared terrifyingly at the muzzle of the gun held by the small man. It was aiming at Tracy, the front-desk attendant because she posed the most threat at the moment. Balancing on her left-hand was the silver tray wreathed with two covered plates, a cream-colored napkin and two miniature containers of salt and pepper. Blaine realized the items could be used as a weapon if she was bold enough. Although, the look on her face assured him she was not, he also knew of the unexplainable strength attributed to cornered animals, so rather than relying on the look of fear on her face, he decided to erase all doubts. He instructed her to drop the tray and move closer to Jenny. Blaine was a bit surprised at how calm his voice was. Just moments ago, he was close to abandoning his wits when Tracy unexpectedly showed up at Jenny's door. He was willing to barge in, guns blazing, and end the scene violently. Now, seeing the look of horror on their faces, he realized they were too scared to do anything. His commands would be obeyed without much qualms. Tracy dropped the tray and moved closer to Jenny as instructed. They sniffled and cried silently. The horror could not be contained as they huddled closely with their grief pouring out in a flood of uncontrollable tears. Blaine grabbed the tray and moved it away from their reach.

He rummaged through his bag and brought out another handcuff and tossed it to Tracy.

"Cuff yourself to the bed just like her," he said still maintaining his calm demeanor.

Tracy, shaky hands and all, did as she was told.

"I thought you were at the front-desk." Blaine asked, "Why are you delivering food?"

For a moment there was no response. Blaine was about to repeat himself when Tracy spoke.

"We're short staffed today," she said, attempting to quiet the fear in her voice but failing miserably.

"So, who's watching the front-desk?" Blaine continued.

"No one is there right now," she said. "I placed a sign that I'll be back in a minute."

"Really?" Blaine said permitting a wry smile across his face.

Tracy nodded nervously.

"What about the kitchen?" Blaine asked. "Who's there making food?"

"The chef," Tracy said. "He should be finishing up in a second. The kitchen closes at 11, so he's probably preparing his last order, then he spends the next hour cleaning up."

"Were you going to deliver that order too?"

"I'm not sure. He didn't tell me anything."

"Is the chef the only one there?" Blaine asked.

Tracy nodded, and then added, "Everyone else called out tonight."

Blaine wanted to ask why, but he quickly remembered the region's obsessive interest in football.

"So, no one will come looking for you for a while?" Blaine asked, with a sardonic expression on his face.

Tracy was unsure on what he meant. "Huh, I'm sorry?"

"Me too," Blaine said in between heavy breaths, "Me too. I'm sorry."

Gently, he squeezed the trigger.

Jenny had been in a trance for the past few minutes. The high hopes that regenerated when Tracy walked in the room were quickly ruined when Blaine showed up behind her moments later. All expectations of living beyond this night were dashed. She subconsciously embarked down memory lane reliving some of the treasured moments from her childhood. She recalled when her family still functioned like a normal one before the toxic appeal for power brought about by politics. She recalled the way her father used to look in her mother's eyes whenever they spoke. She hoped to meet a man with such enthusiasm and dedication to her. That was before Marcella...or "Marcy." That was when her father had just written to their congresswoman, objecting to the municipal's decision to build a pipeline running through their backyard. The letter was incredibly detailed and filled with poignant points that subsequently halted the project. Terry Gibson gained a bit of a reputation from this endeavor. Letters expressing the constituent's grievances on a plethora of other issues raised his visibility amongst the city's leaders. Then, a late-night visit from one of these elites began the end of their close family bond. Terry was nudged into politics and the rest, as they say, was history. He climbed meteorically through the ranks, and upon saving the African-American woman from her abusive white lover, there was no other logical destination than the top. Marcy, once his personal assistant, had taken the spot as the potential future first lady, placing Jenny in a never-ending cycle of contempt for her new parents. But now, with death lurking, she wished she had not spent so much time disliking them. She hoped for one more chance to reconcile. One more chance to let—

Tracy's limp body fall against hers. It took a few seconds for her wits to catch up with the moment before she realized Tracy had been fatally shot in the head. Her immediate reaction was to let out a thin shrilled cry. The cry would have lingered longer than ten seconds if not for the gun aimed at her head.

"Let's not do that again," Blaine said evenly, "or you'll end up like her."

Jenny nodded frightfully. Muffled sounds managed to escape her lips. The waterworks that congregated in her eyes now fell hurriedly in twin streaks of tears down her face.

When Blaine felt the shrill outburst was now contained, he walked towards the dead front-desk clerk and undid the cuff that held her closely to the bed. Tracy's lifeless body slumped further onto the carpeted floor. Blaine grabbed the body bag and laid it measuredly next to her. With great effort, he rolled the body over until it was inside the body-bag. Jenny could see the look on his face and easily surmised he was not enjoying that part. His small frame struggled with the unresponsive body, but he came out triumphant in the end. Tracy's body laid limply in the black body bag that was originally intended for Jenny.

In between heavy breaths and a sweaty face, he said, "That was meant for you. Too bad you'll have to tolerate my presence for a few more nights till I decide on what to do with you."

Jenny did not react, but in her mind she saw an opening. The idea of a few more nights gave her confidence. Despite her feelings for her dad for the role he played in decimating their family, she was grateful to be connected to him. In a few more nights she was certain his influence would have summoned the elite members of the FBI, CIA, and any other agencies deemed appropriate to find and rescue her.

"But," Blaine continued in a raised tone and index finger, "you can play a part in ending it right now if you don't obey my instructions. I am going to uncuff you, and you will walk gently, with my direction as a guide, towards my parked car downstairs. If we run into anyone along the way and you attempt to draw attention to yourself, I have no problem brandishing my gun and killing everybody. I don't know if you've been paying attention to the news report, but killing people gets me excited. The more bodies, the more excitement. Are we clear?"

Jenny nodded.

The idea of her father's power was more encouraging than seeking attention from a stranger along the way. For reasons unbeknownst to her, she believed him when he said she would be alive for a few more nights and she had no intentions of doing anything to ruin the precious gift of life.

Blaine walked towards Jenny and uncuffed her. He instructed her to lead the way. When they came out onto the hallway, he instructed her to make a right rather than a left towards the elevator. Jenny walked cautiously. Her mind raced through a myriad of reasons why they appeared to be going in the opposite direction. It took a few steps along this path before she realized his motive.

They were electing to take the steps.

Chances of running into a stranger were extremely rare with the staircase, especially in a hotel as sparsely populated as this one. She pushed the door open and it griped with a squeaky sound. The space was clean and well lit. Tentatively, she approached each step, and although she didn't have the courage to look, she believed Blaine was behind her matching each stride. His steps were very light, and in spite of the unnerving silence, it was impossible to hear his breathing. When they made it to the final landing, they were confronted with two exit options.

"Wait," Blaine said crisply.

He placed his tiny palm on the door-knob to his right and gently squeezed it. He leaned his tiny body against it and the door budged a little. It was enough for him to poke his head and see where it led. In that instant a thought flashed across Jenny's mind. A brave thought to reach for the other door and blindly continue to wherever it directed. But the more the thought pestered, the more she realized he still had a gun, and despite her bravery, it would be foolish to think she could outrun a speeding bullet. The risk involved was too high to consider. She banished the thought from her head and allowed the little man to run the show. The first door Blaine peered into led to the lobby. It was empty just like Tracy had said. Blaine realized it would be unwise to follow that path. Cameras and chances of running into a hotel guest were extremely high. He repeated the same action for the second door and a look of relief passed briefly across his face. Jenny was unsure on what he saw but was taken aback with his features. He almost looked personable.

"Let's go," he said insistently.

Jenny walked through the second door. It led to the rear parking lot of the building. Midway through their walk, the headlights of a red Toyota Camry in the corner winked.

"Hold on!" Blaine said sharply. The sound of his voice implied concern.

Jenny obeyed and stood still.

Mere moments later, two white girls materialized skimpily clad in short tight dresses and laughing hysterically as they stumbled towards the red car. One was in high-heels and the other was barefooted. They appeared to be returning from a job in the hotel room. One of the girls yelled out "Quick draw McGraw" and a sidesplitting laughter followed. They didn't seem to notice the small man and the lady in front of him. Jenny wanted to get their attention, but the possibility of losing her life as a result was enough deterrence she needed to remain still. The ladies, in their inebriated states, were ungraceful. It took a few tries, but they finally located the car key and drove away seconds later. Blaine heaved a heavy sigh of relief and instructed Jenny to continue along the path towards the dumpster. She feared he was going to get rid of her, but her mind settled when they arrived by a van and Blaine slid open the side door.

"Get in," he snarled.

Besides the front seats, the rest of the van was an open space covered with a black blanket and a flat pillow towards the rear of the vehicle. The space reeked of disinfectant and it almost made her choke. Jenny did as she was told, and Blaine tossed the handcuff to her. She did not wait to be told what to do. She grabbed it and secured herself to a metal bar next to her.

Blaine smiled at her efficiency.

He climbed onto the van and verified that she was set in place.

"I will be back," he said.

He slid the door shut and walked back towards the rear entrance.

A few minutes later, Jenny was roused by a new source of hope. At first she saw the bright light, then she heard the sound of the engine, and a car materialized. It was the same red Toyota Camry that had driven the two girls out of the lot. This time, the car did not pull into a parking space. It stopped in the middle of the lot and one of the girls stumbled out. She staggered about the space, clearly looking for something.

"Did you find it," the driver called out through the window.

"Bitch, if I saw it would I still be looking?" the other girl barked.

Jenny was suddenly alert and seriously considering getting the women's attention. Blaine had been gone for over ten minutes, so she knew her window to react was narrowing with each indecisive second. She looked at the door one more time to make sure Blaine was still not coming before she made her move. Earlier, she had vehemently dismissed the idea of involving anyone else. She would rather depend on her dad's mighty influence over all else, but with Blaine gone for as long as he had been, and with these girls stumbling aimlessly around her, she figured it would be her best chance to ask for their help. Both girls were now out of the car in an intense search of something they dropped during their drunken walkthrough earlier. *But what could they do?* Jenny thought. In their state, they might complicate things even further. They were clearly not at the height of their mental capabilities and that might fatally impact her fate. She decided against getting their attention. She deliberately sunk further down into her space reducing any chances of being seen.

The girls wandered around aimlessly for about three minutes before the one with no shoes exclaimed, "Got it!! It was in my hand the entire time!"

"Bitch!" her friend retorted.

A hearty laughter ensued as both girls got back into the car and drove off.

Upon witnessing the gross ineptitude that just transpired before her, Jenny was thankful she didn't get their attention. She felt she could endure Blaine for a few more nights. She believed her father would have men with big guns to rescue her before then. As Jenny raised her head to check on the door, she saw Blaine struggling to drag the body bag along, and it dawned on her why he took so long. Observing the way he struggled with loading the body bag, she could only imagine the process to roll the body down four flights of stairs. But now his struggles seemed to be over. Blaine was pulling the body across the parking-lot grounds rather easily. He slid the van door open and stared at his high-profile prey.

"You did very well just now," he said proudly, "I commend you for not giving in to the urge to alert those tramps. Although I wished you did so I could have more bodies to play with."

He let out a creepy sound that was meant to be a laugh.

Jenny cringed with fear. She was glad she had not acted on her impulse to alert the girls.

Blaine bent over and grunted as he un-artfully rolled Tracy's body onto the van. He was breathing heavily but was quite proud with his display of strength. Although the night had not neared what he had in mind, he was beginning to appreciate the new findings about himself. First was his remarkable display of calm when Tracy showed up unexpectedly with the tray of food. He marveled at the way he diffused the situation without much commotion. Outside of the impulsive shrill from Jenny, reacting to the lifeless body next to her, he appeared to have carried out this mission without anybody having a workable story for the FBI. The strength he exerted by moving the body down four flights of stairs, then restraining the urge to kill the two drunken prostitutes that delayed his exit were also worth celebrating. What he was most proud of, however, was the way he had trained Jenny to obey his orders. Even in his absence, Blaine had observed carefully to make sure she did not try to get the attention of the two girls. That made him feel good. He translated it as a sign that his reputation was now a source of fear in the hearts and minds of people that knew about him. In spite of his gun, it was a natural human reaction to explore any chance of freedom unless you were gripped by immense dread and anxiety. This was the feeling he wanted from his prey. Their terror and distress fueled him beyond comprehension. As a child it was the opposite. He was the one who possessed this feeling of dread and horror. He feared the bullies in school, his priest, and his stepfather. Most of the major characters in his childhood had imposed some type of fear in him, but they seemed unsure on what to do with that type of power. Their interests resided in, what he considered, menial things such as taking his lunch money, using him for his intellect, or satisfying a perverse sexual desire. Blaine was unmoved by all of this. He numbly participated in their amateurish usury, but when it came time to payback, they all suffered immensely. The bodies of the bullies were never found. The priest was literally caught with his pants down, and in order to conceal all embarrassment, the church hid the true story behind his death. His stepfather was his only regret. He did not get to him in time before his heart attack. At that point Blaine was convinced of how he wanted to spend his time. The look of terror in the eyes of the bullies had excited him beyond any other life experience.

He needed more of it.

The Tilted Grin Killer had been a source of inspiration. Although he admired the disguise with cosmetics and maquillages, Blaine felt he could be better. He saw things in the killer's skillset that speculated reduced intellect. Blaine realized he could do better because he was smarter. What he lacked in size and strength was satisfactorily accounted for in wits and hasty reasoning. Blaine enrolled in a cosmetology school in Delaware to learn about makeup and other skills with the sole intent of disguising anyone. Now, in a van with two girls of almost similar features, Blaine decided he would throw the authorities for a loop. He would disguise Tracy's features to mimic Jenny's and he would see how long it would take them to rewrite the truth.

chapter25

I was a few steps from the elevator when I realized I had the wrong phone with me. Instinctively, I grabbed my regular phone, but I now realized we were only to communicate with Vaishali's contraption for the time being. Slightly perturbed, I headed back up to my room for my other device. It was the only way to communicate to Nikkyta about the condition in the lobby. I dug in my pocket and retrieved my hotel key. As I pushed the door open and prepared myself to explain the reason for my premature return, I saw Nikkyta balancing awkwardly on a stool with a set of wires dangling from a position above her head. In her left hand was a red and black small-sized drill. She turned around in horror when she heard the sound of the door opening. Her inelegant posture and the peculiar tool in her hand made it impossible to hide anything. The look of confusion flooded my face as she lowered herself from her obstinate situation.

"What's going on?" I asked, unable to subpoena a sense of calm in my voice.

"Look, Ebenezer," she said slowly, "please calm down. I know what you're thinking, but trust me it's not what it—"

"You can't possibly know what I'm thinking!" I almost yelled. "I don't understand what's going on here. I don't know what to think right now. What is that in your hands? What are those wires for?"

There was an uneasy silence and I could sense from her expression that she had nothing to say. Through her eyes I felt I could see the inner workings of her brain scrambling to concoct a believable story to douse my boiling suspicions. She had not expected my untimely return, and the look of shock was still plastered all over her face. Her expression was void of the routine look of poise and self-assurance. She appeared helpless. The only time I've seen her this way was during takeoff or landing. For a brief moment, I felt sorry for her, I wanted to walk up to her and let her know everything would be okay in spite of what she might be up to. This feeling, however, was easily shoved to the side. I needed answers, and no amount of dependence on her appearance could dampen my growing rage.

When she realized my inflexible demeanor, the need to say something became a visibly heavier burden for her. She sat down timidly on the edge of the bed with the drill still in her hand. She looked at me for a long second, and then looked away.

"I don't know how to begin," she said.

"How about with the truth!" I snapped.

"I understand your frustration," she began, "but I will need you to please try to be calm, and I promise I will explain everything. Please, lower your voice."

I didn't say anything. My militant posture was unwavering as I waited for an explanation.

"After the leak," she began slowly, "we've been trying to figure out who was responsible. We met—"

"And you thought it was me!?" I erupted, unable to restrain myself.

"Can you please let me finish?" she raised her voice a little.

I was taken aback at her ability to find courage in her defeated state. I admired it.

"Ok," I said, granting her request, "I'll let you finish."

"Thank you," she said, appreciatively. She waited a few seconds before continuing. "Like I said, we—me, Frank, and Antoine—met to discuss this matter about a leak. I guess Frank picked us because we were the only ones he trusted completely. He—"

"Did he authorize you to do this, too?" I exploded again, reneging on my promise, "Whatever it is you're trying to do!"

Nikkyta got up to leave, "Okay I see you're not going to let me finish. I can't communicate this way if you're gonna keep interrupting me."

"Wait a minute," I said, and reached out to grab her. "You don't get to walk away. You were caught violating my space, and now you think you can just walk away. Na, it don't work like—"

In one expert maneuver she grabbed my outstretched hand, pushed the palm back, and gave it a fierce twist. Before I could come to grips with what was happening, my entire body was spun around, and I felt her hand in the back of my head, driving it forcefully towards the mattress. In just a few seconds, Nikkyta was sitting on my back, with my face buried in the pillow. My left arm was twisted agonizingly behind my back. All attempts to free myself only intensified the pain.

"Don't you ever try to put your hands on me like that again," she growled.

I was unsure of how to react. It happened so fast. I couldn't imagine continuing any dialogue after that humiliating debilitation. Nikkyta, who was a good foot shorter than me and almost eighty pounds lighter, had just handled me with the ease and comfort an adult would a child.

"Get off me," I muffled.

"Are we gonna be ok?" she asked. "Do I have anything to worry about if I get off?"

"Get off me," I repeated. I was too embarrassed to say anything else.

Gently, I felt the pain in my arm subside, then her light weight gently disappeared from my back. I turned and stared everywhere else but at her. I was desperately hoping to find someone assisting her so I could justify my pathetic display. My battered ego would relax if it knew a woman half my size did not just handle me like a ragdoll.

"You're lucky I don't hit women," I said, struggling to salvage the ruins of my shattered ego.

"Yea, I thank God for that," she said flatly.

Her words incensed the shit out of me, so I glanced at her. She was struggling to hold her laughter, and it made the situation worse.

"Can you please leave?" I said.

I was no longer interested in what she was up to. My ego needed attention, and I couldn't do that with her around.

"Are you sure?" she asked. "I can explain what I was trying to say before. You just have to—"

"No, it's fine," I interrupted. "You can go. I don't need to hear anything else."

I thought I saw a look of remorse on her face, but then again, I was too distraught to understand what I was seeing. As the door closed behind her, I walked towards the elevated position I caught her in to see if I could determine her motive. The spot had two fresh holes around it, and I quickly inferred it was from the drill she had in her hand. She appeared to be trying to install something in that space. The only thing I could think of was a listening device or a camera to monitor my conversations. This meant they thought I was the leak, and this was their attempt at finding out. Rather than being upset, my curiosity grew. I knew I was not the leak, but this meant someone amongst us was, and if I could discover the perpetrator, it would certainly give me the respect I sought. This realization restored a bit of my belief in the process. Momentarily, the disgrace I suffered from the hands of Nikkyta was replaced by my newfound goal. I was now determined to find the leak. In my mind, I held this mission at the same regard as the pursuit of the Tilted Grin Killer. I would let them chase that asshole while I tried to earn my respect.

I felt good about my new purpose. Now I needed a plan. A place to start. I was going to do this all by myself. The only person I felt compelled to exonerate was Commander Gordy. There was no logical basis to think that he leaked the information and then made a big fuss about it. That would be stupid. Next on my list was Agent Brady, but before I continued with my line of thought, I realized I needed to jot these down. Even though I had a pretty reliable memory, putting it all on paper would definitely organize the plan better. A Chinese proverb that states that "The palest ink is better than the best memory." On top of the notepad, I wrote down Frank's name. I did not have anything to pin on him, so I continued to Agent Brady. I paused and took a deep breath. I knew I had to be objective and clear-minded in order for this to be a success. I held the pen in my hand for about two minutes with nothing to show. I suddenly came to the stark realization that I knew very little about the team. Nikkyta and Vaishali were probably the ones I knew the most, and even that was not enough to populate more than half of the page. Reluctantly, I began with Nikkyta. The thought of her inevitably led to recalling the beating I received earlier. The zeal that fueled my ambition only moments ago was now substituted with disgrace and dishonor. I thought about abandoning the project altogether, but something in me pressed on. My crushed ego would have to endure the shame for the greater good. As I reached this heightened state of understanding, I felt my mind open. I quickly recalled the chummy interaction between Nikkyta and the senator in his home on the day of the press conference. They were certainly friends, and maybe more. The thought of them together fouled my mood a little, but I quickly corrected it. I needed to stay focused. I was getting somewhere with this train of thought, and I could feel it. I needed to feed it, and not allow my unproven feelings for her get in the way. I paused and took a deep breath. It was obvious the senator was somewhat of a playboy, and Nikkyta was breathtakingly stunning, so it made sense that the senator would want to be friendly with her. Powerful men often felt entitled to the company of beautiful women. Now I needed to find out if the feeling was mutual. Was Nikkyta interested in him that way? I couldn't see it. She didn't seem like the type that was easily impressed with power, or at least trade her career path for bedroom thrills. Just at that moment, a contradictory thought occurred to me. Maybe she was interested in him because of the amount of power he amassed and how that could benefit her rise within the ranks of the FBI. But why not call the senator directly? Why go through the media? My inquiring mind turned these questions over relentlessly. I imagined going through the media would shield her better as opposed to talking directly with the senator. From the little I knew about journalists, they could risk almost anything to protect their sources. If needed, she could rely on the media's ability to protect her identity. This development filled me with a mix of jealousy and excitement, but I knew I had to concentrate more on the latter. Jealousy over someone I had no relationship with was silly. Nikkyta had proven, at least with me, that she moved pretty quickly towards what she wanted. I did not consider myself overly attractive, and certainly not in tiptop shape—Joseena reminded me of this after my broadcast in the senator's coat—but Nikkyta still approached me, and we made love. Three times. Nikkyta went for what she wanted, so what if her friendly deportment with the senator was part of a bigger plan to create a rapport with the future president? That was certainly an avenue to explore. It was well within the boundaries of logical reasoning to deduce that she called the media and alerted them of the mistake between Jenny and Tracy. That way, the senator could protect himself as needed. But then, why call the media and not the senator directly? Calling the senator would let him know it was her and he could allocate favors correctly when it was time. Now, I felt like I was going in circles and repeating the same questions. I had no answer to this quandary, but I felt confident in the case I was building against Nikkyta. A part of me wondered if this new obsession was remnants of the animosity I held against her for the disgrace. I wasn't sure if I knew the answer to that question, but I refused to capitulate what I had thus far. I decided to sleep on it and see how I felt in the morning. If the fire still burned as fiercely to investigate further, I would do just that. At the end of the day, my respect with the team was the only goal...I thought.

chapter26

My phone rang at a quarter past seven in the morning. I was shocked to learn that I slept through the night. I was expecting my sad display at self-defense to haunt my dreams, yet I felt relaxed and well rested. I reached for the phone and realized it was Commander Gordy.

"Good morning, Commander," I said, alertly.

"Hello Ebenezer," he responded, sounding like he had been up for hours. "How was your night?"

I was just about to respond when the events of my night came rushing back like an angry river. I recalled Nikkyta, before handling me, tried to tell me how Commander Gordy met with her and Antoine to decide my destiny. I cursed at myself for not allowing her finish her explanations. If I had, I would have had enough ammunition to escort the bitterness I now held for Frank Gordy. I viewed him as a principled man with a knack for telling uncomfortable truths if needed. I did not expect a covert mission to discuss my fate. This was an aggressive departure from who I thought he was. Right from the first day in that dilapidated building, his brutal honesty appeared to set a precedence for the way things would get done. His strong candor was something that equally scared and pleased me. I was scared because I did not want to unknowingly find myself on his bad side. His explicit warnings of stripping me of my position in the team were loud and clear. I took punctilious steps to ensure no leaks occurred on my end, I warded off attempts from both Ray and Todd when they tried to sniff something out of the investigation; so to meet clandestinely at my expense was hurtful. I wondered how much of an ally Nikkyta was at the meeting. Did she try to uphold my innocence, or was she the leading voice behind my persecution? Was I the only person being investigated since the entire team was not in on this secret meeting? Did they try to install hidden cameras in the other rooms as well? These thoughts stalked my mind and I forgot I owed Frank a response.

"Are you there?" he said.

His voice snatched my mind away from my wayward thinking. I responded unsteadily, "Yea....umm.... yea, my night was good. It was good."

"Okay," he uttered slowly, suspiciously, but he didn't linger much on it. "Well, we are meeting at 8:30 in the lobby. It is imperative that you're there. We will be going over some of the plans for the day."

"Sure, no problem." I responded curtly.

I didn't think he noticed or cared about my clipped responses. He simply said, "Great, see you there." And hung up the phone.

I lay in bed, fuming.

The untainted admiration I once held for the man was now mingled with ire. I was still filled with fervor to discover the leak, but I was not sure if I still valued the respect it would garner. It would be self-serving, but I was ready to walk away from the investigation and watch it on the news like the rest of the country. I knew I was acting like a petulant child, but I didn't care. It was disheartening to see the two people I held in high regard conspire to prove my guilt rather than talking to me directly. I knew I probably did not have a strong basis to hold Nikkyta to such regards, but Frank! I signed his goddamn contract stating the details of the investigation would remain amongst us. It was not as if I'd betrayed his trust in the past. I deserved a conversation, not a candid-fucking-camera. The more I thought about the web of betrayal, the more my blood boiled. There would be nothing sweeter and more gratifying to walk away from the case mere moments after revealing the leak from my fact-finding efforts. The thrill of this mission excited me to no end. I spent the next thirty minutes showering and preparing myself for the 8:30 meeting. Ray checked in to see how I was doing. His text message said I should call when I woke up. I did not think that was a good idea. Calling him would inevitably lead to me telling him my new plan, which would then follow an impulsive trip to Delaware to try to talk me out of it. Ray, for the most part, only saw the dollars and cents equivalent in a situation, and there was no doubt that being in this case until the killer was apprehended would surely yield top dollars once the book was written, along with the accolades and, dare I say, Oprah's Book Club. That was an argument I had no retort for. He would remind me of how it had been my dream to be taken seriously in this genre, and here I was trying to tear it all to shreds over something small. I knew there were no amount of words in the English language to ease his concerns, so I made the decision not to call him just yet.

When I arrived at the breakfast meeting, they were all there. I noticed an obese man with dark eyes and puffy nose sitting with them. At first, I was unsure who he was, then my mind raced back to the video conference meeting we had with the senator. It was Agent Jeff Cumberland. He was taller than what his image on the video call suggested.

"Ebenezer," Jeff bellowed, in a guttural voice akin to the sound of a gathering storm, "Nice to finally meet you. How do you like being an FBI agent?"

I hate it! It's the dumbest job ever to be around so many dishonest people.

"Not bad," I said, "it's been interesting so far."

He let out a hearty laughter.

"Alright guys, let's get started," Frank interrupted.

We all sat around a moderately sized round table. Frank sat at 12, Jeff at 6, and the rest of us were evenly distributed on either side. To my right was Vaishali, and across from me was Nikkyta. I had yet to make eye-contact or even acknowledge her presence. It was true that remnant of last night's beating was still lingering in my head, but I was more focused on revealing the leak and she *was my* leading suspect. She *was my* only suspect. As a behavioral scientist, I was concerned with her abilities to read my mind by making eye-contact, so for the sake of my plan, I avoided it.

"This meeting is just a quick recap on what has transpired," Frank began, "and what we hope to accomplish today. The trip to Wilmington yesterday was a good one. We've been able to determine the place of death for Tracy, the front-desk attendant. We have a lead on a name: Blaine Grubber. We've checked our database and there's very little on this guy."

Frank paused because for reasons unbeknownst to all of us, Vaishali found his last statement hysterical.

"I don't get the joke Agent Kumar," Frank said, not sharing in her guffaw.

"I'm sorry," she said, with her hand on her mouth, trying to muffle more laughter. "It's just that you said there's very little on this guy, and he's 5'2" and 110 pounds, so yea. There's literally very little on him."

I didn't think it was funny to the point where you had to muffle your laughter, but I saw and appreciated where her mind went. The rest of the table offered a weak smile, then Frank continued.

"Anyway," he said, "we have NOTHING on this guy." He paused and the table chuckled a little louder this time. "He paid his way in cash, and did a good job cleaning up after himself. We have partial or no prints to work on so far. But I think he can't be too far from Wilmington so being in Dover might be counter-productive. We need to be closer to the action. I will keep our reservation here for one more night while we do some serious investigation today. Ebenezer and Agent Kumar, stay behind because you're the only two without a decent amount of field-training hours. We will need you two to help assist on any computer-related issues. I want everybody else in Wilmington today. The plan is to scour the entire area, ask questions, and reach a consensus on whether we need to move this party to Wilmington or remain here in Dover. Any questions?"

The room was silent.

In my mind, I was on a different mission, and his spiel did very little to deter me. When the crowd dispersed to their respective rooms to retrieve essentials for the day, I pulled Commander Frank to the side.

"Do you have any information on the leak?" I asked.

"So far," he began, "I haven't had the time to investigate that. Why, do you know anything?"

"No, I was just curious," I said, then boldly added, "have you met with any members of the team to discuss the matter?"

"No, I haven't," he said. His face showed no signs of deceit. "Why your sudden interest in this?"

I wanted to tell him badly about Agent Nikkyta, but his response about not meeting with any member of the team about it made me think twice. I believed him. I had no basis to do so, but I did. He appeared to be telling the truth. This development only buttressed my inclination that Nikkyta was the leak. She had lied to me about Commander Frank orchestrating the meeting along with Antoine. She had to be hiding something.

"No, just curiosity," I said calmly, hoping to sound believable. "I just don't like the idea of a mole amongst us."

At that moment, the elevator door opened and Nikkyta walked out. I made eye-contact with her for the first time that morning. I was unable to hide my contempt for her, and I was sure she noticed it. I saw a look of concern on her face, especially upon seeing me with Commander Frank.

I shook the Commander's hand and said in an audible tone, "Thanks for the information."

I walked past Nikkyta and headed towards the elevator to take me to my room. I knew she was burning with questions and that made me smile inside. Moments later, the team drove away in a blue and gray van leaving Vaishali and I alone for God knows how long.

chapter27

There were some things I needed to do that would require leaving the hotel premises, but with Vaishali sitting in the lobby, it was impossible to avoid her. I tried engaging her in a conversation to get a sense of what she had planned for the day, but that happened to be a mistaken attempt. She incessantly and effortlessly weaved through topics. The only interruption was for five minutes when Frank called to know how everything was going.

"He loves playing a fatherly role," she said fondly of him when she hung up.

I wanted to ask more about him, but Vaishali was intelligent. She would quickly know my questions had an ulterior motive and either get to the bottom of it or leave with a level of distrust for me. In order for my plan to work, gathering enemies was the last thing I needed. I smiled and allowed her merge back into her conversation. She was speaking rapidly about an event that happened in her chess club in the fifth grade. I guess the story was interesting and filled with plausible twist and turns, but I was not interested. I needed to be alone so I could drive to my appointment. Earlier, I had contacted my journalist friend at the Delaware News Journal, the same journalist that wrote a glowing review about my first book and how persistent writing could juxtapose my collection with the great Walter Mosely's. I had a few questions to ask him about informants and the newspaper's obligation to protect their identities. He was in Dover covering an event with the Governor, and he offered me a slight window into his busy schedule. We planned to meet at 11:30 a.m.—which was only in an hour. I decided I needed to act now or miss the opportunity. I interrupted her swift chatter when she was saying something about running across the hallway with the rook piece while being chased by members of her own team. The story appeared to be nearing its crescendo and the look of hurt was evident on her face when I halted her pace.

"I'm sorry," I said, "I really need to go. I have something I need to take care of."

"Really?" she asked sprightly, "Where?"

I was not expecting her to pry. I was stuck. My mind had not prepared me for this, and in an act of desperation, I blurted out, "In my beach house. I'm expecting a repair man in about two hours, so I need to leave now so I don't miss him."

The more the words escaped my lips, the more confident I felt about the lie.

Vaishali was speechless and I felt a sense of pride for my accomplishment. If Nikkyta and I were on speaking terms, I was sure she would find value with the fact that I was able to silence Vaishali. As I relished my accomplishment, I saw her expressionless stare turn into a smile. My heart sunk. She looked at me and she said, "I'm coming with you. It'll be nice to see your beach house."

I had not anticipated this move on her part. I stared stupidly for a few seconds before managing, "What about Frank, won't he need you here?"

"No," she said frivolously, "I can do anything he needs remotely. I don't have to be here. All I need is my laptop and a cell."

I forced a smile.

"Great. I'll go grab some stuff upstairs."

"Cool, I'll be here." She said, readily.

When I got back to my room, I slumped dejectedly on the bed, trying to figure out how I managed to botch that the way I just did. It was never part of the plan. Even with Nikkyta as my main suspect, I felt it would have been safer to approach this alone because at the end of the day, they were all part of the same team and their loyalties resided in the same corner. I was the stranger here. I needed to be in this alone.

This realization caused me to rethink my plan.

I called the journalist and informed him I wouldn't be coming as planned. He sounded disappointed. I was not sure if it was authentic, but I appreciated the gesture. We agreed to meet the next time our schedules permitted. Now, I realized I had to go to my beach house to maintain the lie I started. I looked about the shabby hotel space for anything else I might need. Nothing else besides my original phone seemed appealing, so I grabbed it and headed down.

Vaishali sat on the passenger side as we meandered through the small development and onto the highway. The little bit of time it took for that vehicular maneuver, Vaishali was about to finish her story and was laying the groundwork for a next story. I realized this would be my reality for the next hour, so I prepared myself. The girl was smart, but sometimes I wished she could voluntarily take time to reflect silently. The ride was smooth. This part of Delaware only saw busy traffic during beach season. In December, there was nothing but the open road that stretched as far as your eyes could see. Once in a while we zipped past a gas station or an auto repair shop. In some ways, I was glad Vaishali was with me to liven the trip, but this would be a day wasted in my quest for vindication.

About thirty-five minutes into the journey, I realized I was running low on gas. Although we had enough to make it to my beach house, I needed a break from

Vaishali's running mouth, and I needed the autumn breeze to reinvigorate my body and my senses. The monotony from the ride was beginning to dampen my spirits. I found a Shell gas station about a mile after my thought for a break, and I made a right to ease softly into it. The place was rundown. It had two working pumps and the other four were in various stages of disrepair. Thankfully, the traffic was very light, so the decrepit state of the place did not affect our wait time. My gas pump was on the passenger's side of the vehicle, so I pulled up to the pump that was closer to the road. I walked around the front of the car. The credit card reader at the pump looked neglected, and its deteriorated sight made me extremely reluctant to swipe my card. Gratefully, I had cash in my wallet, so I decided to go inside to pay. On my way in, I heard the window wind down and Vaishali's voice chirped.

"Are you getting anything in there besides gas?"

I hadn't planned on it, but I elected for the gentlemanly thing to say. "Yea, you want anything?" I asked.

"Awesome!" She said excitedly, "I'll have beef jerky and a bottle of water, please."

"No problem."

A few more steps brought me to the entrance. I pushed the door open and I was immediately greeted with the sounds of the bronze wind chimes that hung on the door. To my right was the payment counter. Behind it was a man about 5'9" with unkempt facial hair and what appeared to be engine oil smeared about his face. He fitted every stereotypical image I had in my head about people that lived in rural areas. He wore a pair of blue jeans overalls and beneath it them a dingy white shirt—that looked more like brown— with black vertical stripes. The man was thin and the plain red hat on his head was clearly a size or two larger than his peanut head.

In an excitement that did not match his appearance, he asked, "How's it going, Buddy?" as if we were old acquaintances.

I nodded respectfully and continued along my path to the back of the store in search of Vaishali's orders. The sound of country music blared from a loudspeaker perched next to the attendant. The space was small, so the sound filled the room with ease. I stopped by the tall refrigerators in the back of the store for a bottle of water. The task took longer than I anticipated. The refrigerator was packed with anything but water. It had columns of Monster, Red Bull, Starbucks bottled coffee, Coke, Fanta, Mountain Dew, and a myriad of iced tea flavors. I had to look at the far end of the fridge to find an unimpressive collection of bottled water. I shook my head and grabbed two. The beef jerky wasn't that complicated, and within a minute, I was ready to check-out.

"Is that all, Buddy," the man asked in a southern drawl.

"And, umm," I said, staring out the window, "let me get thirty on where that white car is."

"Pump seven," he muttered.

The numbering made no sense to me. There were two working pumps and four in disrepair, so to have a pump number above six was illogical, but I was not in the mood to learn the twisted reasoning behind it.

"Thirty-six dollars buddy," he said after scanning the products.

I reached for my wallet and brought out two crisp twenty-dollar bills.

"Do you need a bag?" he asked as we exchanged money.

"Yes, please," I said.

"Do I know you?" the man said suddenly.

Oh Lord!

Just when I was almost out, he decided it was time for small talk.

"No, I don't think so," I said politely. "I've never been here before."

"I get that," he continued, "but I think I've seen you before, Buddy."

"Well," I said, offering a practiced smile, "It's a small world, so you might have."

Inside, I was battling to hide my impatience. He looked like one of those people who were under the belief that all black people looked alike. I was not in the proper state of mind to stand on some moral intellectual high ground and lecture him on the mistaken path he had allowed his sense to wander. There was a time and place for such conversation, and neither parameter was fit at that moment. I just wanted to pay for my goods and continue the voyage down to my beach house and let him wallow in his ignorance.

The man was unrelenting.

"No, Buddy," he said, with a confident look on his face, "You're that writer!"

I was taken aback when he said that. I did not consider him a reader. In my mind, I had placed him with the pile of people where menus and road signs were the height of their literary exposures. I realized I had committed the same debauchery I just accused him of. I had inaccurately lumped him with such group of people only because of his accent and appearance. I felt bad for my hasty conclusion. Although, he did not know the inner workings of my mind, I felt like I owed him a little bit of my time as penance for my erroneous assumption.

"Yes, I am," I said, as I placed the bag of goods on the counter giving him the impression that I was open for discussion. "So, I'm guessing you read my book?"

The man shook his head, and immediately, I felt the need to resurrect my unsubstantiated assessment of him.

"I just saw you on CNN the other day that's all," he said, smiling from ear to ear. "You was standing next to our senator, Terry. You know I went to school with that fella. We used to be very close. Closer than two fat guys in a phone booth. It's a shame what that asshole did to lil' Jenny. She was a nice young gal. Sweet, sweet little gal. Terry really loved that gal, you know? Make no sense to take a man's baby like that. For what!? Me, personally I think Terry should've never entered politics. We was tryna warn him to leave that life alone, but he aint hear us. He boneheaded. The attention got good to him. He kept on goin till the point where he had to divorce Margrett too. Now he got him a new woman. Jalapeno Spanish mami! I guess you need somethin' like that when you enter that world. As for me I like my women fat and ugly, and if I'm lucky, missing a few teeth. That way their standard is low, am she sure gon' be faithful. She aint goin' nowhere! Hell, if you turn off the light, they all look the same anyway. They all got the same pot of gold in between them thighs. I don't see no reason to leave somethin' you know for somethin' shiny like that Marcy lady. Who knows, maybe this asshole wanted her, so for backup he settled for lil' Jenny. Anyway, where you folks headed anyway? Beach season over."

I stood there in awe, struggling to mask my confusion and trying to make sense of his erratic patter. The entire time, I was trying to picture the senator being friends with this guy. The senator was known for his clear and precise reasoning when discussing the most complex issues of the time, and this guy was unable to arrange his thoughts to rollout a lucid sentence.

"Umm," I hesitated, "we're from New York. I have a beach house in Rehoboth."

"New York City huh!" he bellowed boastfully, "I been there before. Not for me though. Too packed. I don't even have room to change my mind when I was there." He snickered. "Everybody was always going somewhere.

No time to relax and enjoy the small things in life. I wanna move to Texas. They got enough land and country living that makes me happy."

I realized I had tolerated enough self-punishment. Whatever sin I might have committed should have be absolved by now. I needed to plan my exit.

"We really gotta go," I said as I reached for my things. "We are on a tight schedule."

"Alright, Buddy," he said, "you take care out there. Hope the FBI is treating you well?"

His question sent a chill through my body. I don't recall ever telling him I was with the FBI. There was no way he could have known that. Not my appearance, not my car.... nothing!

"How do you know I'm with the FBI?" I asked challengingly.

He stared at me for a loaded second with nothing to say. The look on his face was like that given to a child by a disappointed father.

"Hey buddy, what's the problem," he said contemptuously, "didn't I just tell you I saw you on CNN with Terry. He said you was gon' be a consultant or somethin' because the asshole was using tricks from your book."

I did recall him saying that in the beginning, and a part of me now felt embarrassed with the way I acted.

"I'm sorry it's been a busy week," I said, "We're still in the middle of figuring everything out. I'm sure you understand I can't share anything."

"Oh, trust me I get it buddy," he said energetically, "even the other fella on the case don't say much about it either whenever he comes around."

"What other fella?" I asked, suddenly interested in a conversation with him again.

"I forgot his name now," he said, appearing to be in a deep thought. "He's a short fella. Kinda round. Built like a basketball with hands and legs."

There was only one person on earth that I knew matched that description beyond a reasonable doubt. Now, I had fresh set of questions on why Agent Tomkievich would come to this store. From what Nikkyta told me, he lived in Smyrna. Although, my knowledge of Delaware was marginal at best, I knew Smyrna was almost an hour in the opposite direction. There should be very little reason why Agent Tomkievich should have to make regular stops at this gas station. It would be a gross discomfort having to do that. Unless... he moved, and Nikkyta was unaware? I could not think of any other reason why she would lie to me about where he lived. In the midst of my mental tussle, another thought occurred to me. Why not ask him and do away with the guessing game.

"Does he live around here?"

"I believe so," he said cautiously, "I don't know for sure, but he comes around here most mornings."

"And he just came out and told you he's working on the case?" I asked shiftily.

"No," he said. "It didn't just happen in one day. In the past, he just waddles in here, buy his stuff and go. He pays with cash every time. One morning when he came in, I was watching Terry on the news. This was before Jenny got killed. I was telling my other buddy I went to school with him. I guess FBI guy heard me. The following day, we began talking about him. He asks me questions and whatnot."

"What kind of questions?" My interest grew.

"You know, like what kind of student he was and whatnot. I guess he was trying to figure out if he'll get his vote. I aint gotta worry about that myself. Terry gon' get my vote. Behind all that style and beauty, the man is a good man. At that press conference the other day, the nation saw the real Terry. It's a shame it took for this to happen for people to see that."

I felt a fierce urge to tell him that was all for show. I wanted to tell him the Terry he knew had traded his childhood morals for the allure of the office he sought. But that was a truth I knew this guy was not ready to accept. It would only add more distraction to our already overstretched time. I needed to ask targeted questions to gain a little more understanding.

"What does he buy when he comes in?" I asked.

"Sometimes gas, chips, soda... shit like that."

"Has he been here since Jenny?"

The attendant appeared to think about the question for a while before answering.

"Yea he came in the day Terry gave the press conference. That was when he told me he was assigned to the case."

I recalled we were all in D.C. that day except for him. It was the day he told Tristan and I that he went to the Delaware Learning Institute for information about the killer. At that moment, all I could think of was a line from one of my favorite literary characters, Harry Bosch. He never believed in coincidences, and I found everything thus far too convenient to be a coincidence. Something seemed wrong, but I had no idea where to begin. I was just a writer, and before today, I was operating solely on the whims and wishes of Frank Gordy. I only did what he ordered, and if not for Nikkyta's strange behavior, it would have remained that way for the duration of the case. Now I had to do some information gathering to clear my name from the list of people that might have caused the leak. This investigation led me to this shabby gas station where I have gathered a little more information. There had to be a way to exploit this new path. It had to lead somewhere with substantive information.

"Is the Delaware Learning Institute around here?" I asked hastily.

"Yea," he said. "My daughter goes there. It's about five miles down the road. You can't miss it."

"Really," I said. "Ok, thanks. But now I really have to go. Thanks for everything... ummmm what's your name?"

"Kyle," he said confidently, "but they call me Butch!"

I reached out and shook his hand. "Thanks, Butch."

"You got it, Buddy!" he responded.

As I turned around to leave the store, I heard the sound of the bronze wind chimes, and moments later, Vaishali appeared.

"Are you okay?" she had a worried look on her face.

"I'm so sorry about that," I said, "I got carried away with Butch. I'm all set though."

"How you *doing*," Butch called out, now interested in Vaishali.

I could see the look of lust in his face as he stared intently at Vaishali. I felt a cynical urge to remind him that Vaishali did not fit his requirements. Of the three criteria he gave me, her physique was the only criterion she might qualify for, and then even narrowly. She had all her teeth and she was certainly not ugly.

"I'm doing well," Vaishali responded politely, then returned her attention to me. "We have to go. Frank just called."

I could tell it was serious and she was not ready to share whatever it was in front of Butch. I grabbed the bag and pushed through onto the brisk air outside.

"What did he say?" I asked impatiently.

"They seem to be sure this Blaine Grubber guy is our killer," she said in a voice barely surpassing a whisper, "and they believe he is still in the Wilmington area. Starting tomorrow, we are all moving closer."

"Wow, really?" I felt a surge of excitement race through me. "That's great news!"

"Yea," she said.

I thought I sensed a little bit of dejection in her response.

"Don't you think so?" I asked.

"Oh, I do," she said, "Trust me I do. I just...I mean it's just selfish reason on my part. I had some technological ideas and I knew I could really test it out with this team, but once this is over, I won't have the chance to really do anything. I'll return to the archaic procedures the Bureau uses."

I understood where she was coming from. The selfish feeling was similar to what I felt when the original Tilted Grin Killer was captured. I wanted him to remain at large so I could exploit the situation to my benefit.

"It's okay," I said unconvincingly, "I'm sure Frank noticed everything you've done. He's not blind to it."

"I hope," she said.

I heard the gas pump click indicating my tank was full. The pump reflected I had $4.76 left. I thought about going inside for my change, but that would mean more chatter with Butch. I had had enough of him, and the $4.76 was too low to suffer another moment of his time.

I eased the car back on the highway towards my beach house. Vaishali was pulling on her beef jerky after securing her bottle of water on the holder between us.

"What took you so long in there?" She asked after about a minute of silence.

Her question had no traces of hostility or aggression. It was an innocent curiosity that any normal caring person would ask. I was in there for over twenty minutes. It was not as if the store was packed like what I was used to back home in Brooklyn. Vaishali and I were the only people that materialized in the whole twenty minutes. I figured I owed her a little bit of explanation, but I stopped at expressing my personal opinion about the whole thing. I did not share my feelings about coincidences. I just told her, verbatim, what we talked about. At certain points in my explanation, I tried to talk like Butch or use some of the peculiar phrases he used to describe things. Vaishali found it side-splittingly hilarious when I told her about the two-fat-guys-in-a-phone-booth line. She confessed she had never heard that before and she made a vow to use it when describing the closeness of things. It felt good to be the one talking. She was actually a phenomenal listener. She did not interrupt my flow unless to clarify something that might have not been recalled correctly.

When we got about four miles away from the gas station, I saw a sign for the Delaware Learning Institute. A feeling tugged at me to visit and talk to them. Just as quickly, another thought invaded my mind, reminding me of the rude reception we received when I accompanied Agents Taylor and Tomkievich. There was no reason to believe this would be any different.

It was now one o'clock in the afternoon. It was the perfect time of day to interact with people. They would have just returned from their lunch breaks, so they should be in good moods. There was no scientific backing for my conclusion; I was just trying to find a reason to overcome the doubt lingering in my mind. When we got within three-tenths of a mile from our exit, I shared the sudden change of plans with Vaishali.

"But I thought Earl went there when we were in D.C?" she asked.

"Yea he did," I said. "I just want to see for myself. I went to the other three spots. I just want to get the image of all four spots. It's more for my writing than anything."

I was a little worried with the ease at which the lies came to me. I said all those things as if they had been premeditated, and they appeared to have done the trick. Vaishali nodded obediently.

The building was similar to the three we visited the day before. It was pink but in desperate need of repainting. It was located in a meagerly populated space with an antique shop and an auto repair shop across the street. A sign on the side of the road read "Big Mommas

Fried Chicken" with an arrow pointing to the left. There was a huge parking lot with a few cars but most were pickup trucks. The building looked uneventful. If not for the few cars in the parking lot, my decision would have been to return to the road and maintain my lie.

A thin lady with wiry blonde hair sat behind a black table. Upon seeing us, she offered a huge smile and welcomed us. It was already a great departure from our visits the day before, but I tried to suppress my enthusiasm. I was certain once she learned we were not there to enroll for the next semester, her hospitality would wither and die.

"How are you folks doing today?" she said, exposing her uneven brown teeth.

"We're doing great," I said, returning her smile. "We're just here to ask a few questions about one of your former students."

I had debated if we should introduce ourselves as FBI agents. I decided against it at the last minute. We had taken that approach the previous day and that seemed to dampen their initial friendliness. I decided we go as regular people with good intentions. Although, Vaishali brought up a good point that they might not divulge student's information to unauthorized people and using the FBI seal might be the only way to coerce any type of information out of them. It was a good point and was strongly considered—at least for the three minutes it took to park—but I chose my method. I was a little surprised she yielded willingly. Nikkyta would have been inflexible. I concluded that it was because Vaishali was more like me than an FBI agent. Her strength was in computers and behind the scenes stuff. The hardened exterior was not needed because she rarely interacted with perpetrators.

"Okay, have a seat and I'll get someone with you shortly," the thin lady said as she disappeared into a small room within the establishment.

The lobby area had ten chairs arranged in pairs of five at either side of the space. A thirty-something-inch television hung on the top-left corner of the room. A documentary about John D. Rockefeller was on the screen, and I panically remembered I was yet to do my part for the show on the ID network. I thought about calling Todd and controlling his rage, but I knew that would not be smart. I could not envision a scenario where he would be willing to listen to anything I had to say. I decided I would spend the time at the beach house handling that instead. I realized that would have been a better lie to tell Vaishali than what I ended up saying.

"How are y'all doing?" A heavyset black lady appeared before us interrupting my thought. "My name is Linda Cummings."

"Hi, my name is Ebenezer," I said, refraining from using my surname in fear that I might be recognized.

Vaishali also used her first name.

We stated our intentions, and without many qualms, Linda ushered us to her office. My heart jumped with happiness with the way everything has transpired thus far. The reception had surpassed everything we experienced the day before.

Linda's office was cluttered with mountains of papers and manila folders. It smelled nice, and the sound of smooth jazz emanated from a Bluetooth speaker on top of a bookshelf. We had to move a pile of paper on the second chair to accommodate both of us.

"So, who is the student?" She asked, with a smile on her face.

I hesitated a little before saying, "Blaine Grubber. I'm not sure the year he graduated, but it is probably around—"

"Oh my God Blaine!" Linda exclaimed. "What is he up to these days?"

The look on her face suggested she had fond memories of him.

"Oh, so you know him," Vaishali asked excitedly.

"Of course, everybody knows Blaine," Linda said, still maintaining her smile. "Blaine is probably the most gifted student we've ever had. See, Blaine is an introvert, so he did not interact with people too much. But in spite of all that, his work was so good, that you couldn't help but know him. Blaine could make you look like her and her like you. He is so talented with makeup! He has a real future in Hollywood if he can ever get over his shyness." When she realized she had allowed her fond memories of him disrupt the way she should have handled the conversation, she paused and righted herself. She straightened her posture and asked, "How did you guys know him anyway? Is he doing okay?"

It was too late. Her blunder had benefited us immensely. I wanted to jump over the table between us and give her a kiss. She has strengthened our suspicion that Blaine was the Tilted Grin Killer. The story about his inimitable disguising skills was all I needed to hear. Although Frank had informed Vaishali of that earlier, this was definitely a loud endorsement to that fact.

I thought about her question for a few seconds and the perfect lie came to me.

"We are with a talent agency in New York City," I began, "and we are just here following up on the information he gave us. It's a very important job that will surely take him places, so we are just here talking to people that might attest to his character. Is there any more information you can tell us about him? You know like family? Friends? Hobbies?"

"Oh really?" Linda's excitement re-emerged, "I don't feel bad anymore then. I thought I might have spoken too soon without asking who you guys were. Like I said, Blaine was very quiet. He rarely talked to anybody. He definitely had no friends that we know of. We even had to create a joint project one time just to force him to interact with people. He enrolled as an adult, so there was no reason for him to provide guardian information. And for emergency contacts, he used his father, which we later found out had been dead for over ten years. But I knew Blaine would make it. With him, you might not get a chatterbox, but trust me, he would do great work for you guys. What's the name of your company again?"

"I'm sorry say that again," I asked. I heard her perfectly well, but I needed the time to come up with a lie.

"Your company," she said, "What is it called?"

"Oh, it's called Restore NYC," I said confidently, "It's a subsidiary of Sephora. It's a fairly new company and we are trying to introduce some of the cinema enhancing techniques to New York. For the past five decades, Los Angeles has cornered that market, but

New York City has the money, people, and enthusiasm to lead the charge. We need some talented people to make this a reality, and based on what I've seen and what I'm hearing, Blaine appears to be our guy."

"Yes!" Linda screamed innocently.

A part of me felt bad for misleading her this way, but I convinced my mind it was for the greater good. It was going to save lives. I stole a glance at Vaishali, and she maintained a stoic expression. I was impressed with the level of commitment she had devoted to this endeavor. She might talk too much sometimes, but we definitely worked well together.

"Well," I said, pushing my chair back, "thank you for everything. You have been extremely helpful."

"No problem at all," he said. "You have no idea what this would do for enrollment—especially when Blaine's work gets the national exposure it deserves."

You have no idea. It already has!

"Definitely," I said, maintaining my smile. "I look forward to a great working relationship with him."

"Yes!" Linda continued. "Do you guys have business cards I could hold on to?"

"Uh," I panicked.

"Actually," Vaishali barged in cleanly, "we have a slightly different approach to the business card idea. We pride ourselves on being an earth-friendly company, so no paper or plastic cards. We will be using an app on the phone for that type of information. Unfortunately, we are still finishing up on a proprietary software that will take care of all that. Do you have an email address? I can send you the information once the app is ready."

"Wow," Linda was mesmerized, "that's awesome. Yes, I do have an email address, but now I feel bad sharing it because it's on my business card."

We all erupted in a hearty laughter.

"That's not a problem," Vaishali said permissibly, "that's still the norm."

When we got back in the car, we rode in silence for about thirty seconds, but I could feel Vaishali's stare on me the entire time. It was as if her eyes would burn a hole through me.

"So, you'll just sit there and act like nothing happened?" she said, smiling. "Is your name even Ebenezer? Where did you learn how to lie like that?"

I chuckled and then retorted with, "What about you and your proprietary software? That's an amazing lie too."

"At least I'm within my known parlance. Software is my world, so I can easily maneuver through that. You went into makeup and a New York company and Sephora..."

"I'm a writer," I said defensively, "it's what we do. I make up stories all the time."

"Well, you're a very good writer," she commended. "I just hope your art is not an imitation of your life."

"Not all the time," I said, "but everybody lies."

"Well, you do it so well. I'm impressed."

I was glad Vaishali came along for the ride. Her comment of me being a very good writer sent tingles of excitement through my body. I didn't know her endorsement meant so much to me, but as the words left her lips, I felt myself wanting to hear her say more. In that moment, not even the explosive discovery of Blaine Grubber's identity could disturb what I was feeling.

chapter28

BLAINE GRUBBER opened the door to his three-bedroom home and ushered Jenny in after instructing her to remove her shoes by the doorway. It was now two in the morning, but trepidation made it impossible to feel any form of fatigue. Jenny was wide awake, in fear that she might never wake up if she went to sleep. She was unfamiliar with the new space, so she took a few steps in and stopped awaiting further instructions. The floor was cold, and it looked like no one lived in the house. The expanse had only two chairs, a stool, and a television mounted on the wall. A faint smell of pumpkin clamored for attention.

The directions came almost immediately.

"Make a left," Blaine said, "and go down the stairs."

She did as she was told and ended up at a door that led to a very dark space below. Blaine noticed her hesitation and quickly instructed her to flip the switch to her right. The dark abyss was immediately filled with a bright burst of light. Cautiously, she took the first step. The wooden staircase creaked causing her to pause and determine if she should continue. She could feel his presence behind her, so she disregarded her concerns and continued down the stairs. The soothing smell of lavender invaded her nose with each step she took. By the time she made it to the bottom, she was confronted with a very cozy feeling. It was unlike the thinly equipped space upstairs. It rebelled against all logical rationale to have the living room, the main point of entry, looking threadbare, and all efforts concentrated in the basement. But Jenny recalled she was dealing with an unbalanced man, so commonsensical reasoning must be discarded when trying to relate with him.

The basement was a large and exquisitely furnished space. It was an open floor plan with demarcations around the corners that appeared to be hasty additions. One of the demarcations was a weakly lit area. It was a secluded space with a bucolic looking chair and table. A floor-to-ceiling-sized bookcase fed with an array of titles stood on one corner of the room. Her bare feet sank deeply into a remarkably soft cream-colored rug on the threshold of the dimly lit space. Again, Jenny allowed her mind revel in its luxury. It bore a similar quality to what her father had in his Washington D.C. home. Jenny had vowed never to return to that house after he married Marcy, but that was ages ago. Right now she was willing to relax her stance for a chance to be there and enjoy their company. The past five hours had terrified her beyond belief. To still be alive at this moment only reinforced her confidence in miracles. A part of her felt bad Tracy had to die for her to be in this moment. Outside of being a senator's daughter, she couldn't identify a reason why she deserved this fate over Tracy. *What makes me so special over her?* She thought. It was a question she may never know the answer to, but she vowed to maximize every moment of her time.

"Here," Blaine said, interrupting her thought.

He handed over the handcuff and pointed to a general area, near the dark space. As Jenny walked towards his pointed finger, a spurt of light occupied the space. Slightly startled, Jenny turned around and saw the little man by a light switch. Her steps packed a little more confidence now that she could see her path. As she was about to perform the handcuffing routine, she heard him say, "Wait a minute."

She paused.

"I need you to take off your clothes and face me."

Jenny thought for a second. A look of confusion spread across her face. The man did not appear to be the type that pursued joy from sexual acts with a woman. *Maybe a little boy or girl, but certainly not a grown woman.* Jenny was not exceedingly voluptuous, but she had enough curves and bends to prove her femininity. *Maybe I didn't hear him,* she thought as she stood there waiting for him to repeat his request.

Blaine had anticipated this, so rather than asking again, he simply made a waving gesture with his weapon, as if to say, "Get on with it."

Terrified, Jenny quickly did as she was told, and mere moments later, she was naked. Her body was visibly shaking as she tried persistently to shove the thoughts of what was about to happen away from her mind. But the more she looked at him, the more she disbelieved he was interested in her that way. Moments later, a chilling thought crossed her mind. Jenny had heard of men that got off on sodomizing women with foreign objects. The thought gripped her with terror. If this little man was not sexually aroused by her bare body, being sodomized seemed to be the only other reason he would have her naked. She tried frantically to recall any of the news reports on him for anything on sodomy. She could not remember that being a part of the narrative, but that did very little to put her mind at ease. She feared the worst as she stood vulnerable without her clothes on.

Blaine could see the confusion in her eyes, and it thrilled him. He wanted to allow the moment to linger but he realized he was pressed for time. He had a few things to take care of before the senator's presidential announcement in the morning.

"Stand there," he said coldly.

Blaine reached for a Nikon camera that was sitting on a shelf next to him. To an average-sized man, a simple stretch of the arm would have been sufficient to retrieve the device, but Blaine had to extend his arms to its max while making sure his weapon was still trained on Jenny. He flipped another switch and the light above Jenny shined brightly. She was now under a magnificent lighting, and the walls around her were pure white. The scene instantly transported her mind to the days when she was trying out as a model.

It was during her sophomore year at Drexel University. She recalled enjoying the process, but more importantly, she recalled it being a phase in her life. It was one of the many things suggested by her friends to ameliorate the effect of her father's decision to choose Marcy over her mom. That chapter lasted for about three months, but Jenny held on to the memory as fondly as most of her life's feats. Her present condition, however, in spite of the comparable scene, was miles apart from her amateur modeling days. For one, she was never naked, and the photographer never aimed a gun at her. Jenny was utterly confused, so she decided to stop trying to figure things out and just allow time unfurl at its own pace. So long as she was breathing, the mighty force of her father's influence would surely prevail.

"Stand still," Blaine's voice sounded gently, "I need you to keep a straight face."

He lifted the shutter and two flicking sounds, accompanied by two bright flashes, emanated from the camera.

"Good, good," he said, and then added, "go ahead, you know what to do."

Jenny grabbed the handcuff and looked about her surroundings for a place to secure it. A tall rusty pole was next to her. The structure appeared to stab through the ceiling and beyond. It was sturdy. Jenny felt weird being handcuffed with no clothes on, but she quickly remembered Tracy's fate and her mind settled a little. She wondered how long this mad man would keep her in this peculiar space. She had a lot of questions for him, but she was still trying to get over the shock of her reality. She did not want to hold so much fear in her voice when she worked up the nerve to speak. She watched him as he moved. Now with Jenny cuffed to the pole, Blaine felt comfortable moving around without the need to threaten her with the gun. He placed the weapon on the shelf where the camera was taken from earlier, and walked to another segregated corner of the room. The space was dark and unnerving. The superb lighting in the basement space was cordoned from the area. The small room consisted of a water-hose that snaked its way from an unknown source outside into a till-colored sink. Photographic equipment, like a print enlarger, film-developing fluids, a dryer, and even photographic papers that are sensitive to light, were neatly arranged in the small room. The enlarger had a height-adjustable head containing a red lamp and a film holder. On the wall were different prints of past photographs. Blaine worked quickly but carefully. He placed the photographic paper on an easel and projected the lens to focus on the image. To ensure the images were sharp, he made use of the focus finder. He used timers to control the length of the exposure. Multi-grade filters were used to adjust the contrast to reveal the beauty of each primary color. When he finished, Blaine walked out of the dark room with a satisfied grin on his face. The negatives were perfect. He let them dry, and with the enlarger, he made three complete sets of 15 by 11 prints. He felt a sense of euphoria as he saw the images slowly appear at the bottom of the developer. Jenny was still in the same sorry state he left her in a while ago. He walked up to her and smugly showed her the results of his work.

"You're very beautiful," he said sincerely, "now I have to make a twin out of you."

Jenny was infuriated with his short ambiguous statements. She wanted to understand what he meant by that, but she refrained from asking. Like everything thus far, she would find out soon enough.

Blaine walked back to the dark area, and moments later, the sound of the running water hose stopped. He walked back upstairs leaving his prey alone to wonder privately. Jenny looked about the space hoping to commit its details to memory just in case there was an opportunity to describe her condition to someone on the phone. The thought warmed her heart for a brief second, but gloom quickly returned the moment she heard Blaine struggling with something down the steps. When his petite body appeared, Jenny saw the cause for the commotion. He was dragging Tracy's lifeless body across the room. Jenny felt her body go rigid once again. The only other time she had been next to a corpse was that of her grandmother eight years ago. Jenny recalled recoiling and wanting to be away from that space. Now with Tracy, she was forced into the same situation again, but she appeared to be numb to it this time. She knew she couldn't do anything, especially if she wanted to maintain her alive-status.

Blaine walked to a wardrobe near the secluded space and wheeled out a truncated table that only rose up a few inches past his shin. He locked the wheels of the table next to the cadaver, and in a sorry display of strength, he managed to roll the body bag onto the table. Breathing heavily, he unzipped the bag. Next to the wheels of the table was a remote control with green and red buttons. Blaine pressed the green button, and slowly, the table rose close to his chest area. He scrutinized the height for a second, and then pressed the red button, and the table let out a pneumatic hiss before dropping in height. Blaine released his finger from the button when the descent was close to his abdomen. He walked into the dark room and emerged with a tripod stand and a small makeup bag. On top of the tripod was a flat rectangular metal. Blaine gently placed the naked pictures of Jenny on the rectangular surface and held it tightly with the clamp. He glanced at Jenny and offered a scornful smile. Jenny was fully privy to what he was up to, and the fact that she was naked no longer affected her as much.

Blaine reached inside his makeup bag and brought out a brush. He stared at Tracy's body briefly as if he was paying respect to the dead. Then he began brushing off the dry blood splattered across her face. The water-hose in the dark room was rerouted to a bucket near the table, and from it, he took a rag soaked in water and isopropyl and gently wiped her face. When he was done, the gash from the gunshot was the only visible blemish on the cadaver's face. Blaine paused again and venerated his work. He only allowed himself to gloat for a second before returning to his duties. A look of unflinching concentration rested on his face as he worked. Next to the thrill he got from killing, this was Blaine's second favorite part of the process. His attention to small details when working with makeup brought him unexplainable joy. He recalled when he was still in school and the way his classmates marveled at his work. They often left class in open-mouthed awe upon seeing the excruciating details of his work. Now as he traded stares between the corpse and the naked picture on the tripod, Blaine aimed to relive some of his past glory. He typically moved from head to toe. Jenny's hair was black, and Tracy's was blonde. He thought about dying it, but he soon disregarded that idea. He knew, from months of trailing her, that Jenny had just recently dyed her hair to black. She was a natural blonde just like Tracy, so he decided it was not of the utmost importance to waste time on that. He moved to her head. The huge wound from the gunshot was the main difference in their facial landscapes. He felt like the gods had given him a gift with Tracy, because she shared similar features with Jenny. They were both of the same height, similar proportions in terms of breasts and hip sizes, and were both natural blondes. Blaine was only able to spot out three main differences between the living and the dead women. Tracy had an old cut on her right cheek. The wound had since healed, but a keen eye could easily spot this anomaly and quickly conclude it was not Jenny. Their noses were also dissimilar. Tracy had a wider nose that could simply be spotted by an acute crime scene investigator. The third difference was a heart tattoo missing from Tracy's wrist. It was an indelible mark that a seasoned detective would look for, when identifying a popular victim like Jenny.

With a course of action in place, Blaine prepared himself for the task ahead. He reached in his makeup bag and grabbed a small container with foundation and concealer. As he was about to apply it, he paused and looked closely at the scar. He leaned forward and touched it with his gloved hands. He realized it was not a new scar, so redness and hyper-pigmentation were not an issue. It was an old scar, so the foundation and concealer could not do anything to hide the uneven texture. To help smoothen the area, he needed to start with a foundation primer. He used a silicone-based formula so the skin texture would appear more even. He patted a small amount of the primer over the scar and rubbed it consistently around the area. When he was satisfied, he brought out a color-corrector to counteract the skin discoloration. He used a color opposite the skin color on the color wheel. He applied it gently and rubbed it smoothly in the area. He then covered the color-corrector with the concealer. The thick creamy formula was able to bring it all together, and for precision, he used the brush to balance the appearance. He applied a translucent powder to lock it all in place, and he allowed the mixture to set in. Fifteen minutes later, there was no trace of a scar on Tracy's face.

Blaine smiled.

Next was to try to make her nose smaller. Blaine was well versed with the contouring process. It was a procedure he found useful and he took painstaking measures to reach the height of the practice. He brought out a marker and drew two thin lines down the sides of Tracy's nose. The lines began at the brow bone and all the way down to the end of her nose. He made sure the lines were light because he knew it was easier to build on it than to erase. Next, from his makeup bag, he chose a highlighter which was two shades lighter than Tracy's natural skin color and applied it to the bridge of her nose. The application was from the top to the tip of her nose. The lines that were drawn earlier were blended away leaving subtle shadows in its place. He stepped back and exchanged multiple stares between the picture and the dead body. He smiled because he realized both images were almost alike.

As if he suddenly remembered he was not alone in the room, he turned to Jenny and asked, "So, what do you think?"

She did not say anything. She did not know what type of answer he was expecting, but in her mind, she marveled at the lifeless body on the table. It was just like staring at her own face. The body looked exactly like her. She was terrified of his abilities. With everything she had seen, she could not imagine leaving this luxurious dungeon on her own volition. It would require great effort from people, whose services, her father wielded. She had seen too much to think he would let her leave. She was already terrified but seeing Tracy's transformation added layers of terror to her existing fear.

"It's okay," Blaine said, "I get that a lot. I leave people speechless."

He thought about taking a break but following the perfect execution of the first two tasks, he felt he should ride the wave of success for the next task. He was well ahead of schedule, and this kept his mind at ease. The shopping center where he planned to dump the body was only a few miles away. He could do that and be back well before the senator was scheduled to make his announcement. Gently, he grabbed Tracy's wrist and observed the area for several seconds. He was grateful the tattoo was not a multifaceted artwork with profound artistry. It was just a solid black heart tattoo on the back of her wrist. Using a thick sharpie, Blaine drew an outline of the image. He applied baby powder over the dead skin and lightly dusted it off. He sprayed liquid bandage on top and it was all done. He got up and stretched his small body. He realized he had not slept all night, but that was not much of a bother. This was not the first time he had gone an entire night without sleeping. It never seemed to affect him at work. Plus, the commotion his antics would cause the following day was enough adrenaline to keep him going.

He reached for the table's remote and pressed the red button to drop it below his shin. He rolled the body into the body-bag and zipped it up. He walked determinedly to Jenny's handbag. After seconds of rummaging through its contents, he came out with her wallet and a few random items. He dragged the body upstairs and loaded it in the van. He came back downstairs for one final appraisal of the area before heading out. He made sure Jenny was away from all foreign objects that might inspire an act of bravery just like in the movies. He was not concerned about any shouting. He spent a lot of money making sure the room was properly soundproof.

The ride to the empty parking lot was uneventful. It was almost four thirty in the morning, and the inhabitants were still in the comfy confines of their bedrooms. It was a brisk morning, and over in the horizon was a faint hint of the morning sun. Blaine obeyed all the road laws because the last thing he needed was something as stupid as a traffic infraction. He arrived at his destination within five minutes. He had canvassed the area multiple times in the past, so he had a keen knowledge of where the working cameras were located. There was only one working camera and it was located on the north entrance of the shopping center. He recalled during his fourth murder how he deliberately revealed his physique and masked face for the authorities to work with. He was bored back then, and he needed a little more challenge. That was not the case with this mission. He had spent the better part of the last six months preparing for this task. Jenny was not like his usual preys. There were powerful people that would make it their business if she came up missing, so he knew he had to take scrupulous measures for his preparations. But even with all his efforts, the sudden appearance of Tracy appeared to have decimated the entire plan. He credited his quick thinking for the way things turned out. Now he could derail the authorities for a day or two, maybe more if he was lucky, but in the meantime, he would watch the uproar while he decided on what to do with Jenny.

Blaine parked on the south entrance of the shopping center and reached for his mask. It fit his face perfectly and altered his appearance considerably. He struggled with the body bag, thankfully for the last time, and dragged it to the north entrance of the shopping center. He paused to make sure he was in the camera's view and he unceremoniously dumped the body in the middle of the lot. He beleaguered the area with Jenny's belongings before entering his van and drove to a mail collection box on his way home. This was part of his plan. He had drafted a letter and addressed it to Thirty-Mile Zone tabloid news, better known as TMZ. In the letter were gory images of some of his past killings. He also included images and facts to contradict the news of Jenny Gibson's death. He knew her death would be widespread and expected the news agency to release the report while Senator Gibson was mourning the death of his daughter. It would be a delightful distraction to confuse the entire nation, including the FBI, that way.

It was now 5:15 a.m. and the morning sun felt bolder announcing its presence. There were a few more cars on the road, but not enough to resemble the midday flow. When he got home, he walked straight to the basement, and to his mild surprise, Jenny appeared to be sleeping. He liked that. He wanted her to be well rested so she could withstand his torture much longer. He tried to walk lightly, but the presence of someone else in the room was loud enough to awaken her. She jerked up and sat upright. Slightly disappointed, Blaine went about his business at his usual pace. He opened the wardrobes and returned everything to their proper places. In thirty minutes, the room was tidy, just like it was when they first arrived. Jenny watched as he moved about the space. She was still concerned, but her thoughts were now a mystifying web of a lot of things. As if that were not enough, she watched as he walked towards the closet. He brought out what appeared to be a bodysuit that was about five times the size of his body. Smoothly, Blaine slid into it and placed a wig on his head. He stood before a short mirror and applied a little bit of makeup on his face. The little application was enough to cause a radical change to his looks. Then he grabbed a blue double-breasted suit and wore it over the bodysuit. The outfit was perfectly designed for the bodysuit. He looked odd; like a wigged basketball with arms and legs as an afterthought.

"How do I look?" He asked, in a wimpish voice.

chapter29

The reluctance to bring Vaishali along now sounded like a stupid idea. I could not imagine enjoying the day without her. Her company, in spite of her endless tales, was exactly what I needed. As we pulled into the driveway of my beach house, I stole a glance at her, and for the first time, I saw her in a different light. I found her platonic beauty irresistible. I entertained a strong yearning for her touch. Her voice. Her smile. Everything about her now aroused my desire in ways I could not measure. I stayed in the car longer than I had planned with hopes that an explanation for this new feeling would emerge, but nothing was forthcoming. I had gone from warding off her presence a few hours ago to trying to suppress a powerful magnetic attraction to her. The only thing that changed within that span of time was the new information we got about Blaine Grubber. But I struggled to find the parallel between that and what I was feeling. Then another thought occurred to me. Prior to this day, Nikkyta was the one that riled me up this way. Now I wondered if our rift the night before had opened me up to new opportunities. I was so infatuated with Nikkyta that I failed to see and appreciate Vaishali's perfect blend of beauty and brains.

"Are you coming in?"

Vaishali's voice snatched me out of my dilemma.

"Oh, yea sorry," I said hastily. "I was just thinking about something."

"Obviously," she said, smiling. "Are you thinking what I'm thinking?"

My heart skipped a beat.

She could not possibly be thinking the same thing as I am, I thought.

"What are you thinking?" I asked curiously.

She darted a suspicious look at me. "Whoa, why do you look like that? What are YOU thinking?"

I cursed at my face for having betrayed me. I quickly relaxed my expression before asking, "Look like what?"

"You look very eager to know what I'm thinking, so now I'm curious, because the thought I had did not warrant that kind of expression."

I breathed a sigh of relief. From her response, she did not seem to have fully reached an inference about the lewd nature of my thoughts. I realized I needed to share something that would discourage any hint of lecherous thoughts.

"I'm just thinking about everything we've learned today," I said vaguely, "I wonder how it all connects."

She seemed to buy my explanation, and for that, I felt a pang of displeasure. It hurt me to lie to her. I recalled earlier when she asked if my art was an imitation of my life as it pertained to lying. My response had been tempered to paint me in a favorable light.

"Well," she said, as we walked towards the front door of my beach house, "I was thinking something similar but it's not as vague as yours. I was thinking why Agent Tomkievich was unable to get the information we just got. If he went there like he claimed he did, there should be no reason why he wasn't able to get the same information. I didn't think we did anything special, minus the lying of course. But that lady was really nice. She would have shared that information even without the lie. She was very proud of Blaine Grubber and she was eager to praise him and the school."

I thought she made a good point. That was where my mind needed to be. Her return to the topic was exactly what I needed for my brain to stay on track. I considered her point in silence for a while. We were now in the living room.

"I think that might be something to consider," I said doubtfully, "but I might have an explanation for that."

She looked at me inquisitively, urging me to continue.

"When all three of us went out the other day," I began slowly, "I noticed that as soon as we introduced ourselves as FBI agents, they stiffened. And their friendliness from that point went down the drain. I'm guessing the same thing happened when he went there. He probably introduced himself as an FBI agent and they just withdrew. It's probably the M.O. for these schools because they might have students with questionable backgrounds, and they don't want to ruin their effort at rehabilitation."

"Hmm," Vaishali said. I was unsure where she stood with my rationale. "I guess you might have a point. I know I wanted to bring it up when we were there, but I didn't want to mess up the flow we were on. Our story with the fashion agency in New York was yielding so much information, I didn't want to bring up Agent Tomkievich and possibly interrupt our good fortune. But I couldn't help but think how odd it was though. She was very nice. I couldn't imagine her not sharing with people, including the FBI."

"You should've seen the other ones we went to," I countered, "they started off nice just like Linda. Their greetings were hearty, and they appeared genuinely happy to see us there, but as soon as they learned we were the FBI, they just changed. The transformation was swift and lingered throughout the duration of our stay."

My explanation seemed to be ineffective.

"Do you mind if we call her? Just to be sure."

I didn't see any harm in it. We'd already gotten key information about Blaine. This attempt would just be to tie all the loose ends.

"Sure," I said.

I fetched her business card from my wallet and handed it over to her. She brought out an exact replica of the phone she gave me. She dialed the number and placed it on the table for both of us to listen. I appreciated the gesture.

The phone rang four times, then the familiar jovial voice sounded on the phone.

"Linda Cummings speaking. How may I help you?"

"Hi Linda," Vaishali said readily. "This is Vaishali Kumar. My colleague and I were just there about an hour ago inquiring about Blaine Grubber."

"Oh, yea of course I remember you two," she said cheerily. "How may I help you?"

"Umm, my colleague and I were just wondering if you, or anyone on your staff, got a visit from our other colleague on Monday. We were just talking to our director, relaying the information we got, and he mentioned sending someone over there on Monday. With the move from Los Angeles to New York, we are trying to maintain a streamlined communication pattern, but sometimes some small details are overlooked. I'm sorry for the inconvenience."

"Oh, it's not a problem at all," she said. "Trust me, I understand. Umm let me see, what day did you say again?"

"Monday."

"Hmm," she said doubtfully, "do you know what time on Monday?"

"I'm not quite sure, but I can get that information if you need it."

"No. I'm just asking because on Monday we had to close down the building around eight in the morning, and we did not reopen until the next day. We had a bomb threat that ended up being a hoax, but I can assure you that any time after eight, the building was empty."

I felt my body stiffen. I recalled Agent Tomkievich saying he had been there in the evening. This would mean he lied. But why?

"Oh, wow ok," Vaishali sounded unmoved. "I'm glad it was just a hoax. Has this happened before?"

"Yes, it has," Linda said, "but thankfully, both instances have been hoaxes as well."

"Well, I don't want to take up too much of your time. Thanks for your help."

We stared at each other intently, trying to articulate reasons why Agent Tomkievich would lie about going to the Delaware Learning Institute.

"Was it because he felt embarrassed for not going," Vaishali said, "so he lied? But he probably would go later?"

"It couldn't have been that," I said confidently, "when we were out, we drove past it. I reminded him about it and he simply said he already went there the previous evening."

"Really?" Vaishali let out. "I'm out of options. We have to definitely let Frank know about this."

"Just Frank," I blurted out, a little louder than I planned, "not the team."

Slightly taken aback, she said, "Of course it'll be just Frank. It'll be easier to tell only him. If we try to tell the team, we might risk Agent Tomkievich finding out."

I felt a little embarrassed with my tone. I realized my premature outburst was from remnants of animosity I still held against Nikkyta, her deceit, and how I was easily discarded like a toy. It was still nagging at me, so I hid behind 'the 'team,' but in fact I meant Nikkyta. I remained silent for a while.

"Well," Vaishali said, illuminating the mood again, "let's not let this dampen the mood. Give me a tour of the place while we wait for the repair guy!"

It took a few seconds, then I recalled the original lie for coming over to begin with. I realized it would be wise to distract my thoughts from the discovery thus far. It appeared to be something monumental, but neither one of us had the skills nor power to make any real decision. We needed to talk to Frank Gordy alone for the proper way to deal with this.

"Sure, no problem," I said, as I walked towards the kitchen. "This is obviously the kitchen space. It's rarely used because I only come here in the Fall and Winter. I know it's weird. Beach houses are summer spots, but I prefer it around this time. The area is quiet, and I write better in that type of seclusion."

"I see," she said, nodding her head. "It's really roomy. Such a waste of space. You can make some really good stuff here."

As we were about to walk to the next part of the tour, she stopped and focused her attention on a patch on the wall.

"What happened there" she said, pointing to a crack on the wall. "For a space scarcely used, this looks like some serious wear and tear."

"Oh that," I said with a tinge of anger in my voice as I recalled the memory, "It's when I made the mistake of renting the spot out to college students in the summer. They left my place in such disorder, that I rarely rent it anymore. And the few times I do, it's to an older couple with better appreciation for the property. They messed up my bedroom door too. You'll hear the squeaky noise. It sounds really creepy. I've been telling myself I'll fix it, but I never seem to find time for it."

Vaishali chuckled as we continued the tour.

We went back to the living room and I properly reintroduced the space to her. I pointed to where Agents Taylor and Tomkievich sat the morning they visited me. It was hard to believe that was only four days ago. With all that had happened, it was difficult to accept the fact that I was insulated from all these five days ago. A part of me wished I could go back to that. I understood the unique opportunity I was being offered, and most of it thrilled me. I enjoyed the idea of working closely with the FBI and then using the material in one form or another for my next book. It was the level of access I needed, but the stress involved was not something I anticipated. In fact, I was under the impression that I would be a muted observer with very little to say. At least, that was what I deduced from Frank Gordy's speech in that awful building. I did not expect to be thought of as the leak. Now, in an attempt to vindicate my name, I came across Butch, which then led to the Delaware Learning Institute and Linda, and then the inconsistencies with Agent Tomkievich's story—it was getting too much for me to handle. And all the aforementioned sources of stress had not included the senator and his shenanigans!

These developments weighed heavily on my mind as we walked around the house sluggishly. I could not tell with full certainty, but I suspected Vaishali was feeling the same. The elapsed time between her smiles was a clear indication that she was feeling something as well. I decided I should do something to lighten the mood.

"Do you want something stronger than that bottle of water?" I asked.

"What do you have?" she asked gamely to my delight.

"Umm, it depends. Are you a wine person? Light or dark liquor?"

"Do you have brandy and coke?" She asked.

I was taken aback. I've hastily judged her as a wine drinker at most. I did not envision her even knowing the

names of anything else. She could see the look of disbelief on my face, so she added, "I hung out a lot with my brother and his friends. That's how I got this level of understanding."

"Oh, I see," I said, as I walked back to the kitchen to make her drink.

She came along with me to watch me make the drink. I walked towards my collection and scanned the options before me. I realized I was running low, and I decided my next visit from Brooklyn must include a restocking.

"Is Cognac okay?" I asked, holding the bottle up high.

She nodded.

"What about Pepsi instead of coke?"

She nodded. I found it odd that she was not speaking. Her eyes concentrated intently on me and the task of making her drink. For a while I thought she was making sure I didn't add any foreign object into her drink. I wondered if that was a safety training in the FBI. I wanted to ask her, but I could not find a way to make it sound ordinary. I mixed the drinks, with the brandy occupying about seventy-five percent of the glass and the Pepsi filling the remaining quarter. I offered it to her to let me know if it was a satisfactory ratio. As she reached for the glass, our hands brushed slightly.

Neither one of us felt the need to apologize, nor did we feel the need to ignore the mood. I enjoyed the feel of her touch. A deafening silence overcame us. The way she stared at me made me safely conclude she was harboring the same feeling inside. Her eyes were a pool of glistening light piercing right through my soul. It was filled with a raw desire that appeared to prevail over anything that was happening at the moment. I was determined not to repeat the indecision I displayed with Nikkyta. Aggressively, I grabbed her hand and pulled her forcefully towards me. She quickly dropped the glass aside. She let out a slight moan, as she allowed her body to be controlled by my force. There was a sizable height difference between us, so I bent a little to meet her elevated lips. The contact caused millions of small tingling sparks to detonate within my body. We kissed closed-mouthed for a few seconds, then I charged my tongue out from hiding causing her lips to part ways. With fierce urgency, my tongue eased into her mouth wandering freely and causing us to move in wild unpredictable motions. It was a sudden, shocking intimacy I found thrilling and she responded similarly. We kissed passionately as my hands swam at will across the voluptuous terrain of her body. I settled my hands on the front hook of her capris pants and undid the zipper quickly. At that point, she had already tossed my shirt on the kitchen floor and was making due of my pants. I assisted her efforts and soon we were both down to our underwear. I lifted her on top of the countertop and parted her thighs with force. I quickly realized my countertop was a little too high, and I would need to be slightly elevated for a smooth entry. She realized my predicament and slid down from her raised position. She turned around and leaned on the counter, with her butt protruding out. She gave me a look of yearning and I felt I was about to explode. I grabbed her underwear and slid it down to her knees. She parted her legs, and I drove into her.

chapter30

The first time the phone rang was in the middle of the ferocious lovemaking, so neither one of us deemed it important enough to interrupt our plans. It was over an hour since we finished, and Vaishali and I were cuddled on the couch. With our breathings now regulated, we were flirting with the idea of taking a nap when my phone buzzed to life again. It startled me a little. I reached for it and realized it was Nikkyta.

"Oh shit," I said. "It's Nikkyta! Should I answer it?"

"Sure, why not?" Vaishali was confused with my indecision.

It made sense for her to be confused. She had no knowledge of my intimate sessions with Nikkyta, so in her mind it was just answering a call from a colleague. My mind raced frantically trying to find a lie to normalize the situation. Even though Nikkyta and I were not in a great place at the moment, I still cared about her feelings and how she would interpret what Vaishali and I just did.

"Hello," I said, slowly.

"Where the hell are you guys at?" Her voice was filled with rage. "I've tried Vaishali's number about five times and yours twice. What's going on? We need to head off to Wilmington tonight."

"We're at my place," I said carefully. "I was expecting a repair guy at my beach house and Vaishali decided she wanted to come along, rather than staying back with nothing to do."

"So, you guys are in Rehoboth?!" she said, angrily. "We're supposed to be leaving in about thirty minutes. You guys are at least two hours away. And why is Vaishali not answering her phone?"

"I'm not sure," I said. The words came out faster than I planned. "I've been outside doing some yard work, so I didn't hear my phone. I can check with her inside to see what's going on."

"No need for that," she said dismissively, "I'll text you the hotel information in Wilmington. You guys are expected there tonight. Frank went back to D.C. at the request of the bosses at Quantico, but we're having a meeting tonight, around 8 p.m. Tell Vaishali she would need to be there much earlier than that for the setup. I'm heading up now with the crew. I recommend you guys hurry back and join us."

All I heard was, Frank was in Washington. This meant we would not have the opportunity to share what we learned today... at least not during the conference call.

Maybe Vaishali and I could call him privately and share our news.

"Alright," I said. "We have time. We will be there well before the meeting time."

She hung up the phone without any proper parting words. I wondered if she knew what had happened and the thought had incensed her to the point where she had nothing else to say to me. I was not sure, but the idea of Nikkyta enraged over my carnal interaction with Vaishali gave me a sense of pride. I enjoyed the idea that I was valued that much to stir up that level of emotion within her.

"Everything ok?" Vaishali asked.

For a second I was consumed with my thoughts that I forgot she was laying naked next to me.

"Yes," I said, then realized it was a lie, so I added, "Umm, not really. We are moving to Wilmington and they need us there well before eight tonight so you can setup the video conference for a meeting with Frank Gordy tonight."

"What do you mean a meeting with Frank?"

"Apparently he went back to D.C. at the request of the bosses at Quantico."

"Really? That sucks." She sat up and drew her legs closer to her body essentially covering her breasts and abdomen. "I wonder what's going on. This would mean we probably can't talk to him about any of this tonight."

"I was thinking the exact same thing," I said, "but maybe we can call him privately tonight."

"Yea that's a possibility," she sounded unsure, "but we have to be careful. We can't be seen alone talking on the phone. Especially not by Earl Tomkievich. The man is smart, and he might sense something is up."

"Well," I said, "you can come to my room that way no one can see us."

"Yea, but what if I get caught on my way before I get in? I'm thinking we should try to call him on our way back because it sounds like he's not with the team right now, correct?"

"Yea that's the impression I got," I said. "Nikkyta sounded like he was already in D.C."

"Did she say anything about us leaving the hotel?"

"No, she didn't say anything, but I think she might suspect something."

"What makes you say that?"

I refrained from telling her the wordless departure on the phone with her. It would only lead to more inquiries and expose my extremely lewd conduct of sleeping with the two female agents on the same team.

"I don't know," I said instead, "it's just a feeling I got from the conversation. And the fact that she called you at least five times, and me twice. She's smart. She might suspect something."

"Is that a problem?" She asked.

Yes! I thought.

"No, not at all." I said confidently. "At least for me. I'm not sure of the policy at the FBI and sleeping with other agents."

"As long as it doesn't interfere with the job, they're typically relaxed over stuff like that. It might not apply to me because I'm not heavy on field work or the other consuming aspects of this job, but FBI agents typically marry each other because that's the only place to find someone with similar schedule and a good understanding of what you do. Of course, the marriage rarely lasts, but the weddings occur regularly. Anyway, did she ask what we were doing at your beach house?"

"I told her I was here for my repairman and you decided to come along because you didn't want to be in the hotel alone. And then for the missed calls, I told her I was doing yard work, so I didn't hear my phone ring."

"Yard work, huh?" she said, smiling seductively. "Is that what they call it now? I know I'm a little hairy down there, but yard work though. That's original."

"I didn't notice any hair down there," I said, mimicking her sensuality, "Do you mind if I take another look?"

She smiled.

Slowly, her legs parted ways and she gradually traced her middle and index fingers down the opening beneath her navel.

"Is this what you wanna see?" She asked, as her fingers glided softly around the area.

"Oh yea," I said as I pounced on top of her.

chapter31

Both calls to Commander Gordy went straight to voicemail. This gave an indication that he was probably on the flight to D.C. and had his phone on airplane mode. Vaishali and I were about an hour into our ride from my beach house to the hotel in Dover to move our things to the new location in Wilmington. Despite our spontaneous intimate sessions, we were still on course for a timely arrival. She had since discovered that I lied to her about the repairman. In order not to look as if I lured her to my beach house just to have sex with her, I had to share a little bit of why I wanted to be away from the hotel. Of course, I did not tell her about the way I was handled by Nikkyta, nor did I volunteer to share our lovemaking sessions. I gave her just enough information to douse her curiosity and still maintain my character in a favorable light. To my slight antipathy, she sided with Nikkyta. She advised that if it was her belief that I was the leak, it had to be coming from a place of strong conviction and not the whimsical standards of a hunch.

"Nikkyta is very smart and thorough," she said, "I don't think she would do anything shady just to hurt you. Even at the morning meetings, before you joined the team, she was one of your most ardent supporters. She and Agent Tomkievich actually."

I listened carefully, but my pride was still unwilling to relent on the grudge I held for her. Perhaps if she knew the entire story, she might not be as vociferous in her favor. We rode in silence for another half hour before dialing Frank again.

This time, she was rewarded with the sound of his voice.

"Frank!" she almost yelled. "I'm so glad I got you! You're on speaker phone with Ebenezer and me."

"Hi, Vaishali," his deep voice emanated with his usual poise and confidence. "Are you guys all checked-in?"

"No not yet," Vaishali continued. "We're on our way back to Dover to get our things and head to Wilmington."

"What do you mean back to Dover?" His voice revealed his confusion, "Where did you guys go? Aren't you already in Dover?"

Vaishali paused before continuing.

This was another reason to be glad Vaishali was with me. I could not imagine myself talking with so much poise. Perhaps if our working relationship was of considerable length... but in just four days I was yet to understand enough about the man. I respected him because he came off as a man of integrity, but mastering the intricacies of his demeanor was something that eluded me.

"Sir," Vaishali began, "we had an intuition earlier today and we followed it. It led us to a gas station, on the way to the beach. We met this guy named Butch..."

Vaishali was flimsy on the facts concerning the premonition that led us to Butch, but she made up for it with exhaustive details about what we discovered. When she finished, Frank Gordy was speechless for almost a minute. She had to confirm the connection was still live.

"Yea, I'm here," he said. "I'm just trying to understand what's going on that's all. You guys did great work, but I won't be doing my job if I didn't reprimand the decision to act on this hunch. You cannot go around doing fieldwork. It's dangerous. There's a reason why you have your assigned role. It's for your own safety. If something had happened to you guys, there would be no way to make sense of it to the guys at the top. I appreciate the effort, but please do not make this a habit. Give me some time to mull through this. Continue your journey to the hotel. I will be talking to you directly when I need something done. And also, please try to be normal around the team. He is a behavioral specialist; he can detect when something is wrong. I will do some investigation and talk to the team tonight."

"Alright," Vaishali and I said in unison. "We'll talk later."

The rest of the ride was uneventful. Occasionally, Vaishali would share a story about something from her past, and I would offer a reaction to match what I anticipated she expected of me. It was obvious that the weight of what we discovered was beginning to take a toll on us. Especially with the way Frank Gordy treated the information. He must have viewed it as a big deal. He needed time to mull it over before reaching a conclusion. It had to be big, if not, he would have either dismissed it as a non-story or offered a quick decision to calm the situation.

When we arrived at the hotel, we both walked insistently to our respective rooms to retrieve our things. We met at the front lobby ten minutes later, ready for Wilmington. The ride remained uneventful. The only thing I felt compelled to say was to reiterate Frank Gordy's advice to remain inconspicuous with our deportment. We needed to act the way we normally would. As the words fled my lips, I realized we had crossed a crucial line in our relationship and it might be difficult to act the same way. I wanted her in my bed, and I safely assumed she wanted the same. That would mean sneaking to her room or vice versa, and that was the antithesis of Frank's recommendation. But I could not imagine spending the night without her.

She was perfect.

Beauty and brains.

Am I being absurd? I thought.

I had not lost sight of the fact that I slept with two FBI agents in just four days. That was never my intention when I walked into that dilapidated building to meet with Frank Gordy for the first time, four days ago. It was supposed to be a unique experience to apply to my next novel. Sleeping with Nikkyta, and now Vaishali, was never part of the plan. Matt had known this would happen. He tried to warn me, but I was already enamored by Nikkyta's beauty. My deterrence had been a fragile one. The appeal for Vaishali came late. I was not captivated with the same haste as Nikkyta, but the effect on me was of equal intensity. Other than being a mildly successful author, I could not think of anything to make the appeal for me worth exploring, yet, I was able to bed two FBI agents in four days. An immature side of me beamed with pride, but I did not let it show. In spite of how it might be interpreted in the shallow minds of men, I refused to revel in it. I needed to concentrate. Being involved in this love triang... What the fuck am I saying!? It's not even love! And it might not even be a triangle. Why couldn't it be just two consensual adults choosing to explore the physical pleasures of the flesh? My mind bounced erratically, trying to locate a rationale for my libidinous behavior. I guess a part of me was feeling guilty after championing women's rights at seminars I'd attended. I realized the conflict within me was something that had to be solved at a later date. At the moment, I needed to focus on the case. I needed to refrain from sleeping with Vaishali and Nikkyta until this was over and I was no longer under the watchful gaze of the bureau.

We arrived at the hotel in Wilmington around 5:30 p.m. I spotted the blue and gray FBI van as soon as we pulled in. It was parked at the side parking lot. I thought about parking next to it, but I noticed there were a few people in it, so I decided to park elsewhere. I decided to park as far away from it as possible. Just in case there was a need for a hasty escape, I wanted my assailant to suffer every disadvantage possible. Our rooms had been reserved when we arrived at the front desk. All we needed to do was to show forms of identification and our room keys were immediately handed to us. I was in room 331 and Vaishali, 435. That meant we were on different floors, so sneaking into each other's rooms would not be a walk in the park.

Suddenly, a thought occurred to me.

"Can your phone make three-way video calls?"

"Yes, it can," Vaishali said proudly as we walked towards the elevator. "Why do you ask?"

As I was about to explain my thought process, the elevator yawned open, and standing there, was Nikkyta and Agent Tomkievich. It was the first time seeing Earl away from Tristan. Together, they looked equally as strange as the real odd couple. This was the first true test to reveal if we could really adhere to the warning to act normal. Here we were, standing before two of FBI's behavioral specialists, attempting to end this segment without a hint of suspicion.

I felt my body congeal.

I tried forcing a smile, but I quickly realized it would be detected, so I stifled it. I spoke instead.

"Hey guys," my voice was high, like a guilty person. "What's going on?"

What the fuck! What's going on? You might as well have said, "I know about you, Earl."

"Nothing much," Nikkyta said, and then added sarcastically, "Nice for you two to finally join us."

I noticed Vaishali was not talking. She had the perfect facial expression to combat their analytical prowess. She was better prepared for this role than I was.

"Yea, it's been a long day," I said, as the odd pair stepped out and Vaishali and I stepped into the elevator.

Before the door closed, Nikkyta alerted us that they were going out to dinner. "The rest of the crew are in the van. Are you guys interested?"

"No, I'm good." I said.

Vaishali said the same thing.

"Ok, well we'll be back in about an hour. We are having the meeting in the conference room on the first floor. It's open, so when you have time, please set it up. Frank said he'll call around 8 p.m."

"No worries," Vaishali said confidently. "Let me drop this off and we'll get to it."

The door closed and the elevator ascended.

"You're terrible," Vaishali said, smiling, "you almost told on us."

I chuckled at her words. I knew her assessment of me was incorrect. Of course, she sensed my nervousness, but she thought it had to do with the inconsistencies of Earl's story, but in reality, I was edgy existing in a space with two women that I had just slept with a day apart. There was no way she could know that because I deliberately omitted that part when I brought her to speed on things. I gladly accepted the incomplete charge and offered a practiced smile.

The conference room was much bigger than what I had expected. It had enough room to hold twice the size of our team. A large 70-inch TV was perched high-up at the north end of the room. A long table with smooth curved edges sat in the middle of the room, with about twenty chairs evenly spaced around it. The room was carpeted, and a flowery smell of some sort dominated the scent in the room. Vaishali brought out the projector and a bunch of blue Ethernet cords. I was impressed with my ability to assist without much directions from her. The small time I spent with her in Dover revitalized my love for this world. A part of me still missed it, but I knew I could never give up writing. Not at this stage, not with all the attention. Ray would kill me. In about 30 minutes, the room was set, and all the sound checks were confirmed.

It was 6:30 p.m.

"What do you wanna do while we wait?" she asked.

"I know what, or better yet, who, I wanna do," I said playfully.

She smiled.

"We can't do that," she said as she moved closer towards me. "Trust me I really want to, but I've been thinking. It'll make sense to pause on this for a bit, at least till the end of this case and you're no longer on the team. That will flow better."

I felt rejected even though I had reached a similar conclusion earlier. It took some effort, but I was able to maintain a smile on my face as I accepted her polite refusal. Thankfully, her phone buzzed to life inviting a necessary distraction.

Her facial expression turned serious as soon as she saw the caller.

"It's Frank," she said in a near whisper.

"Hello," she said, "what's up?"

I couldn't hear him on the other side of the line, but I noticed Vaishali nodding a few times, and then she mentioned the whereabouts of the team. She nodded a few more times and the line went dead. In all, the call lasted about ten minutes with Frank doing most of the talking. In my eyes, she could see the severe thirst for information, so she began speaking almost immediately.

"That was Frank," she said in a measured tone. "He said he has conducted a quick investigation on Agent Tomkievich. He pulled out his file and reviewed some of his old cases. He said nothing suspicious is currently jumping out at him, but it's early. He is convinced Agent Tomkievich is a little more involved with these deaths. He wants us to be away from the area. Us as in just you and me. He said he'll tell Nikkyta and Antoine about it, and the steps going forward. He didn't think it would be wise for Gabbert, Brady, Taylor, and Cumberland to know anything about it for now. Tomkievich is too smart. If everybody knows something, he could easily detect trouble."

I realized that I did not experience any hint of hostility upon learning that Nikkyta was one of the people Frank deemed important enough to know about this. Ever since the physical squabble between us, and her erroneous inference of labeling me the leak, I harbored a pang of bitterness whenever her name was mentioned. But this time it felt completely normal. The name did not affect me. I wondered if it was because of the imminent bombshell with Agent Tomkievich, or my recent romantic interest in Vaishali. Whatever it was, I was perfectly unmoved by the reference to her name and I liked it. I wanted to be over it and concentrate on the case, my book, and whatever lay ahead between Vaishali and me.

The rest of the team walked through the front lobby about twenty minutes after the call with Frank. From their vantage point, they were able to see me and Vaishali in the conference room, so all but Jeff Cumberland walked towards our direction.

"All set?" Agent Gabbert said.

For his standard, his beard was not as untidy as the previous days. He even had on a dress pant and an ironed plaid shirt.

Vaishali gave him a thumbs up.

They all took their seats around the table. Tomkievich and Taylor were the only two sitting together. For the first time, I now entertained a deep interest in their relationship. The hazy details of Tomkievich's story had now implicated Agent Taylor. It was well within the confines of logical reasoning to wonder about him. They rarely spoke, but they were always within an arm's reach of each other.

"So, you guys had a good day?" Agent Brady asked in an attempt to end the silence.

I looked up and realized his question was directed to me and Vaishali. He had a mocking smile on his face like he knew of the carnal pleasure we had experienced.

Nonsense! A logical voice bellowed in my head, *there's no way he would know that!*

"Eh, not bad," I said, unwilling to participate any further into whatever he was driving at. "Just a regular day."

He noticed the lack of zeal in my response, and that discouraged him from advancing with the small talk. The room was unusually quiet with everybody consumed in their own little worlds. Vaishali was scrutinizing complicated lines of code on her laptop. I felt like joining her because I knew I could keep up with the logic, but that might mean revealing too much, so I remained in my corner. Agent Brady was leafing through the day's copy of the Delaware News Journal, and Agent Gabbert appeared lost in thought. Nikkyta was jotting ferociously on a notebook. I wondered what she could be writing and why no one else seemed to care for the concentration she devoted to this task. Agent Jackson was typing on his phone. The smile on his face suggested he was conversing with someone he fondly regarded. Agent Taylor and Tomkievich were looking about the room just like me. The cloud of suspicions hanging over Tomkievich had made it difficult to make eye contact with him. It was almost seven o'clock. I dreaded the thought of being in this uneventful room for another hour before the scheduled call. I would rather be in my room, or better yet, in Vaishali's.

Jeff walked in minutes later. Unlike me, Jeff could not withstand the monotony. He justified placing the call before 8 p.m. as long as we were ready. No one appeared to object to his reasoning, so we used Vaishali's phone. The Commander's voice was heard before a blurry image appeared on the screen. Vaishali quickly sprang up and walked towards the camera device by the television. She adjusted a green knob, and in an instant, Commander Gordy appeared in high definition clarity.

"How're you guys doing?" He asked.

A scattered response spattered about the room.

"Good," he said, leaving no further room for small-talk. "First, let me bring Ebenezer and Vaishali up to speed with our trip to Wilmington. We have confirmed the death occurred at the hotel, and we also know our victim was not Jenny Gibson. There is a very good chance Jenny is still alive. I made the decision to move the team to Wilmington because I think Jenny is still in Wilmington somewhere. We met two night workers today. A hotel employee referred them. Fortunately, they are somewhat of regulars at the establishment. Unfortunately, they were of little help. They recalled seeing a van but no other qualifying features to help identify the vehicle in spite of our push and veiled threats to arrest them for their profession. At this point, the van could be anywhere in the state, or in the country for that matter, but it appears we are dealing with an intelligent man and the intelligent thing to do would be to hide in plain sight. We will begin with a small search radius in Wilmington and its immediate towns, then expand as needed."

He paused, allowing for Vaishali and me to digest the information. The rest of the team already knew about this, and it was evinced by their tamed interests in the Commander's words. I was still unable to look at Agent Tomkievich, so I could not tell if he too showed a dreary interest in Frank's speech.

"As for my emergency trip back to Washington," Commander Gordy resumed, "it was a good one. It helped answer the question about the leak."

He paused, I think, for the dramatic effect.

My body tensed. I felt everyone in the room show similar response. Naturally, my eyes rested on Nikkyta, hoping to capture her full reaction upon hearing who the leak was. I knew it was not me, and in a moment, I expected Commander Gordy to reveal the culprit. At this point, Agent Tomkievich had surpassed Nikkyta as the person behind the leak, but I wanted the redemptive feeling upon seeing her face and knowing that I was not the leak.

"A letter from TMZ came in today" he continued. "it basically ended the suspicions that a leak emanated from this group. The mail contained key information about Tracy, Jenny, and some of the previous killings in the past. It's safe to assume this was from the killer because outside the people in this team, no one else possessed that level of knowledge about the case, besides the killer of course. I am certain it was not from you guys because the mail was sent out on the morning Tracy was murdered. They received the package two days ago and then decided to release the breaking news. My guess is with the Senator's status, they felt a little bit of pressure to send the package to the FBI. So, in all, the case has not been fully derailed. In spite of the untimely report, we think we are closing in on the killer. We have updated the Senator with information we deemed appropriate. We did this mainly to buy his silence and prevent further damage from the media. We are going to review this package thoroughly within the next twenty-four hours, but in the meantime, I need you guys to remain in Wilmington, pending what we discover from the package. Are there any questions?"

The room was deafeningly silent. I could not discern Nikkyta's expression, but I longed to be alone with her—not for sexual pleasure, but to shamelessly celebrate my exoneration, and perhaps if I was lucky, get an apology for the way she treated me. The Commander's words would mark the end of my side investigation on her, so I could return my focus back to the case and embody my role, whatever it was, on the team.

After continuing moments of no response, Commander Gordy continued. He touched on some basic facts, and in a show of force, he openly reprimanded Vaishali and I for the decision to leave the hotel. I had heard the Commander's reproaches in the past, and for some reason, this one was not believable. It lacked the usual fire and surety it was known for. I suspected it was just for show, to dissuade all doubts, and to maintain the narrative that unilateral decisions were not tolerated. I sat with a practiced glum expression and endured the verbal onslaught. When he was done, I saw a look of relief on Vaishali's face. We all planned to meet the same time the following day barring any unforeseen circumstances.

When the call ended, Jeff Cumberland turned to Vaishali and me and said, "Don't take it personal. He means well. He's a good guy. Like he said, you guys are not properly trained in the field, so it's dangerous. If something had happened, that would be his ass."

I appreciated his words although they were not needed. For the first time, I was completely unmoved by the Commander's words. I knew why he did it, and I applauded the genius behind it.

I forced a smile towards Agent Cumberland. "Thanks."

At that exact moment, I felt my phone buzz to life. It was perfect timing, because I was in no mood to continue my involuntary display of remorse. It was a text message from Commander Gordy. The message simply read, "Head up to your room. I will call in ten minutes."

"Sorry I have to call my agent," I lied.

"Oh sure," Jeff said and continued to a different corner of the room.

I wanted to alert Vaishali about the message, but it occurred to me that the Commander would have reached out to her as well. This was obviously a clandestine operation, so alerting Vaishali would risk exposing it all. I glanced at Vaishali and she was busy with Agent Jackson who was unplugging the camera for the video conference. His height was perfect for the job. Nikkyta was staring intently at something on her phone, and Agent Cumberland was giving the impression that he was about to leave. Brady and Gabbert were on one corner of the room, and Taylor and Tomkievich were on the opposite corner. Agent Tomkievich stood with his back facing me, on a raised platform that made him almost as tall as Agent Tristan's broad shoulders. I needed to make my escape without raising any suspicions. They all seemed engulfed with what they were doing. I flirted with the idea of walking out unannounced. *Would they know I got a text from Commander Gordy?* My eyes scanned the room, and for a quick second, they rested on Nikkyta's face. Our eyes met. I noticed a slight but perceptible move in her signaling me to leave. It took a few seconds for my wits to catch up, and then I realized she knew about the text message. She was waiting for me to head to my room as instructed. I quickly announced my departure and dashed to the door. Right before the elevator closed, Agent Cumberland caught up with it.

"Yea I think I'm done for the night myself," he said. "I need to sleep."

I nodded politely. I was not in the mood for a casual conversation, so I curtailed my responses to head gestures and one-word responses. Thankfully, he was on the seventh floor, so my escape to the third was God-sent. I quickly barged into my room and pulled out the massive phone. The anticipation has reached unbearable levels. I checked the timestamp on the message and noticed six minutes had passed though it felt as if it was closer to twenty. I was nervous. I tried everything I could within that period to tame my nerves, but to no avail. I decided to abandon all hope and allow my anxiety to rule me. My phone finally buzzed about fifteen minutes later. I grabbed it frantically and pressed the large green button to answer the call. On the screen were pictures of Vaishali, Nikkyta, and Frank.

"Are the sounds and pictures good for everybody?" Frank asked.

I nodded, while the other two spoke their responses.

"Good," Frank said. "First of all, let me start by saying, I meant every word I said earlier about not making decisions and acting on it in the field. You only do that when it's life and death situation. Any other time, I want you to consult a leading field expert and work through them. It's dangerous out there. But having said that, great work you two. Your discovery has raised enough doubt to discover some interesting things about Agent Tomkievich. If not for your work, we wouldn't have found this out. He was not trying to hide anything. He prefers to operate in plain sight. We were able to recover his records and there have been at least four deaths from his childhood that were suspicious. In 1987 there was a death of a monsignor and the disappearance of a group of high school students. The church quickly disregarded his death because of the circumstances surrounding the monsignor. Notes from the detective working the case detailed that the monsignor was a pedophile, and one of the kids he molested was a suspect. Unfortunately, the detective passed away seven years ago. The case has been closed for a while now, but the true killer remains unknown. And as for the missing group, they were never found. In both instances, Earl was present. The missing kids attended the same high school the same time he did. And the monsignor was the priest at the church he attended with his stepfather. Earl was an altar boy under the monsignor. I think it's too much of a coincidence to be involved in these amount of scenarios. But what's also obvious is that he has an accomplice. The physique of the man on the picture from the fourth killing was that of a skinny man with dark hair. The goal now is to find out who this is. We can arrest him right now, but I don't think he would fold in an interrogation. We have to make him take us to his accomplice. To do this, it will require discipline. That's why I only have three of you. I believe the more people know about this, the less likely its chances. Earl is smart; he can sense when something is wrong. He can easily sense a change in behavior or mood. To avoid this, I would need Ebenezer and Vaishali to be away from the group right now. I'm sure Nikkyta can handle herself, and the rest of the crew would not be a problem because they will have no idea. I need you two to head to Ebenezer's beach house. I have received an authorization for this location over the safe house in Dover. That building was recommended and secured by Earl, so it would be unwise to try and use that. Ebenezer, is that okay for you?"

"Sure," I said nervously.

"It would just be for tonight." He continued. "We will secure a different safe house by tomorrow for you two, but I need you two away from the group tonight. Wait for the commotion around the hotel to die down a bit, then head out. You don't need to check out. We will handle that. Is that clear?"

I nodded. Vaishali did too.

"Do you guys have any questions?"

I had plenty.

But it was of no use. My questions were about Earl and the sudden revelation that he was part of a killing duo. I recalled the morning he was at my place. The thought sent chills through my body. I was no longer excited about our discovery. For the first time in my role, I was afraid for my life. I wanted to call a character from my normal life in order to hear a familiar voice. This life was new to me. It was too scary. I needed to be out of it and return to life as I knew it.

chapter32

EARL TOMKIEVICH was an only child. His mother remarried a bricklayer from Seaford, Delaware in 1973, soon after his father's death. Earl's mother was mentally unstable and spent time in and out of rehab, so he spent a lot of time with his stepfather. He never liked Earl. He blamed him for the fate of his wife, and every chance at admonishment was utilized to disburse the maximum allowable punishment without killing him. Earl was terrified of his stepfather. Coming home from school was one of his least favorite things to do, but as he stayed in school, a group of boys began to torment him. Confused, Earl turned to the only place he knew he could seek refuge. He went to their Catholic church. Although their attendance had waned ever since his mother's condition reached worrisome levels, Earl was still accepted within the hallowed grounds of the holy place. He was allowed to eat, do his homework, and relax a little before heading home. By the time he was home, typically around 9pm, his stepfather would have collapsed into a drunken stupor by the entrance of their three-bedroom house.

The episode continued for several years until he got to the tenth grade. At which point, he felt sufficient enough to fend for himself without the need to hide behind the church walls. He visited his mom at the State

Mental Hospital in New Castle Delaware. Each visit was typically an emotional whirlwind. Seeing his mom in such a deplorable state affected his psyche in ways he never imagined. She was a victim to the rapacious voices in her head. She talked incessantly to no one in particular, and often times she would fling feces at anyone that attempted to make sense of the chaotic thoughts in her mind. Earl tried to help, but his efforts were futile. Nothing in his discipline to prepared him for her condition. After each visit, he left her with a heavy heart. He wanted to do something to change her situation. He felt his mother had been unfairly plagued with mental illness. He did not think she deserved such fate. She was the only person he ever felt genuine love for. His stepfather was naturally his guardian after his mom was admitted to the mental institution. He turned to his friends when he got older, but they took advantage of his waiflike physique and constantly took his lunch money. The monsignor was, on the surface, a kind presence in his life. He provided much needed safety from his abusive stepfather and bullying friends. At first, Earl enjoyed the sacred space, but he soon realized it came at a price. The monsignor would often visit him in the dimly lit room he boarded. He wore his priestly robe with not much else underneath. Earl had heard stories about adults with perverse needs. His mother had warned him about their aberrant desire. But when Earl was confronted with it, he did not know how to react. He feared the monsignor would be upset and cast him back to the life he fought so hard to escape from.

With the psychological damage not as immediate as the blows and slaps from his old life, Earl tolerated the holy man's deeds. He did not anticipate a lifelong mutilation of his being. When he became self-reliant to fend for himself, Earl began to devise ways to seek revenge against people who had wronged him. Earl had since realized he was much smarter than his friends, so what he lacked in power, he believed he made up in wits and cunningness. He was able to lure the bullies to a remote graveyard in Bridgeville Delaware. He devised a hasty treasure hunt that led them there. Earl killed them with his stepfather's gun. It was his first killing. His initial plan was only to discard the bullies in order to secure a semblance of peace in his life, but the act was invigorating. He felt something in him he had never felt before. He was a bit disturbed with the level of satisfaction he gained from the killing. He decided to kill again to see if it was an irregularity or something worth exploring. His stepfather was an easy choice for his next kill, but Earl imagined it would lack the thrill. He suspected the ecstasy was as a result of the difficulty involved. He decided to turn his attention to the other person that had negatively impacted his life.

After high-school, Earl still had the same elfin physique, so he imagined the body type that the Monsignor found attractive many years ago would remain true. His assumption was accurate upon seeing him. He invited Earl to the poorly lit room as expected. They were always alone in the past, so Earl knew he could easily kill him without the risk of being heard or seen. He assumed his position as he had in the past, and the monsignor entered him from behind. Earl placed his right hand on his coat pocket to protect the knife inside. He imagined using a knife would raise the difficulty, and hopefully, the excitement. He felt the Monsignor's rhythm increase and Earl realized he was near climax. Before reaching the crescendo, Earl pulled himself away from the penetration and got down on his knees. He grabbed the Monsignor's person and stroked it for a few seconds. He heard him let out a slight moan, and a white creamy substance spurted through his phallus. It missed Earl's face and landed a few inches from where he was standing. He was regaining his senses when he felt the sharp object pierce through the side of his stomach. He looked down just in time to see Earl wield the knife into him a few more times each time puncturing different points on the side of his stomach. By the time he knew what was happening, he had lost too much blood to react. He fell to his knees, and moments later, his eyes closed for the last time. Earl had never felt better in his life. The act surpassed the feeling from his first killing. His mind and body soared as he moved through this euphoric experience. He left the knife in the monsignor's body and escaped through the door he innocently used in the past. The authorities had several leads on how to approach the case, but it was difficult to ignore the semen at the crime scene. The church would rather concoct an alternate scenario than to admit the carnal sin from a Monsignor. They leaned heavily on the police department to fabricate something believable, and in essence, close the case. The police department was made up of some high-ranking members of the church, and they too understood the disgrace it would bring. The case was swept under the rug, and soon the public's interest died. Earl knew he was lucky. He did not plan it that way. After going months without a killing, he began to feel the withdrawal. He yearned for that feeling again. He thought about his stepfather, but the ease of the mission discouraged him.

He needed more.

He needed a formidable challenge.

He tried to distract his mind by doing something else. He enrolled at a community college and earned an associate degree in Criminal Justice. It was a very easy process, and that made it unworthy. But while at the college, he met with a guidance counselor, Emmanuel

Saunders who suggested he considered becoming a behavioral specialist for the police department. He lauded his unique intellect and quick wits and assured Earl he had what it took to succeed. Earl was reluctant at first, but after years of lackluster activities in his life, he reached out to Emmanuel. At this point, his parents had both died. His stepfather died of a heart attack, and his mother jumped off a building in an apparent suicide. However, when Earl went to get her belongings, an eager employee told him that she was pushed off the building. The employee wanted Earl to stoke the narrative and begin a movement for massive reform in the institution, but Earl was not interested in that. He was desperate for thrill and excitement in his life and pursuing a wrongful death accusation posed to be more challenging than thrilling.

Emmanuel gave him a few phone numbers to call in the state capital building in Dover. Earl was further introduced to two more people, and by the Summer of 2003, Earl was under strong consideration as an FBI Behavioral Specialist stationed in Delaware. The only source of concern for the folks at Quantico was his size and limited ability for physically-demanding chores. But Earl's mind was able to wow them into giving him the job. They felt at ease stationing him in Delaware for the time being because the level of danger was not as high as the other areas in the Northeast. Earl felt a surge in his excitement upon achieving this feat, but it soon faded, and he soon plunged back to the monotony of his day-to-day activities.

Earl's interest was finally piqued in 2008. He was copied in an email about a murderer dubbed Tilted Grin Killer. Earl was only copied in the email because it contained a detailed analysis issued by the head behavioral specialist in the bureau about the killer. Earl's interest in the killer grew beyond control. With his access, he was able to obtain classified files from the killer's folder and saw details of his killings. He observed the killer's strengths and weaknesses. He assessed his ability to perform on par with the killer. Earl read about the novel that inspired the killings in the beginning. It would not go down as one of the classics, but Earl appreciated the author's ability to hold his reader's attention. He noticed some incorrect facts that were hastily glossed over, but Earl respected the author's efforts. He decided he would resurrect the phenomenon eventually. In the meantime, he prepared by learning the disguising powers of makeup. He enrolled at the Delaware Learning Center as Blaine Grubber. Outside of his official FBI duties, Earl Tomkievich fully assumed the role of Blaine Grubber. He realized he wanted both characters to assume two different body types, so gradually he purchased different sized bodysuits. As Earl, he began wearing these suits over the course of five years. He began with the smallest size, and he soon reached the largest one. He did so at a pace that would suggest he was gaining weight. As Blaine, he maintained his small body. Soon, following his degree in cosmetology, Blaine Grubber executed, flawlessly, his first murder. The thrill returned a massive surge of excitement as he stabbed his victims.

As the room dispersed, Earl couldn't help but notice the effort Ebenezer employed to not make eye contact with him. It was something he first observed when they met at the elevator. Then, Earl chalked it up as an attempt by him to be respectful. He realized society admonished individuals for staring at people with odd shapes. That was something he learned when he newly gained the fictitious weight. But as the night went on, Earl realized something was wrong. Ebenezer was trying *too* hard to look away. The moment their eyes met, he quickly turned them elsewhere. This was a swift departure from the past. Over the past four days, Ebenezer had been unable to shift his eyes away from Earl for more than a minute. His physique had been a great source of fascination for him from the moment they met at his beach house. The sudden shift in his demeanor was enough to raise his doubts. He watched him as he looked down on his phone just moments after the video conference call. He looked very uncomfortable from what he read in the message. Earl watched him in that state for about two minutes, and then without warning, he walked out of the room towards the elevator. Soon, Jeff Cumberland followed him. Earl was not concerned with Jeff. He knew Jeff was always trying to be alone whenever he could, but Ebenezer was definitely a source of concern. He needed to know more. There was something wrong, and Ebenezer had it written all over his face. He just needed to concentrate to decipher its meaning. About an hour later, everybody in the area had resigned to their respective rooms. Earl and his best friend, Tristan, were the last to go. Their friendship began three years ago when they worked on a small case in North Philadelphia. Earl appreciated his straightforwardness, and Tristan appreciated his professionalism, and they both appreciated the fact that they could be together without the demand of engaging in small talk.

Earl snuck back out of his room and headed downstairs. He did so just in time to see Vaishali drive off with Ebenezer in his Nissan Maxima. Agent Nikkyta Hunter was seeing them off, but she was not part of the journey. Earl was now completely engulfed with this development. He hid behind one of the pillars outside the establishment. It took a few seconds for Nikkyta to walk back to the hotel lobby towards the elevator. Hurriedly, Earl got in the FBI van, and began trailing the author and the computer guru. His mind raced frantically as he decided on what to do next.

chapter33

I was glad Vaishali and I were able to leave the hotel without being seen. I wanted Nikkyta to come along because she was the only one, amongst the people with the new information, with legitimate field experience: she was familiar with guns and ways to protect herself. Vaishali and I were simply "indoor talents" with very limited field expertise. I tried to conceal my fear as we parted ways. I assured her we would be okay.

It was unusually cold with almost no stars in the sky. The forecast called for rain much deeper into the night. My hope was to be at the beach house before then. The road was thinly populated with a few cars. While we snaked through the city of Wilmington, the streetlights and bright Christmas decorations kept the roads well lit, but as we merged onto the interstate, a coat of darkness descended upon us. I had to adjust to the high beam for additional yards of sight.

Vaishali had been quiet the entire time and I assumed she too was afraid. A part of me wanted to console her, but I knew nothing of this world, so my words would lack authenticity. I reached for her hand and she rested it comfortably in mine. She was soft and warm. I was looking forward to our time together at my beach house. The thought of wrapping her tightly in my embrace was comforting.

"Do you want anything?" I asked.

She shook her head.

I cursed at myself for ever feeling tired of hearing her voice. There was nothing I needed more at this moment than to hear her speak.

"Are you sleepy?" I asked.

She shook her head again. I safely assumed she did not want to be bothered, so I decided to focus on the task of getting us home.

At that moment, she spoke. "Are you scared?" she asked.

"Yes," I responded truthfully.

"Me too," she said softly.

I squeezed her hand.

"We'll be fine," I managed, gently. "We will be all good by tomorrow."

"I hope so," she said.

The rest of the journey continued with very little dialogue between us. When we arrived, I placed a call to Nikkyta to notify her of our arrival.

The phone rang twice, and her voice came to life,

"Hey, are you guys there?"

She was a bit louder than anticipated. I was going to ask what was up before she started speaking.

"Are you guys okay?" She spoke rapidly, "We can't find Agent Tomkievich. The van! The FBI van is gone. No response from his room."

I felt my body turn rigid. There was no other way to interpret the concern in Nikkyta's voice. Earl must have followed us. Instinctively, I looked about my surroundings for the familiar van, but everything was still and pitch black.

"What's going on?" Vaishali facial expression had quickly taken a worrisome appearance.

"What do you think happened?" I asked.

"I don't know," she said, then quickly added, "are you guys in the house?"

"No, not yet," I said. "We literally just pulled in. I'm about to grab our luggage."

"Hurry inside," she said grimly, "and activate your alarm. I'm about an hour away from your beach house. I got a rental car. I should be there soon. Go inside and lock up!"

The dire nature of her voice was enough to obliterate all my remaining lethargy. I hung up the phone and quickly briefed Vaishali on the new development, as I grabbed our luggage. I opened the front door and urged her inside. I noticed she was a bit hesitant.

"Come in," I said impatiently, "I need to lock up."

She did not move. The look on her face suggested she was deep in thought. I wanted to grab her and yank her in, but the luggage in my hand would require extra effort on my part.

"Come inside Vaishali," I repeated, almost screaming.

She still didn't move, but this time she was speaking. Carefully, she said, "I saw you activate your alarm when we left earlier."

I was unable to make the logical leap she seemed to have made, so I said irritably, "What the fuck does that mean?"

It took a few seconds, but my mind quickly reached the same conclusion before she had the chance to explain.

My heart, the phone, and the luggage, dropped.

Someone had deactivated my alarm, because there was no alert when I opened the front door. In that exact moment, I heard the cantankerous squeak of the faulty door. From where I was standing, the door was about fifteen meters away. I knew whoever just caused it to move was most likely unaware of its defective state. The sound must have startled the intruder as well. I turned to Vaishali and screamed, "Run!!"

I heard a booming sound, and in an instant, the glass in front of me shattered. The impostor must have been propelled by the sound of the door. In an extremely brief moment of reflection, I hailed my decision to leave the door in its deformed state. The sound gave me the necessary warning to run for cover. Vaishali and I ran down a lit pathway and made a sharp turn, almost doubling back on the same road we came from. I looked behind, and trudging determinedly was an oddly-figured man. He was moving a lot quicker than what his body suggested. Vaishali was a few steps ahead of me as we continued to run. After minutes of running and multiple turns, it appeared we lost our assailant. We decided to pause to catch our breaths.

"Did you see anybody?" Vaishali asked, in between breaths.

I nodded as I tried to control my breathing.

"Agent Tomkievich," I whispered. "He found us. He must have followed us."

"So, that means he's been here before?" Vaishali asked.

I nodded frightfully. "I mean, he was here with Agent Taylor."

"What about before that," she asked.

"I don't know." I said dolefully.

"Do you have your phone?" She asked.

I shook my head. I dropped it along with the luggage back at the entrance to my place.

"Where is yours?" I asked.

"In your car," she said dejectedly. "We need to find a way to escape."

In the near distance, I heard the noise of a car engine. The sound began considerably far from us, but as each moment passed it grew louder. There was nothing but tall grass dividing us from the open road. We realized at the last second that the automobile was heading in our direction.

"Run!" I screamed.

The car barged into our safe space, splitting the shrubbery between us. Vaishali and I dove in opposite directions. The FBI van came to a halt a few yards in front of us. I was trying to regain my bearings when I saw a

tiny figure exit the van. The only thing this new actor shared with Earl was his height. The rotund basketball shape and long hair were nonexistent. *This is the accomplice Commander Gordy was talking about,* I thought. I felt overwhelmed with the fact that we were now being chased by two men. Two peculiarly short men, but two nonetheless. I wondered if Agent Tomkievich was also exiting the passenger side of the vehicle to torment Vaishali, but I couldn't hear any screams from the other side of the van. I needed to save her, but first I had to escape this new figure I assumed was Blaine Grubber. He moved noticeably quicker than Earl. He walked unwaveringly towards my direction. I wanted to run, but the gun in his hand crumbled the courage within me. I never imagined my life ending in this weed-infested space from the hands of a serial killer that mimicked the methods I laid out in my book. *I created a monster,* I thought.

As I was about to close my eyes and accept my fate, I saw the silhouette of a woman walking slowly towards the gunman through my peripheral vision. I thought I saw a long wooden plank grasped in her hands. It took everything within me to remain calm and not betray her location. I wondered where Earl was if he was not with Vaishali.

"Ebenezer," Blaine said. "You didn't have to do this. I never planned on killing you, but now you must fall." He tilted his head to the side and offered a derisive grin. Besides the vast difference in their physique, he sounded exactly like Earl. The similarity was eerie.

"I promise I won't tell," I said the first thing that came to my mind. "Please, anything you want. Money?" I knew my pleas were useless, but I was hoping to buy enough time for Vaishali to make it within striking range. She had to move slowly to guard her position.

"I don't think you can afford me," he continued. "I might be a tad bit too expensive for you."

I realized Vaishali was now within striking distance from him. I stopped pretending and urged Vaishali to attack. It happened in a split second, but Blaine did not have enough time to react before the plank smacked squarely across his left cheek. The impact was spectacular, causing the elfin figure to misshape immediately.

"Let's grab his gun and keys," Vaishali said hastily, as she bent over to search his pocket.

I joined her in the search almost immediately. I found it extremely odd that his pant, held by a long belt, was at least five times his size. Vaishali confiscated the gun, but we were unable to locate the keys in his large pants pocket.

"Maybe it's in the van," I said.

Vaishali sprang up and ran to the van. "Yes it is!" she called out.

I left the collapsed body and joined her.

"We can't go back to the beach house," I said. "Earl would still be there."

I saw a look of miscomprehension on Vaishali's face. "What do you mean? Who's that on the ground then?"

"That has to be Blaine Grubber," I said unsurely, "He's much smaller than Earl."

"Wow you're right," she said. "I only noticed his voice. They sound just alike."

I nodded as I climbed onto the passenger side of the van. In a few seconds, the vehicle coughed to life and she reversed the car to make it back onto the main road. We had no plans of going back to the beach house for fear of encountering Agent Tomkievich. We only travelled about a tenth of a mile before I heard Vaishali blurt out a curse word.

"What is it?" I asked frantically.

"There's no gas in this car," she said dismally, "We can't use it."

"Can it at least take us until we get to the next gas station?"

It was as if the van heard my words, it sputtered and came to a complete stop. The parted grass, where we left Blaine Grubber, was only a few meters away. He was still well within our line of sight. In spite of Vaishali's impressive strike, I knew it would be only a matter of time before he woke up. We needed to act fast. We needed a car and a cell phone. These were two things waiting for me in my driveway, but the fear that we would encounter Agent Tomkievich was too risky to consider making a dash for them. Our only choice appeared to be to walk to the nearest gas station and ask to use their phone. However, with the possibility of Agent Tomkievich lurking, we had to refrain from using the main roads because they were well lit which would make us sitting ducks. We needed to remain behind the cover of the tall grass. I thought about knocking on the neighbors' doors, but it was no longer beach season, so most of the houses in the area were empty. I knew some were occupied, but it was impossible to tell which one. We would be risking too much going from door to door. I shared my thoughts with Vaishali, and she agreed. We decided to walk to the gas station. We had a gun, and a wooden plank for protection.

The rain started almost immediately. It was more of a drizzle, but it was enough to add more obscurities to our night. The gas station, as I recalled, was about a mile away, but that was with travelling the way it was meant to be. I had no idea of the distance going by our convoluted path. Due to the rain, the plants and small tree branches were not as loud as we stepped on them. The night was pitch black and I depended heavily on my outstretched hands, and the plank, for guidance. Vaishali held on to my shirt with one hand and the gun in the other. After about ten minutes of walking, we arrived at a dead-end. My heart skipped a beat as I halted my movement. I felt Vaishali's soft body bump into mine.

"What is it?" she said, delicately.

I could sense the fear in her voice.

"We're at a dead-end," I said.

"Oh no!" she reacted, "what are we gonna do?"

I cursed at myself for being the cause of this new dilemma. I looked around my surroundings for a place we could hide for the night. The space was stock-still. A cacophony of nightly creatures dominated the sounds in the area. It was hidden, but if either Blaine or Earl ever made it here, it would be impossible to escape. But going back the way we just came from was also a very dangerous proposition. We could easily run into them, and that would result in the same ending as being caught here. To my right was a modest-sized building with waist-high fence around its perimeter. The house did not look inhabited. I realized our only hope to continue would be to climb over the fence and run across the compound to the other side. There were no lights on the porch, so I safely assumed the space had not been inhabited since the end of the beach season.

"Let's go across this building," I said. "It's our only option if we don't want to go back where we came from."

Vaishali did not protest my plan. She nodded and urged me to lead the way. Her face was very close to mine, and I could see the fear in her eyes. Even with everything happening, her beauty was impossible to ignore. My fear... being alone with her, the adrenaline... all of it exhilarated me. I grabbed the back of her head until our lips touched. She did not resist. I wished our condition wasn't so dire. I wanted nothing more than to have her on that shrubbery ground. With all my strength, I pulled away.

"We have to go," I whispered painfully.

She nodded.

As we neared the fence, I made sure there were no foreign sounds outside of the customary nightly organisms. The house came into view. In my mind, even if someone was inside, I hoped to make it across without alerting anyone. I climbed over first. The drop at the other side of the fence was onto a smooth terrain. I paused and stared. The area seemed secure enough. I grabbed the gun from Vaishali to help her chances of making it over. Vaishali was a bit heavy, so the activity was not as effortless as I made it seem. She landed with a little less grace than I did. We paused to see if anything or anyone had been roused.

Thankfully, all was well.

I led the way, as we trekked lightly across the other side. The opposite fence was about fifty yards away, but it felt like ten miles. When we got within thirty yards from our goal, I heard two sounds in rapid successions. First, was the sound of a window opening, and then the undeniable boom from a gun. Fear gripped me as we threw caution to the wind and ran with abandon towards the fence. I could hear a voice screaming obscenities as we dashed across the land. I was unable to discern its gender or what was being said, but I knew it was not liberating. The fence was the only thing on my mind. I could feel Vaishali close to me, so I assumed she was safe, and I didn't bother to turn around. As I was about to jump the fence, I heard a shrill cry from her. I assumed the worst. I turned around, and to my horror, she was on the ground, unable to move. Tears rushed down her beautiful face as she winced in agonizing pain. I ran back towards her and noticed the bullet tore through her right ankle.

As I was about to apply pressure to the wounded area, I felt the earth around me ruffle from the bullets. I flinched and pulled away.

"Go ahead without me," she said, through her gritted teeth.

I ignored her. There was no way I was going to continue without her. I pulled her towards a metal drum that was sitting in the compound. The barrel was large enough to shield us from the shooter. The shooting subsided, but I knew it would not be for long. I was breathing heavily. A blend of fear and courage ruled me. I needed to do something before the shooting resumed. We were caught between fences, and with Vaishali's current state, it was impossible to elude the gunman.

Out of desperation, I screamed, "We are not intruders! We need help. Please dial 9-1-1. We are being chased by the Tilted Grin Killer!"

I held no hopes that the strategy would be effective, but it appeared to be the only option at our disposal. We were indeed trespassing, so the homeowner's decision to shoot at us was warranted. I was hoping to make him think by invoking the Tilted Grin Killer. Over the past week with Jenny Gibson, the killer had been a household name. I prayed this was not the only house that had not heard of him.

As the seconds amounted into minutes, and without much activity, I imagined my words struck something within the shooter. Vaishali was breathing heavily and trying valiantly not to let out a cry. I needed to get some help before she lost too much blood.

I decided to try something new. Slowly, I walked out from behind my shield, with my hands in the air. The expanse was still dark, so I had no idea whether my show of surrender could be seen from the shooter's view.

"My name is Ebenezer Cosmen," I said slowly, and loud enough to be heard. "I own a property about half a mile from here. I just got home when I realized I had an intruder at my place. The man had a gun and was—"

I stopped abruptly when I heard the sound of gunshots. I instinctively withdrew into my protective space. The homeowner seemed to be unconvinced by my act. Another gunshot sounded. And another. And another. I noticed the sound was not coming from the same place as the first few shots. I turned towards the fence and I could make out the shadow of a little man running towards me. I felt stuck. But during this entire ordeal, one thing remained odd. There had been nearly no reaction from Vaishali. I was too consumed to notice it at first. I glanced at her and realized she was not moving. Nervously, I reached to grab her, that was when my hands felt the slippery feeling of blood on her stomach. My heart sunk. I was no longer concerned with the little guy or the homeowner. Vaishali appeared to have been shot and her immobility made me fear the worst. I shook her vigorously, and her body slumped lifelessly on the ground. It was the most terrifying moment of my life since the death of my mom.

"Noooo!!!" I screamed, no longer concerned about giving up my location. "No, no, no! Please, wake up. Please, I need you. Please! Please... please!"

My cries went unanswered. Vaishali had taken her last breath, and I too found it difficult to breathe.

chapter34

EARL TOMKIEVICH was in a daze when he woke up. He had faint memories of what transpired over the past two hours. As he staggered across the bushy surface, his retentive abilities began to strengthen. He recalled taking the FBI van to trail the author and the computer genius. It had been an act of desperation. It was a fierce departure from his modus operandi.

Unplanned.

He had no clue what they were up to, but he could not allow the pair drive off into the night. As the miles began to mount, he gleaned ideas on what they might be up to. His mind was fully made up when they passed the last exit that would have taken them to the safe house in Dover. The only logical destination from this point would be Ebenezer's beach house in Rehoboth. With this in mind, Earl overtook the black Nissan Maxima to set the scene before they arrived. His plan was to kill them and concoct a quick scene to mimic the Tilted Grin Killer. He believed it would make for a great story. Maybe not the same level of attention as Jenny Gibson's, but it would still be enough to cause a stir, and most importantly, a distraction. The thought excited him. This had not been part of the plan, but he reveled in its existence.

Well before the 4:42 a.m. visit with Agent Taylor, Earl had visited the beach house on numerous occasions in the past. He knew of a vulnerable entrance through the back door, and it would give him enough time to reach and disable the alarm system. In several disguises, Earl had rented the beach house for the summer, and he was able to learn of these deficiencies. The author had informed him of his willingness to rent to older tenants because of their appreciation for the property, so Earl adopted the look of an aged man in search of a summer hideout to enjoy his maturity. With his unmatched skills at masquerading his looks, the author was unable to differentiate between the men that approached him for the four-bedroom space. He innocently assumed they were different people and he appreciated the fact that they paid in cash. Earl learned how to disable the alarm from these trips. He rarely stayed at the house. He only used the time to learn about the security system. He had several dry runs, making sure he was able to disable it with enough time left to spare. Still, Earl had not anticipated utilizing the skill so soon. Ebenezer Cosmen was supposed to be the final death, after he had brought down the entire FBI team working on the case. He planned to fake his own death as well and then revert to his true body but under the name Blaine Grubber. It was a perfect plan that was now unfolding well ahead of schedule.

He arrived at the beach house thirty minutes before Ebenezer and Vaishali. He parked the van away from their anticipated entry route and went to the susceptible spot at the back. The entire exercise took about three minutes; he made it safely in the house and disabled the alarm system. He waited behind the last door to the front entrance for them to come in. The space was dark, but he was confident that his gun aimed directly at the door. The sound of Ebenezer's car sounded fifteen minutes later. Earl heard some imperceptible chatter between Ebenezer and someone on the phone, but he didn't bother to listen. His concentration was staunchly on the mission at hand. As the door yawned open, Earl could hear Ebenezer urging Vaishali to come in. This development was a little strange. He did not see a reason why Ebenezer would have to do this. When Ebenezer reiterated his command, this time a little more forcefully, Earl realized something was wrong. The computer geek had discovered something. Rather than wasting anymore precious time, he decided to act. He pushed the door in front of him and it opened with an infuriatingly squeaky sound. It was something Earl had not detected in his many visits as a renter. It threw everything into disarray. He realized he had to act because his cover had been betrayed. He squeezed the trigger, and moments later he heard the sound of the shattered glass but no one was laying on the floor. His targets darted down the road behind the building. He gave them chase, but the darkness of the night made it difficult to locate them. His bodysuit was also impeding his progress and he noticed he was losing ground at an alarming rate. He paused and removed the suit. He loosened the pants and wore it on his small physique instead. He tossed the bodysuit into the bush nearby and began walking slowly. He had lost track of his targets, but he was unwilling to give up. He had begun something that needed to end. There was no way he could return to his dual roles as Earl and Blaine without suffering the consequences. It was obvious they knew something. Earl was curious as to how that happened, but this was not the time to reflect. He needed to kill the runaways above all else. As he walked towards the logical path, he thought he heard something. He paused and strained his ear. He heard the whispering of two people, and he could only imagine them to be his targets. Thankfully, his van was parked in the area, so he softly climbed onto it and sped towards the direction of the voice. He crashed through the shrubbery and jumped out with his gun. He left the key in the ignition. Standing unsteadily before him was Ebenezer Cosmen. Earl was glad he saw him first. He appeared to be a greater foe than the girl.

Earl almost chuckled when he insinuated to exchange money for his life. Money was not worth the amount of joy Earl derived from killing. The smile on his face widened as he observed the look of fear on the author's face. Right as he was about to pull the trigger, he noticed a slight shift in his expression. It was as if the fear was instantly vanished and in its place, bravery. Earl realized it too late. He did not have time to react. The plank smacked across his cheek, and everything went black.

When Earl recovered, he walked about a tenth of a mile and saw the FBI van abandoned by the bushes. There was no key in the ignition. Earl peered in the glove compartment for an extra gun that was stowed in there. He was happy to see it. Disheveled, Earl tried to correct his bearing. He was now fully aware of his surroundings and how and why he ended up here, but he was unsure on what direction to turn to. He was trying to figure this out when he heard the booming sound from a not-too-distant location west of him. He turned, and as if to reward his movement, the sound occurred again. And again. And again. With determined steps, he raced towards the direction. Before he got to the source of the gunshots, the booming sound had subsided. To replace it, however, was the sound of something better. He heard the unmistakable voice of the author announcing his presence, in hopes that the shooter would relent from protecting his yard.

Earl smiled.

This was a gift, and he was determined not to waste it.

As his head reached over the fence, he could see Ebenezer with his hands up hoping to influence the shooter. Earl took aim at him and squeezed the trigger. The first shot did not seem to make contact because he saw him move freely back to the corner where he was hiding. He fired two more shots in that general direction. Earl did not want to keep firing in fear of running out of bullets. He cleared the fence and ran towards them. He noticed they were not moving. This development was promising. Their immobility would imply they were either dead or badly injured. Both prospects were delightful. As he neared the author and the computer prodigy, he heard, "Noooo!!! No, no, no, please—"

Earl smiled.

chapter35

E arl Tomkievich was standing over me. The need to live was now of little to no importance. I felt empty inside. I held Vaishali closely to my body as I rocked back and forth. The tears were relentless.

I looked up at Earl, the new and improved Tilted Grin Killer.

The scene was surreal. It was as if I was staring at my own creation. In my book, I had written a dreadful death for him, but this time life appeared to be defying art. He, the villain, was the one with the gun. Standing over me. It was as if he was taking revenge for the way things ended in the fictional depiction of his life. There was nothing more I could do. All I had was my IBM computer and my imagination. I had been able to amass an illusory account of a psychopathic killer. However, he was the one with the real gun, and the real intent to kill real people. He held all the cards. The narrative would flow anyway he pleased.

I closed my eyes and waited for my end.

I heard him take a deep breath and a deafening sound arose.

Everything went black.

chapter36

AS NIKKYTA Hunter neared her destination, she slowed almost to a standstill, inching the vehicle slowly. When she reached the driveway, she saw that the front door was wide open. That was a bad sign. Nikkyta had enough field experience to know something had gone awfully wrong. She tried to avoid the worst thoughts and conjure up a viable reason for the scene before her, but nothing was forthcoming. Everything suggested a gruesome sight inside. Slowly, she tapped her holster to make sure her weapon was in place. She had turned off the headlights a few yards before arriving. Gently, she pulled the door lever and nudged it a little. The door budged silently creating enough space for Nikkyta to exit. She did not bother closing the door. That would cause unnecessary noise. She approached the front door cautiously. Early signs of her surroundings suggested nothing out of the ordinary. The black Nissan Maxima was parked sensibly. The doors appeared to be locked, and the lights were off. Two steps past the driver-side door, Nikkyta heard the crunchy sound of broken glass on her feet. Naturally, she looked down and noticed the ruins of shattered glass all about her. Her faith plummeted, but she still maintained her composure. She could not allow her emotions to influence her reaction. As she neared the entrance door, she was expecting to see at least two lifeless bodies, but to her relief, there was nothing. She did not allow the joy to linger beyond the moment. She focused on the task at hand as she edged further into the house.

She soon realized that besides the front door, the rest of the house was immaculate. She walked to the kitchen, but nothing seemed out of place besides a condom wrapper on the floor. She did not allow this discovery to sway her emotions. She was about to continue to the rest of the house when she heard rapid sequences of gunshots in the distance. Mechanically, she changed course. She stormed out of the space and ran towards the sound. Her bearing was solely directed by the sound of the gunshots. When the sounds ceased, she still gained on the general vicinity. After about ten minutes of silence, she began to guess which way to go. Her guessing was soon enhanced by renewed sounds of gunshots. Nikkyta realized the second round of shots were from a different gun. She did not know what to make of the information, but it came to her naturally. As she neared a short fence, she heard the sound of a familiar voice. It was Ebenezer. He was establishing his presence to someone. Nikkyta was about to run towards him when she noticed a small man jumping over the fence.

Her pace slowed almost to a halt as she observed the situation. She quickly realized it was Blaine Grubber from his physique. He was the only logical guess. From what she knew of him, she knew he was not on his way to liberate the screaming author. She had to act fast. She quickly closed the gap and observed for a second. If she scaled the fence, she would definitely give off her location, and the result could be catastrophic. With nothing else left to do, Nikkyta aimed her gun at the little man. She could see him standing over a slumped figure. With no time left to think, she squeezed the trigger.

epilogue

It has been almost a year since I lost Vaishali Kumar. Her death violently reshuffled something within me. The joy I used to derive from writing now eluded me. The therapeutic appeal it used to bring is now a chore. I tried to force the process once, but it showed. Even Ray, my biggest supporter, found it difficult to stand behind my work. I am a mess.

The events of that night had haunted every day of my life. Unable to cope, I pulled out of my contract with the ID Network because I could not offer the required focus it needed. I never did call Todd, the producer, for the final episode, but they cleverly put something together that garnered a good-sized audience. I sold my beach house in Rehoboth with everything in it. I alerted my realtor to discard anything she could not sell. It was a part of my life I wanted to remain in the past. My realtor called to let me know I left my cell phone at the front entrance, but I knew I couldn't handle the emotions it would summon. Vaishali's brainchild was not something my mind could handle. I told her to add it to the things to shed.

Living a hermit life in Brooklyn meant I was completely out of touch with everyone besides Ray, my dad, and sister, Caroline. Occasionally I would hear from Joseena, but I knew she was risking too much for that.

She was engaged to, what appeared to be, a nice guy named Michael. I was happy for her, and I told her that much the last time we spoke. I urged her to refrain from reaching out so she would not put her great situation in jeopardy.

She was thankful.

I cut ties with my FBI family a week after Nikkyta saved my life. The shot that killed Earl Tomkievich was hailed as a heroic feat, and I agreed. I owed Nikkyta my life for what she did. I wanted to be with the team. I wanted to relive the days we spent together, but the pain it summoned was too much to bear. The last I heard from the crew, the team had been dissolved. Commander Frank Gordy was demoted due to the fact that a person like Earl Tomkievich existed under his watch and killed one of his agents. It was bullshit, but I understood the need to have a fall-guy. Rather than carrying out his new post, Commander Gordy decided to retire after thirty-seven years of dedicated service. He was properly hailed for his service and a befitting sendoff was organized on his behalf. He personally invited me to the affair, but I could not accept the invitation. I had to be away from them. The memory of Vaishali was too powerful when around them. But the gesture suggested he regarded me favorably. At the time, Nikkyta was unsure about how to proceed with her life, so she planned a two-week vacation to clear her mind. She invited me to go to New Orleans with her, but I politely declined. A part of me felt like I was being unfaithful to Vaishali. It's stupid I know, but that was how it made me feel. Nikkyta and I were able to repair the fissure in our relationship. She expressed regret for suspecting I was the leak, and I assured her I held no grudges—which was the truth. Vaishali's death had forced me to concentrate on things that counted in life, and holding on to pointless rifts did not qualify as one.

Agents Brady and Gabbert moved to Colorado to head a newly formed taskforce. Jeff Cumberland remained local in D.C, but he was near retirement as well. Agents Jackson and Taylor shared the responsibility left behind as a result of Commander Gordy's retirement.

The case with Earl Tomkievich did very well for my book sales. It was a stronger surge in sales than the original killer from ten years ago, and I finally made it to the coveted Book Club. I was approached by top Hollywood studios for the right to adapt the novel into a movie, and renewed talks with Hulu began almost immediately. I was offered an inordinate sum of money as a consultant and an executive producer for the project, but I declined. Ray was unhappy I did, but he understood. For the first time, he allowed his need for my success to take a backseat to my wellbeing, and for that, I thanked him. I promised him I would be back.

Although, it's been a year and I have shown no signs of returning. Lately, in the privacy of my thoughts, I have felt a familiar tingle within me. I have parlayed this feeling into a few thousand words on my IBM computer, but I am still unwilling to share it. It feels like the early days of my writing career when I patiently told my impatient friends, "Once I feel it, I'll publish it."

I felt it almost a year later.

"Pittsburgh, Pennsylvania!" a stubby-looking man on the television screamed, "please put your hands together for the president-elect Terry Gibson!!!"

The crowd went wild.

I noticed Terry, Jenny, and Marcy walk across the stage. A genuine smile splashed on their faces as they stepped on yet another stage, on their thank-you tour to the American people for granting them the opportunity to be the first family for the next four years.

I grabbed the remote and muted the President Elect's booming voice.

I placed my noise-cancelling headphones on to drown out the dissonance sounds originating from the Brooklyn streets, and I began typing...

"IT SOUNDED like something from a dream. The thumping was rhythmic, but after many seconds of no response, it became erratic, close to the point of madness. Rapid successions of exasperating knocks ensued. The noise yanked me cruelly from a slumber..."

Edmund Okocha

inPlainSight